Echoes of Orpheus

by

Tammy Lowe

The Acadian Secret

Cover Art by *The Wild Rose Press, Inc.*

The Wild Rose Press, Inc.
PO Box 708
Adams Basin, NY 14410-0708
Visit us at www.thewildrosepress.com

Publishing History
First Edition, 2025
Trade Paperback ISBN 978-1-5092-6246-5
Digital ISBN 978-1-5092-6247-2

The Acadian Secret
Published in the United States of America

Chapter One

"Overcome with unbearable grief over the death of his wife, Orpheus traveled to the underworld to bring her back."

"Oh, the irony." Elisabeth adjusted her head-lantern, its beam revealing nothing but more darkness. She led the way along another pitch-black tunnel. The air clinging to her was thick and stale, as if it had been trapped here for centuries.

While Elisabeth focused on David's familiar story, her heart pounded in rhythm with their footsteps. She fought to keep her grip on reality from slipping, but it seemed like they were already lost, adrift in this soundless abyss.

"Orpheus crossed the river Styx, made it through the gates of Hell, defeated Cerberus, the giant three-headed dog, and survived every obstacle in his path." David grabbed Elisabeth's waist. "Careful." He shuffled in front, through a flooded section of the abandoned mine. "I'll go first here, but stay close. The limestone absorbs all the sounds. There's no echo, so if we become separated, it will be that much harder to find each…other." He groaned after stepping into a submerged hole and then turned, extending an arm. "Jump."

Elisabeth climbed atop a protruding rock and jumped, clutching onto David to steady herself.

He tilted his head to the side, his headlamp casting its glow. "You all right, *cor meum*?"

The unbearable silence was a void, a vacuum that sucked away any semblance of life. It was unbearable because it was unnatural, unnerving. It gnawed at her sanity, urging her to scream to break the stillness. "Yeah. As long as you keep talking. The silence down here is the worst part of all."

He offered an understanding nod and then turned, sloshing down the corridor through ankle-deep water. "When Orpheus finally found himself face to face with Pluto, the god of death, he begged him to let Eurydice return to the land of the living." David's breathing became heavier, his voice more animated. "Moved by such an incredible act of love, Pluto relented on one condition; Orpheus was forbidden from looking back at Eurydice as she followed him out of the underworld. Finally, Orpheus saw the sunlight and was so overcome with joy they made it out that he turned around to look at his bride." David looked back at Elisabeth, his eyes widening dramatically. "But she had not yet stepped across the threshold from the underworld."

Elisabeth gave him a playful swat.

David confined laughter to a snort and continued leading the way through the abandoned mine. "Horrified, Orpheus lunged for Eurydice, grasping nothing but the cold, stale air. She'd fallen back into Pluto's domain."

As they reached dry ground again, Elisabeth glanced over her shoulder. The inky darkness swallowed every trace of light, while the walls seemed to inch closer. The chill in the air seeped through her clothes.

David pressed forward, his hands moving with theatrical flair, engrossed in his story-telling. "In desperation, Orpheus tried to follow but was not allowed back in. So, he wandered the earth broken-hearted, waiting to die so he could be reunited with Eurydice in the afterlife."

Elisabeth slowly shook her head. "Yeah, still not a fan of that story's ending." She let out a nervous laugh and jogged to catch up, not realizing how far she lagged. "Can I go in front again? I'm less scared when you're behind me."

With an easy nod, David stepped aside. The backpack he wore squished against the wall as Elisabeth scooted ahead.

"You know what scares *me* most down here?" He adjusted his own headlamp.

"What?" She tried not to think of all the possible ways they could die in this underground labyrinth.

"This clothing you've thrust upon me."

With a bemused smile, Elisabeth stopped and spun around, her headlamp illuminating the fleece hoodie, blue jeans, and rubber boots she'd brought from home—along with other necessities needed to get through these endless cave-like tunnels.

"What's wrong with it?" she asked, staring into his blue eyes that pierced through the darkness. David's brown hair was tousled and unkempt, but he grinned with his typical roguish charm. "Your feet are dry and you're warm and comfortable. We'll change back into our other clothing once we're safely out of here." She paused and stared into the void behind him, unable to shake the feeling something was watching them. She glanced over her shoulder, half-expecting to see ghostly

3

figures lurking in the shadows. "It's not like we've run into anyone the entire time we've been down here."

"We've run into *nothing* down here. Not even spiders, bats—"

"Bats!" Elisabeth's breath caught in her throat, the word conjuring images of leathery wings, sharp fangs, and beady eyes. "I didn't even think about *bats.*" Her boots scraped against the rocky floor as they continued down the narrow passageway. The walls seemed to press in on her, suffocating and oppressive. She imagined the creatures swooping down, tangling in her hair, their claws scraping her skin. "They're flying *rats*, you know."

In the eerie silence, she heard David suppress a wheezy laugh.

Her gaze darted up to the ceiling and she bit her lip. Here, the tunnel opened into a large cavern from which several more tunnels branched off. Elisabeth strained to catch any hint of life, but there was only dampness and the weight of the earth above.

David stepped next to her. "It's unlikely we'll encounter any *winged rodents* at this point," he said, pulling her into a side hug.

She forced a smile and then wrapped both arms around his waist. When he lowered his head, anticipating a kiss, she reached into a side pocket on the backpack he wore to grab the canteen instead. "I hope you're right." She pulled back and took a long drink before handing it to him. "Have some."

He snorted in amusement, glanced around the cavernous space, and took gulps of water before returning the canteen to the side pocket. "If you're tired, we can rest here and get a few hours of sleep."

Elisabeth's brow furrowed; her attention focused on the entrance of a nearby corridor. The darkness seemed to seep from its depths. "I'm all right," she replied, her determination unwavering. "Let's keep going."

"You sure?" he asked, pulling out the map Nicolas gave them. It crinkled in his grip.

"Yeah." She rubbed the back of her neck. "I'm desperate to see blue sky again. Just the thought of spending yet *another* night down here…"

David nodded. "I'd give anything for the world above at this point."

Glancing down at the map, Elisabeth traced her finger along the route they'd taken beneath Paris. "We must be right *here*." She looked up at the tunnel they'd just come through. "If we continue this way," she said, her voice steady, "we'll keep heading north through the main tunnels for several more days." But then Elisabeth's fingertip tapped a different spot on the parchment marked in faded ink. "Look, there's a closer exit *there*."

David studied the map, its lines sketched with uncertainty.

"Do you think it's safe to start heading to Ghent above ground now?" Her question hung in the air. The world above, with its blue skies and open spaces, seemed like a distant dream.

David's gaze met hers, their shared longing unspoken. "We *are* a long way from Paris."

"A *really* long way," Elisabeth agreed. "Surely to God, Cato and his men won't be looking for us *this* far away?" Her determination surged as she wandered to the opposite end of the cavern, but then her posture slumped. "Unfortunately, *this* is the quicker way out."

"What's wrong?" David stashed the map into his back pocket, and with wide steps, marched closer.

The entrance had collapsed, leaving only a small opening of barely two feet by two feet. She pointed to scattered rocks and limestone dust. "It's caved in."

David bent down to inspect the hole. "We'll fit through there. I'll wager it's undisturbed beyond the entrance."

"We'll fit through *there*?" Elisabeth's muscles tightened while mentally calculating the width of his broad shoulders. "Are you kidding me?"

David stood, quirked an eyebrow, and then leaned closer to plant a kiss on Elisabeth's furrowed brow. "Plenty of room, love. Wait here. I'll see what it's like ahead." He dropped the backpack to the ground and crawled, head first, through the hole.

It wasn't long before she was shrouded in the absolute stillness. The air hung heavy, devoid of any sound except her own heavy breathing. The headlamp's feeble glow barely sliced through the thick darkness, leaving her wrapped in a silent void.

Every nerve in Elisabeth's body seemed electrified, her senses on high alert. She turned, her gaze sweeping over the rocky walls, half-expecting a hell-bound Reptilian to stalk her from the shadows now that she was alone. If it had been winter, they might have crossed paths with a farmer down here, looking to earn extra money by mining limestone. But being summer, it was completely abandoned, as everyone tended to their crops in the world above.

"If you own the land, you also own everything under the land," Perenelle had said to them—while

warning *never*, under any circumstance, to enter these mines.

However, now it seemed as if they'd left the mines beneath Paris behind and ventured into the *real* tunnels.

"There are endless passageways, connecting all of the lands—from here to Cappadocia, from the North Sea all the way down to the Mediterranean," Perenelle whispered to them. *"Nicolas doesn't know who built them, but says they've probably always been here, beneath the earth."*

The hair on Elisabeth's arms stood on end and she forced herself to look away from the insatiable darkness. Bending down, her headlamp pierced the blackness, its weakened beam revealing a narrow passage.

"Aquarius?" she called, but her voice was swallowed by the abyss. Her heart pounded, each second stretching into eternity.

And then, a flicker of movement.

David reappeared.

"Well...?" she asked, her voice trembling.

"It's clear ahead. *Mostly*. However, I can't help feeling like Orpheus leading Eurydice from the underworld down here."

Elisabeth handed the backpack to David. "I know, right?" She grunted while wriggling through the small hole, trying not to scrape her face against the rough stone. "I just hope there isn't a giant three-headed dog ahead."

"Cerberus?" David's voice floated back to her, a lifeline in the night. "Don't worry, love. I'll distract him with a belly rub."

Elisabeth's lips twitched into a half-smile.

She emerged from the tight squeeze into a slightly wider section of the tunnel. Hunched over, they scooted along the crumbling passageway, avoiding dislodged rocks and stones, until the ceiling lifted, allowing them to stand upright. David's headlamp cast long shadows on the uneven ground and he moved with skillful ease as the tunnel twisted and turned, seemingly for miles.

When the passageway narrowed once again, they dropped to their hands and knees, and Elisabeth became unnaturally quiet.

"You all right, *cor meum*?"

"Yeah," she said with a shaky voice while crawling behind him.

He laughed…but it went on longer than normal.

Elisabeth's heart clenched and a lump in her throat refused to budge. "What's wrong?"

"Wait here." David's voice echoed in the narrow passage as he sat on the rocky floor. His legs extended, and he flipped onto his stomach, creeping feet first through the small opening. The rough stone scraped against his chest as he disappeared into the void. "There's a ledge to stand on right here."

The opening resembled a window and was the height of David's torso. Elisabeth remained outside, her breaths shallow as she watched him reach back, his fingers grazing the edge to retrieve the backpack.

"Wait…a *ledge*?" Her voice trembled. "Don't tell me we're going down even deeper?"

David turned, the beam of his headlamp casting eerie shadows. "Yes, it—"

Elisabeth's eyes widened, listening to something tumble and fall—down, down, down—smashing against rocks along the way.

8

When David let out a heavy sigh, Elisabeth gasped. "Was that the backpack?"

"Yep."

She froze, rooted to the spot. "I think we should go back the other way instead."

"We'll be fine. We've come *this* far. If the map is correct, it will be a *much* faster route to an exit out of here. Who's to say the other route is any better?"

"But…it doesn't even feel like we're in a mine anymore. It's more like a cave now." Elisabeth forced a watery smile and lay flat on her tummy. Her fingers scraped against the stone as she wriggled through the narrow opening, feet first. Emerging on the other side, she turned and paused, her gaze fixed on the abyss below. It felt like the cave had transformed into something more—a passage to the center of the earth.

"I'll go first." David's voice cut through the stillness. He flashed Elisabeth a reassuring smile, but it faded too quickly, replaced by a furrowed brow. He began his descent, inching down the nearly vertical shaft.

Elisabeth bit her nails, watching.

"All right, just take your time, *cor meum*. It's not as bad as it looks," David said in a soothing tone when he finally made it to a narrow ledge almost halfway down.

"Liar," she mumbled, knuckles white as she wiped sweaty palms on her jeans. She followed, using protruding rocks as stepping stones. Each foothold was a gamble as her heart pounded in her ears.

"You're doing great," David's voice echoed from below. "There's a rock by your left—"

And then it happened. Her grip slipped. Panic

surged through Elisabeth as she lost her footing and let out a sharp scream. Down she slid, the walls blurring into a chaotic haze of stone and darkness. She reached out, desperate to grab something (anything!) to break her fall.

Suddenly, David's arm wrapped around her waist, yanking her onto the small ledge with him. Her breaths came in ragged gasps as she clung to him.

"Gotcha, love," he said, his voice shaky but relieved.

Elisabeth's watery smile returned, and she pressed her forehead against his chest. She then fought back tears, trying to steady wobbly legs while following David down through the remaining portion. When they eventually reached a spot where the shaft bottle-necked, she grabbed the backpack.

David's face tightened with concentration as he turned, lay flat on his stomach, and carefully eased through the next tight squeeze, raising his arms beside his head to fit through.

Elisabeth handed him the backpack and couldn't help whimpering as she followed.

"We're almost there."

She let out a sigh of relief when reaching the bottom of the pit.

After they crossed the small cavern, the passage wound its way back up again.

David adjusted the backpack and glanced around. He then placed his hands on Elisabeth's shoulders and gave a reassuring squeeze while positioning her ahead of him. "You first this time, *cor meum.*"

Elisabeth nodded as her eyes fixed on the uneven footholds. She pressed her boot against the rough surface of the rock, testing its stability. As she climbed, David followed closely, his presence the only reassuring thing in this place. Adrenaline surged through her veins and she focused on the scrape of his boots behind her, along with the occasional words of encouragement.

At the top, the floor leveled out into another small cavity. Elisabeth's eyes narrowed when the light from her headlamp bounced around the enclosed space. "Aquarius…?" She gritted her teeth. "It's a dead end."

"No." He shook his head vigorously, glanced around the empty cavern, and then pulled out the map. "It can't be."

She leaned in, her finger following the intricate path on the map. "All right, so we traveled through this section, followed this route, and descended here…"

David's fingertip hovered over the parchment. "We're here." He then drew a brief line, emphasizing the exit.

They both glanced around the small cave, searching for an opening.

A moment later, David swore under his breath. When Elisabeth turned to look at him, he forced a smile. "Found it."

Her head flinched back slightly before scanning the space again.

He then pointed down to where the wall met the floor—or so it seemed. What looked like a jutting rock wall rounded out and didn't *actually* connect to the floor, but created a tiny crawlspace beneath it.

A cold chill ran up Elisabeth's spine. "You have *got* to be kidding me."

David cleared his throat and dropped the backpack.

"It'll be fine. Someone *made* this map so we're not the first ones to pass through here."

Elisabeth's brows knit together as she lay flat on her stomach, peering through the gap. She then took a deep breath. "Wait here. I'm going first."

David's protest was swift. "Certainly not. I'll—"

"I'm smaller than you and need to make sure you'll fit."

Before he could stop her, Elisabeth slithered through the tiny opening, using both elbows to propel herself forward. She took deep breaths, trying to remain calm while moving an inch at a time, sandwiched between layers of cold stone. The passage was a mere fissure—a seam in the ancient rock. "I feel like I've been here before," she called back to David. "When I was being born."

His nervous laugh followed her, like an invisible string connecting them.

"This must be what a baby feels like going through the birth canal." When Elisabeth reached a spot where she could lift her shoulders enough to look at the space, she saw it bent slightly to the right. She paused; her forehead pressed against the stone. Dizziness swirled around her, threatening to pull her back into the darkness. "Dear God," she whispered, her voice swallowed by the rock.

"You all right?" David called out.

"Yeah." Her chest tightened. "I hope you're not the slightest bit claustrophobic."

As if in response, the tunnel constricted further. Elisabeth squeezed her eyes shut, willing panic away.

Breathe.

Stay calm.

Take deep breaths.
STAY CALM.

Elisabeth retreated slightly to readjust her arms before making a hard left turn.

It worked.

She sighed in relief seeing the space open up—this time into what looked like a normal mine again. Using her feet to thrust forward, she belly-crawled through the final tight squeeze. When free, she stood and stretched, taking in a deep breath before her eyes caught sight of some old mining tools scattered around—rusty pickaxes, weathered shovels, and chipped chisels. The tools seemed ancient, covered in dust and cobwebs, yet sturdy enough for use. She crawled back inside, just enough to guide David through. "Can you hear me?"

"I can hear you." He cleared his throat. "Are you still unharmed?"

Elisabeth's heart raced. The walls pressed in, unyielding and cold, and she could almost taste the damp earth in the air. Her own escape had been a desperate scramble, fueled by adrenaline and fear. Now, David had to get out safely too.

"Yes, I made it. Come through like I did," she called back, her voice echoing off the stone. She strained to hear his movements, the scrape of fabric against rock. "You'll come to a point where…I got my arm caught, so keep your hands straight up in front of you, and you'll fit. It's going to be tight for you, though." Elisabeth's fingers brushed the uneven surface, remembering the moment when panic threatened to overwhelm her.

The sound of David's heavy breathing reached her ears, almost drowned out by her frantic heartbeat. "It bends to the right, and then you have to make a hard left. There's a spot where you can raise your shoulders and take a break." She imagined him inching forward, muscles straining, the darkness swallowing him whole.

Finally, she saw the faint glow of his headlamp, growing brighter as he pushed forward. The backpack scraped against the walls—a stubborn companion. "By the gods, this is madness," David grunted, his voice echoing her own thoughts.

"You're almost done." Elisabeth crawled closer, her fingers brushing the edge of the passage. She pulled the backpack out and then slunk back inside, her breath hitching as she waited for David.

His arms poked out of the tightest spot—but then he stopped moving.

Elisabeth's stomach knotted. "Aquarius…?"

He cursed under his breath. "I'm stuck."

A surge of panic threatened to overwhelm her sense of reason. "Just—"

"No. I'm *really* stuck." His voice was strained and desperate.

Elisabeth let out an uncontrollable whimper. "Try and see if your—"

With a guttural roar, David's trapped arms disappeared from view. "All right…let me try this one more time," his muffled voice called out.

Elisabeth watched, breath held, as one arm reappeared, and then the other. His face emerged, eyes wide and wild. Then, with all his might, David squeezed through, one shoulder at a time. His upper body was free and he stared at Elisabeth, dazed and bewildered.

She let out a huge sigh of relief. "Thank God, you

made it out."

David managed a shaky laugh and rested his head on his arm. "Barely."

Elisabeth emerged from the narrow passage, her body scraped and bruised from the earlier fall, but adrenaline still pumping through her veins. The mine's corridor stretched ahead, and she leaned against the wall, waiting for David.

And there he was—a disheveled figure. He scrambled to his feet, closing the gap between them in an instant. Elisabeth barely had time to react before he pulled her into a tight hug. His warmth enveloped her, and she clung to him, feeling the weight of their shared survival. She squeezed her eyes shut, and for a moment, everything else faded away—the darkness, the danger, the uncertainty. It was just David and her, two souls entwined in this underground labyrinth.

His lips brushed against her hair, and she could hear the ragged rhythm of his breath. "Let's keep moving."

Elisabeth nodded, her heart still racing.

He lugged the backpack over his shoulders and led the way down the narrow passage, brushing spider webs away from his face.

"It doesn't look like this mine's been used in a long time." Elisabeth stared at the rough walls that encircled them. "This isn't limestone, is it?"

David ran a hand along silver specks in the rock. "It looks like…lead."

Elisabeth's head jerked back, listening to water dripping. She took in a deep breath. The once still, stale air now smelled of must and mildew. Something fluttered in a soft breeze. "Do you hear that? Those are the first sounds we've heard in days. We must be near the exit!"

When David turned a corner and abruptly stopped, Elisabeth crashed into him.

"Turn off your headlamp." His whispered demand cut through the darkness as he switched his off.

Elisabeth's heart pounded. "What's the matter?" she asked, her voice barely audible while extinguishing her light.

Chapter Two

Elisabeth held her breath, cautiously peeking out from behind David. Her pulse raced as she clutched his shirt. "What do you see?"

"Give your eyes a moment to adjust to the darkness and you'll *see* for yourself."

Eventually, Elisabeth saw the outline of a small alcove, with a faint sliver of daylight seeping into the space.

With a gasp, she stepped beside David.

After countless days trapped in this subterranean *hell*, a ray of sunshine sliced through the darkness. Her heart surged, craving the touch of open sky, the scent of fresh air, and the freedom of the wind in her hair. Overwhelmed, she couldn't contain her emotions—a raw, uncontrollable sob escaped her lips.

"That's daylight!" Her voice echoed off the mine's walls.

Elisabeth flicked her headlamp back on, its weak glow competing with the newfound brightness. Without hesitation, she sprinted toward the light, leaving David behind as he tried to hold her back.

"Elis—!"

"Come on!" she interrupted with a booming laugh, turning around to wave him over.

In that heart-stopping moment, hundreds of startled bats erupted into flight, their squeaks and scratches filling every inch of space around Elisabeth. Black leathery wings flapped against her head, her legs—their ungodly screeching in her ears.

Elisabeth's primal scream reverberated within the damp confines of the cavern.

Time stretched, each millisecond an eternity trapped in a nightmare. A huge, hairy bat, its sharp fangs bared, hovered before Elisabeth's face. She staggered back, her steps quick and jerky, eyes bulging, mind paralyzed.

Elisabeth raised her arms, a futile attempt to shield herself from the monstrous swarm. Her legs felt weak, but David ran toward her, seemingly in slow motion.

He lunged forward, wrapping his arms around her as they crashed to the ground. Shielded beneath his body, Elisabeth's heartbeat thundered in her ears, drowning out the chirping and squeaking of the bats.

Gradually, the stillness settled over everything once more. David lifted his head, scanning the surroundings before looking down at her. "They're gone."

Her heart continued to pound, and she stared at him, wide-eyed.

"You drove them *all* out of here, love."

As David rose, Elisabeth clutched his shirt, pulling him back. "Wait…" A nervous giggle escaped. "My heart's still racing. I don't think I can move yet."

He let out a sympathetic sigh and leaned down to kiss her forehead. "As soon as you're ready, we'll leave these mines behind forever."

Elisabeth gasped, playfully pushing him away, and sprang to her feet. "Quit stalling. Let's get out of here!"

David stood and, with long strides, led the way

down the passage. The daylight filtered through a small grassy opening where the bats had flown out. "I can see outside," he said, his laughter both throaty and relieved. "This mine's clearly been abandoned. The entrance is grown over and…"

His voice trailed off as he tore at grass, dirt, and stubborn roots, widening the gap. Within a few moments, the opening was large enough to squeeze through. David wiped dirty palms on his jeans, then reached for Elisabeth's hand, pulling her closer. Happy tears streamed down her cheeks and he squeezed her fingers. "Why do I still feel like Orpheus leading Eurydice out from the underworld?"

Sniffling, Elisabeth wiped her nose with the back of her free hand. "Then don't turn to look back at me," she teased, "until we're completely out of here." Following David into the light, she added, "I'm *never* coming back in h—"

With a sudden shriek, she squeezed her eyes closed and grasped her head, a sharp flash of pain radiating behind her eyelids.

David groaned and covered his face with both hands as well.

Elisabeth blinked rapidly, unable to keep her eyes open. "I can't see anything yet."

Within a few minutes, she was finally able to look at David long enough to watch him squinting. His arm extended toward the sky to ward off the sun's rays.

Elisabeth burst into laughter as she continued blinking. "We've waited so long to see the sky and now we can't even look at it."

David snorted in amusement, and as his eyes adjusted to the sunlight, his posture straightened.

Side by side, they stood in a small clearing. Behind them, the entrance to the old mine was set into the hillside, half hidden by wild grass and untamed plants—evidence that few had ventured here in years. As their eyes adjusted, the landscape slowly came into focus—the forest edge not far away, and the faint sound of a stream somewhere nearby, concealed by the thick undergrowth. An old wheelbarrow lay abandoned, its wooden frame decaying under a layer of moss and fungus, marking the slow passage of time.

Atop the hill, an ancient smelting chimney rose against the sky, its stones blackened by years of fire and smoke. The structure was a relic of the once-thriving industry that had long since faded. Vines crept up around its base, their vibrant green twisting against the gray, weathered stone, further proof of nature reclaiming what had been left behind.

Elisabeth's heart swelled with relief. "We did it!" Unable to contain her excitement, she jumped up and down, squealing with delight. "We've slipped through Cato's net."

"*Under* Cato's net." With a booming laugh, David lifted Elisabeth into his arms and spun around. "Now that we're safely out of Paris, I want you to promise me something, *cor meum*." His tone was suddenly serious after putting her down again.

"What?"

He lowered his head and quirked an eyebrow. "Never again," he grumbled, "will I be *encased* in these trousers. They're thick as armor!"

Elisabeth let out an amused snort while staring at his blue jeans. "Fine. Give me the backpack. I'll get your *tights* for you, Robin Hood."

When David's eyes narrowed in confusion, she broke into a fit of giggles, reached for her crystal necklace, and thought of home.

****

"You know…" Elisabeth ran her hands down the fine linen gown she now wore, after bathing and changing at home. "One good thing about the number of layers wealthy women dress in here is that I still ended up with something suitable to wear."

David, having found the nearby stream to wash up, adjusted his hip-length azure blue tunic and charcoal gray leggings that he'd happily changed into. "What do you mean?"

"Well, I can't exactly wear the enormous gown *Lord Cathon* "buried" me in if we're to remain inconspicuous, but can you believe this—" She gave a twirl, showing off a pretty lilac-colored dress with a scooped neckline. Worn over a crisp, white cotton shift, the bodice was laced tight and tied with a dark purple satin ribbon. "It was part of the undergarments I was wearing. I think it's called a kirtle? Something like that, anyhow." She flashed David a sweet smile and extended both arms playfully, as if asking for a hug. "Come here. I need you for a minute."

He strolled to her with a mischievous grin. "What do you *need*?"

She swallowed her laughter. "I can't button the sleeves myself."

"Oh…" His smirk remained. "I see."

Elisabeth's tummy fluttered, watching David smile at nothing while fastening the buttons that ran from her elbow to wrist.

"There you go," he said, his touch lingering.

Her gaze dipped briefly, then lifted to meet his. With a light bounce onto her tiptoes, she gave him a quick kiss. "Thanks."

"Anything else?"

She shook her head, now weaving her dark brown hair into a simple half-up crown braid.

David whistled a merry tune while collecting a handful of stones from the ground.

"It's still a bit fancy, but it'll pass as a *somewhat* casual dress; don't you think so?" Elisabeth let out a dejected sigh after tying the ribbon to the braid. "The blush pink dress is still at Cato's."

David slipped the stones into his belt pouch. Then, with a gentle touch, he clasped Elisabeth's fingers. "As long as you are here, the other dress can *stay* at Cato's." His playful wink accompanied the soft press of his lips against her hand.

Elisabeth felt heat rush to her cheeks.

"Now, we need to keep moving, love."

"I know. I know." She yawned as he led her by the hand along an old overgrown trail.

Eventually, David looked up at the sky and then gathered a handful of sticks. "Sit here and rest a while," he instructed before using a rock to hammer a long stick into the ground.

"Gladly." Elisabeth flopped down and crossed her legs. "What are you doing?" she eventually asked.

"At night, we'll use the stars to navigate, but during the day, we'll use the sun."

"I'll bring you a compass if it's easier," she said before yawning again.

Where the shadow of the stick ended, David placed a stone on the ground. "A what?"

"A compass," she said with a sleepy smile. "It'll tell you which way is north."

His brows squished together as he sat next to her. "What do you think I'm doing?"

Elisabeth pinched her lips together to keep from laughing. "I have absolutely *no* idea." She then slumped against him, putting her head on his shoulder.

David responded with a protective embrace and kissed the top of her head, a silent promise of safety. "You rest while I keep track of the sun's journey across the sky."

Elisabeth exhaled a contented sigh, her eyelids fluttering closed. "I just need a little catnap," she whispered to the rustling leaves.

Time slipped away, and when her eyes blinked open again, they were both lying down. David's arm was still around her and the soft sounds of the forest were now a gentle lullaby. Above her, the canopy parted to reveal a sky of the purest blue, where the sun played hide and seek with the clouds. Elisabeth watched as the leaves above swayed in a slow, graceful dance, casting fleeting shadows that caressed her face.

Listening to David's slow, rhythmic breathing, she knew he'd fallen asleep as well. With each breath, Elisabeth felt more at peace. She lifted her head to glance at David before snuggling closer, seeking his warmth.

His smile was slow, deliberate, but radiant, and he opened his eyes. His fingers stroked her hair, a tender gesture that made her heart beat faster. "We should go."

With a grin, she nestled even closer, her head finding the perfect nook beneath his chin.

He took a long, savoring breath and neither moved

to get up. Cradled in David's arms, Elisabeth felt the world outside their embrace melt away. The forest's lullaby continued, and David's fingers traced patterns on her back. "Let's stay a little longer," she whispered, her voice barely rising above the rustle of the leaves.

David nodded, his movements reflecting the same desire to linger in this stolen moment.

Finally, Elisabeth eyed David's makeshift compass. Her lips parted slightly and she pulled herself away from him to check it out.

Near the stick he'd hammered into the earth, several stones were placed in a straight line. Against the stones, two more sticks lay criss-cross on the ground.

She couldn't help chuckling. "What sort of sorcery is this?"

David stood and stretched before sauntering over. "It's quite simple really. If one tracks the direction the sun's shadow moves, you will soon learn which way is east and which way is west." He pointed to the criss-crossed sticks. "The top one is north-south. Which means Ghent is," —David turned slightly and pointed— "this way."

Elisabeth gasped. "Oh! Alrighty then." With a bemused smile, she walked alongside him, across the clearing and into the woods. Within a few minutes, David caught sight of an old trail leading off to their right.

They continued until the path eventually came to an end at a dirt road. "This way's north," he said, flashing her a wink as they turned left. The road meandered downhill through the trees, leading to a simple bridge made of wooden planks.

Elisabeth watched a squirrel dart into the

underbrush. "A bridge is a good sign we're not *too* far from civilization, don't you think?"

"Yes." David fiddled with his sling. "Perhaps we're near a village."

The stream flowed over rocks, its soft trickling blending with the forest sounds. A skittish doe, her brown coat camouflaged in the sunlight and shadows, quickly disappeared into the trees, her ears twitching with alertness.

David cocked his head to the side. "Do you hear that?"

"Yes." Elisabeth's gaze wandered around. "It was a doe." Her grin widened and she burst into song. "A deer. A female dee—"

"No, listen." David, oblivious to the reference, stopped walking. "It's getting louder."

Her smile faltered, the notes dying on her lips as the humorous moment passed unshared. Leaves and twigs snapped and crunched, faster and faster, as someone, or some*thing*—ran through the forest, heading toward them. While they searched for the source of the noise, David's hand moved instinctively to his pouch, fingers wrapping around a stone, his sling ready for action.

Suddenly, they both gasped, spotting a woman racing through the trees. She leapt over a fallen branch as something chased her.

"Stay here," David ordered before bolting toward the woman.

That's when Elisabeth heard the familiar squeals and grunts of an angry boar.

Oh, crap!

She sprinted after David. "It's a boar! Be careful,

Aquarius, it's a wild boar! Those things have tusks that can kill a grown—!"

David jerked his head around, nostrils flaring. "GET BACK!" he roared while still running.

Distracted by David and Elisabeth, the woman tripped over an exposed tree root and stumbled to the ground.

The ear-piercing squeals of the creature grew louder as it neared.

Elisabeth's pulse raced and she scrambled behind a tree. Her mind darted back to that day when she was twelve. She'd inexplicably found herself in the Scottish Highlands—far too close to a huge hairy boar with razor-sharp tusks.

"Dinnae move, lass!" Malcolm had ordered while reaching for his dagger. The seventeenth-century Highlander then ran at the beast, as if he were a wild animal himself. Jumping on it from behind, he'd grabbed its ear, yanked its head up, and slashed its throat.

Elisabeth's breath now burst in and out, realizing David's rocks wouldn't be enough to stop an angry boar. He'd need his dagger in order to—

The creature finally came into view and Elisabeth's head flinched back slightly.

Wait...

Her eyes narrowed.

It wasn't a boar chasing the woman.

It was a very angry, very pink pig, with swollen teats swinging wildly beneath its rounded belly as it charged, snorting and squealing with surprising ferocity.

The woman scrambled to her feet, now wielding a

thick branch she'd grabbed from the ground.

David, always quick on his feet, stopped abruptly. He raised his sling to shoulder height, eyes locked on the charging pig. His shout aimed to lure it away from the woman. Then, in one fluid motion, he extended his arm back over his shoulder, rotated the rope, and released an end as he lunged forward.

The rock shot out of the sling, finding its mark— the sow's shoulder. The creature let out a high-pitched, ear-piercing squeal, but instead of veering away, it changed course. Now, it tore through the trees, heading straight for David.

He swore under his breath, quickly reaching into his pouch. Stone after stone rained down upon the angry sow, each impact pummeling its thick skin. Elisabeth watched, her stomach twisted in knots, as the mama pig finally turned and retreated, snorting indignantly as it disappeared into the trees.

David waved Elisabeth over, stashed the sling into his belt, and hurried toward the woman. "Are you all right, milady?"

She rocked back and forth for a moment and then tossed the heavy stick aside. "I will be. Once I catch my breath," she said with a shaky laugh.

The woman spoke in the (now) familiar dialect—a sort of cross between Latin, which Elisabeth and David were fluent in, and French. They'd both picked it up easily after being immersed in the language with villagers, like Isabeau, who didn't speak Latin very well.

As she drew near, Elisabeth noticed her graceful, feminine features. Her eyes were a deep gray and her brown hair was neatly braided and tucked under a white kerchief that matched her apron. Her dress was plain gray, but somehow still flattering due to her slender figure and graceful posture. Elisabeth guessed she was maybe twenty-three? Twenty-four?

Although still struggling to catch her breath, the woman pushed her shoulders back. "I want that pig arrested immediately and put on trial for attempted murder. I need your help."

Elisabeth's mouth fell open. "You want the *pig* arrested and—?"

"Yes," she said with a curt nod. "It's Henry Gagneux's pig. I need you as witnesses to the crime."

"The crime?" David's brows furrowed. "I'm sorry we're unable to be of more assistance. I'm relieved you are unharmed, but we must continue to our destination."

The woman looked them up and down. "Are you headed to Oudenaarde?"

"Ghent," David replied.

"Well, you obviously made a wrong turn somewhere."

When David let out a heavy sigh, Elisabeth offered him a weak smile.

"You might as well come with me." The woman smoothed down her dress and glanced at David. "I'll give you ale and a bed for the night. It's the least I can do. Then you can both make an official statement as my witnesses before you leave." She turned and walked toward the dirt road, swinging her arms happily.

Elisabeth's brows squished together as she and David stared at each other in confusion before looking back at the woman.

"We are *not* going with her," he whispered.

Elisabeth opened and then closed her mouth. "Why

not?"

His posture stiffened. "We're on the run and must not draw attention to ourselves."

Elisabeth's eyes widened. "*You're* the one who ran in with a *rock sling* to save her. Like *that's* not going to draw attention?"

David briefly closed his eyes and took a deep breath. "*You* saw what happened."

"Well…?" The woman waved them over. "Are you two coming or not?"

Elisabeth let out a long exhale. "I think it'll be more suspicious if we *don't* go with her. At the very least, she can point us in the right direction since we're currently in the middle of nowhere." Elisabeth grabbed David's fingers, playfully pulling him along. When he shook his head in defeat, moving with lackluster steps, Elisabeth bit down on a smile. "We're coming," she shouted back to the woman.

Ahead, on the right, the setting sun reflected on a small lake, turning both water and sky vibrant shades of pink.

David smiled politely. "If you could point us in the right direction, I'm afraid we *do* need to continue to our destination. How far from Ghent are we?"

The woman looked at them both, her gaze sharp but not unkind. "If I offered a bed for the night, it's clear you're still a day's journey away. Night's falling. You'd rather sleep in the woods than my cottage?" Her eyes skimmed over David's azure doublet and Elisabeth's lilac dress—neither suited for travel. A gentle chuckle escaped her lips. "Too fine for my humble home, I suppose." She shook her head, a playful twinkle in her eye. "But don't expect to stumble upon grand lodgings around here. My door's open to you, should you reconsider."

"I'm afraid—" David began, a note of polite refusal in his voice.

Elisabeth cut in; her tone firm yet warm. "Actually, we'd be honored to accept your hospitality." As heat crept across her cheeks, she stole a glance at David.

He turned, raking a hand through his hair in exasperation.

With a shy smile, Elisabeth stepped closer, linking her arm through his. "A comfy bed will be *so* much better than sleeping out in the forest."

David's lips pinched together. "Fine."

She bounced on her toes, planting a kiss on his cheek. "Thank you."

When he grunted, the young woman snickered in amusement. "If you leave at dawn, you'll reach Ghent by evening."

David replied with a small nod. "Many thanks, milady."

"Enough with the milady. Call me Beatrice."

Hand in hand, David and Elisabeth strolled alongside Beatrice by the twilit lake. The rosy sky shifted from pink to hues of orange as the sun, ablaze, descended toward the horizon.

Elisabeth glanced at David. "What a beautiful sunset."

A slight smile formed on his face as an obvious memory danced through his mind. "The magic hour."

She took a deep, satisfied breath and nodded. "That space between dreams and reality."

Beatrice turned away and burst into laughter. "By God's teeth, you're a merry pair, aren't you?" Shaking her head, she looked back at Elisabeth. "What's your name?"

Elisabeth's fingers tightened around David's, a silent signal of their shared predicament, realizing an alias might be needed while on the run.

Cato's reach as Lord Cathon was vast.

Not to mention Guglielmo Tartare's. As the leader of a powerful mercenary army, he was forging an alliance with Cato, sealed by a marriage to Elisabeth.

All of Paris believed her to be Lord Cathon's daughter, so to escape the arranged marriage, she'd pulled a "Juliet" and faked her own death by poison—after secretly *marrying* David.

"Sorry, what?" Elisabeth swallowed a lump in her throat, stalling for time.

Beatrice leaned in, a small smile on her face. "Your name, what is it?"

"Juliet." The word just tumbled out of her mouth. "I'm Juliet."

When David took a deep breath and nodded, pretending he wasn't surprised, Elisabeth let out a nervous laugh.

"And I'm Juliet's husband..." He paused to flash Elisabeth a mischievous grin.

Don't say it. Don't say it.

"Romeo."

He said it.

Elisabeth bit down on a smile and looked away. At least the infamous tale she'd told him hadn't been written yet. As they followed a bend in the road leading away from the lake, she gave him a light-hearted nudge, their shared secret a source of amusement.

Suddenly, David gestured toward a tall fence of

sharpened logs. The enclosure guarded a hidden settlement nestled amongst the trees. "This must be your village," he said to Beatrice.

"Told you it was close," she teased. Then, with a gentle push, the gate swung open and she invited them inside. "Welcome to Lindenhart."

Chapter Three

Directly inside the gate was a tiny village square. To Elisabeth's right stood two thatched-roof cottages, their proportions similar to oversized garden sheds. Made of wattle and daub, bits of straw embedded in the mud-washed walls poked out here and there. Straight ahead, a half-timber building, much larger than the others, sat dark and quiet, its wooden door shut tight for the night. As they crossed the square, Elisabeth's gaze caught glimpses of village life: A cart, its wooden wheels worn smooth by countless journeys, rested near a woodpile. The blacksmith's timber-framed lean-to was tucked away in a corner, and a small shed, its timeworn door slightly ajar, housed pottery. And there, at the heart of it all, was a campfire pit.

Beatrice led the way along a narrow dirt road, its surface paved with wooden planks. As they ventured deeper into the heart of the village, Elisabeth's pulse quickened with anticipation. Some houses were built so close to the road, you could reach up and touch the low thatched roofs. Between the homes were small yards, most containing stacked firewood, a small garden, and an outbuilding or workshop. Meanwhile, chickens, goats, and the occasional pig wandered about freely.

When a sheep bleated hello to them from behind a split rail fence, a curious lamb wandered out of a tiny shed and across the grass, inquiring about the new guests as well. In the distance, someone hammered metal.

The magic hour glowed and an old man wandered ahead of them, lighting lanterns hanging from tree branches and wooden posts. As numerous villagers continued about their business, Elisabeth let out a spontaneous laugh, realizing this rustic hidden place, Lindenhart, was larger and more populated than she first thought.

The planks embedded in the dirt ended where the road widened at a glorious weeping willow. Beyond the tree, a wooden bridge crossed over a stream running through the village. Torches flickered romantically along the length of the bridge, causing the water below to sparkle like emerging stars in the darkening sky.

"I think I like it here," Elisabeth whispered to David while reaching out to brush her fingers through the curtain of long willow branches.

Nearby, crickets chirped and a frog croaked before plunking into the bubbling stream, escaping from three laughing children who waded into the knee-deep water after it.

Beatrice, standing on the bridge, called out to the eldest boy, "Théo!" with a mix of authority and affection.

Théo, his sun-kissed face framed by unruly hair, glanced up from the water. He looked about seven. His eyes, wide and curious, met hers, and he waved in acknowledgment.

"Wilem has lit the torches," Beatrice warned.

The boy's reaction was immediate—a gasp, followed by a muttered curse.

"Théodore! Watch your tongue," she scolded while

laughing. She gestured toward the younger children, their bare feet splashing in the water.

They obeyed Théo's hurried instructions, scampering out of the water, resembling little woodland fairies to Elisabeth.

David, leaning against the bridge's wooden railing, couldn't suppress his smile. "What's wrong?"

Beatrice's reply was matter-of-fact. "Their mother expects them home by the time the torches are lit."

He snorted in amusement as they watched the three barefoot siblings scamper off.

After crossing the bridge, the dirt road continued, winding its way between more cottages and outbuildings. To her left, Elisabeth noticed grazing sheep and a handful of goats in a fenced paddock.

Finally, Beatrice reached her humble home, its timeworn walls made from wattle and daub. The thatched-roof cottage beckoned with an open door, and from within, a flickering glow cast shadows on the earthen floor.

To the right of the yard, a quaint scene unfolded. Beneath a small thatched-roof pergola was a weathered wooden table. An oil lamp graced its surface, its flame dancing in rhythm with the night breeze. Atop it, a black cat reclined, its obsidian eyes half-closed. And there, on the moonlit ground, sat two babies—their laughter filling the air.

The little ones appeared to be about a year old. They sat, banging wooden spoons against a pail while squealing with delight. Although both wore simple leather shoes, one baby was dressed in a tiny bluish-gray tunic with brown trousers, while the other wore a sleeveless green smock over a beige shift.

A boy and a girl.

Elisabeth's posture perked up and she glanced around, wondering where their parents were.

"Mama's home," Beatrice cooed, lifting the baby boy into her arms. "How were my two darlings?"

Elisabeth's head jerked back.

Twins?

She has twins?

Beatrice's brow wrinkled while looking to the left, toward a firepit. She pressed a tender kiss to the baby's forehead and placed him in a square wooden walker. Then, with practiced ease, scooped up the little girl, balancing the baby on her hip.

"Lancelot?" she called out, walking to the glowing embers to check on a cauldron hanging from a tripod. "Lancelot!"

Lancelot?

Elisabeth's lips pinched together to keep from smiling, pushing away the mental image of a dashing knight from King Arthur's court.

A second later, a tall and ruggedly handsome man, roughly the same age as Beatrice, emerged from the shadows, holding kindling in his arms.

Sir Lancelot.

Elisabeth's mental image wasn't that far off.

The man's height commanded attention as he moved with confidence and grace. His dark shoulder-length hair suggested a life spent outdoors, while his short beard and mustache contributed to his rugged charm. Although Lancelot didn't smile, there was warmth in his dark eyes. "Relax. I'm right here, Bee," he said in a low, gravelly tone.

Beatrice let out a sigh of relief, watching him add

wood to the fire. "If you're wondering what took me so long, I was nearly killed by one of Henry's pigs."

The color drained from Lancelot's face and his shoulders tightened as he looked up. "Wh—?"

"Not that you care," Beatrice snapped before marching away.

"Why would I not care?" His gaze followed Beatrice as she marched away, a shadow of disappointment crossing his features.

Still holding the baby girl, Beatrice disappeared into the cottage, continuing the conversation through the open door. "I have two witnesses to my attempted murder, so I'm taking the pig to court."

In the tense silence, Lancelot fidgeted with the kindling beneath the cauldron until David cleared his throat, realizing the light from the campfire concealed their presence.

The man's eyes widened as he glanced up. "Oh, my apologies—I hadn't noticed you there." He straightened his posture, brushing both hands against the coarse fabric of his deep brown tunic. "Here for some ale? I take it you're renting Elias Cohen's place?"

Just as David opened his mouth to answer, Beatrice walked back out of the cottage, now carrying a broom, in addition to the baby. "That's Romeo and Juliet. They're just staying the night."

Elisabeth wiped at her mouth, trying not to laugh, but then her eyes narrowed in confusion, watching Beatrice shove the broom handle into the thatched roof over the door. It stuck out like a flagpole.

Lancelot gestured toward the pergola. "The more the merrier. Have a seat."

David and Elisabeth walked over and sat at the

table, while the sleek cat stretched, leaped down, and strutted away. Meanwhile, Elisabeth couldn't help smiling, watching as the baby boy wheeled the walker closer, steering with his tippy-toes.

Seating himself on a stool, Lancelot's crooked smile hinted at a playful charm beneath his rugged exterior. "I take it you're the witnesses to the attempted murder?"

With an amused snort, David nodded.

"I'm Beatrice's husband, Lance. Where're—?"

"He is NOT my husband," Beatrice yelled from inside the cottage.

Lancelot brushed it off with a conspiratorial grin. "Ignore my wife."

Elisabeth stifled a smile, her lips pressing together in amusement as she shared a confused glance with David.

With a frustrated groan, Beatrice returned. "Here, take her a minute." She handed Lance the baby in her arms and dashed back into the cottage.

Lancelot reached over and lifted the now fussing boy from the wooden walker, cradling him in his arms alongside the little girl. As he stood tall, holding a baby in each arm, he pivoted from side to side, showcasing the twins with a satisfied smile. "Which one do you think looks like me? Jemra?" His eyes twinkled with affection. "Or Hannibal?"

David's posture perked up. "Hannibal?"

Lancelot drew in a deep breath and nodded. "Great name, isn't it?"

Beatrice suddenly reappeared, the cups hitting the table with surprising force as she glared at Lance. "His name is Joseph, not Hannibal, and you know it." With a swift motion, she snatched baby Joseph from his arms. "Now, pay up for your ale." Her demeanor softened slightly as she turned to David and Elisabeth, a forced smile gracing her lips. "No charge for yours."

"Thanks." Elisabeth pulled at her collar and reached for one of the cups as David did the same. She stared down at the dark, murky liquid before pretending to take a sip.

Lancelot chuckled softly, a hint of amusement dancing in his eyes as he placed a coin into Beatrice's waiting palm. Settling back into his seat, he balanced baby Jemra on one knee, shooting a playful smirk at David. "Can you believe my dear wife charges me for ale and a bed?" he teased, his tone light but carrying a faint undertone of some past grievance.

"I am not your wife," Beatrice snapped. With Joseph nestled on her hip, she couldn't hide the pain that lingered beneath her façade. "*We* never exchanged vows."

Lancelot's smirk softened into a gentle smile; his tone soothing as he reached out to calm the storm brewing in Beatrice's eyes. "My dear..." His voice carried a tender reassurance. "Clearly, we did *more* than exchange vows."

Elisabeth's head jerked back, and despite the gravity of the situation, she pinched her lips together to keep from laughing out loud as she caught David's gaze, sharing a silent moment of disbelief.

Beatrice's cheeks flamed red, a mixture of embarrassment and anger flashing across her face as she stomped away with Joseph. In a sudden turn, she pivoted back toward Lancelot, gathering baby Jemra into her arms as well.

As Beatrice left with the babies, Elisabeth's posture perked up, sensing a story here waiting to be unveiled.

"So, where were we?" Lance joked, clearly aiming for humor. "Ah, yes, the weather. Always riveting, isn't it?"

Though he tried, Elisabeth noted a hint of distraction in Lancelot's tone. Nonetheless, he engaged with them, exchanging banter and maintaining his gentlemanly poise.

"Your ale stick is finally out," a cheerful male voice called out from the road.

"Stefan!" Beatrice smiled as a short, chubby man with brown hair shuffled into the yard. He looked about forty, wore a green tunic that was too tight around the belly, and a hat with a feather in it. "I'll be with you shortly."

"No rush, Beatrice." Stefan pulled up a stool and sat at the table. "Take your time."

Lancelot rose from his seat, a gentle smile lighting up his features as he placed a reassuring hand on the older man's shoulder. "I'll be back shortly."

As he made his way into the cottage, Elisabeth caught the soft exchange with Beatrice. "I'll put Jemra and Hannibal-Joe to bed." His voice carried a tenderness that resonated in the quiet space.

Stefan glanced over his shoulder, toward the road. "We were beginning to think there was no brew today. I kept checking for the ale stick, but—" His gaze finally settled on David and Elisabeth, and his reaction was immediate. "Oh!" Surprise etched across his features, followed by a furrowed brow. "You folks must be renting Elias' place while he's off on his pilgrimage."

The gap between his front teeth whistled when he spoke.

David responded with a polite smile and a brief shake of his head. "No, we're just passing through."

"Where are you heading? Oudenaarde?"

"We're on our way to Ghent," Elisabeth added—but immediately regretted.

They needed to remain inconspicuous.

Forgettable.

She looked down, forcing herself to taste the dark ale, its tart, smoky flavor lingering on her tongue.

Beatrice set a cup in front of Stefan. "That's Romeo and Juliet."

When David wiped at his mouth, trying not to laugh, Elisabeth cleared her throat and glanced away.

"They saved my life."

Stefan's eyes bulged as he placed a coin on the table. "What happened?"

"Attempted murder by Henry Gagneux's *pig* is what happened," Beatrice said with a high-pitched voice while slipping the coin into her belt pouch. "I was collecting herbs when Henry's ill-tempered, nasty pig appeared out of nowhere and tried to kill me. Romeo saved my life."

Stefan looked her up and down. "You weren't hurt, were you?"

"No, thank goodness, but what if it hurt or killed Joseph or Jemra? We need Matthias to judge the trial for attempted murder before it really *does* kill someone." Beatrice let out a heavy sigh. "Where's Marc?"

"Wrapping bundles of thatch for Dagmar's roof. It needs repairing."

Soon, other villagers joined the growing crowd arriving to purchase Beatrice's ale. Amongst them was a man with a wooden leg, his movements uneven as he made his way toward the gathering with a distinct thud accompanying each step. Following close behind was a woman with a hunched back, her gnarled hands clasped together as she greeted her fellow villagers with a smile.

The crowd shifted to accommodate more, voices rising with the flow of gossip. Amidst the bustling chatter, Lancelot reappeared, his presence immediately drawing attention. He moved through the gathering with an easy grace, effortlessly engaging each villager. With welcoming nods, warm smiles, and genuine interest in their conversations, he charmed the crowd, his charisma evident in the way he navigated the lively atmosphere.

As Elisabeth stifled a yawn, finishing the last drop from her cup, she thought she saw a monk in brown robes drinking with the villagers. His face was weathered by time and framed with silvered hair, his hazel eyes holding a quiet wisdom. After navigating the subterranean world, fatigue weighed heavily, leaving Elisabeth uncertain whether or not he was real. She lightly slapped her cheeks, trying to stay awake.

David quirked an eyebrow and leaned closer, his gaze solely on her.

"Can you believe I actually drank it all?" she whispered, showing him the empty cup. "It was filling, and I was hungry."

With a gentle smile, David took the tumbler from Elisabeth and set it down on the rustic table. Then he clasped her hand, leading them away from the crowd and toward the flickering campfire.

They settled on a weathered log, smoothed by years of use. The large cauldron hung over the embers, its contents simmering and fragrant. "You look tired." He wrapped his arm around her shoulders. "It's quieter here."

"I'm fine." With a yawn, she rested her head against him.

****

Awakened by a soft touch, Elisabeth's eyes fluttered open. She stretched; her movements reminiscent of a cat stirring from sleep. David offered a steadying hand, helping her to stand. Beatrice, taking the lead, guided the pair toward the cottage. Along the way, they exchanged waves and nods with the villagers, wishing them each goodnight.

Beatrice reached up and removed the broomstick from its perch above the door. Spotting the monk, she called out to him. "Brother Matthias, everyone's talking about the pig's trial. You *will* preside over it, won't you?"

Brother Matthias turned toward her; his face serene yet attentive. "I have been called to the abbey for reflection and prayer. I will return in two weeks' time—"

"Two weeks!"

The man smiled gently. "Yes, Beatrice. I will return in two weeks' time and judge the trial then."

"My witnesses are leaving *tomorrow*." She let out a heavy sigh. "They won't be here in two weeks."

Elisabeth smoothed down her dress, feeling awkward. She wanted to get to Ghent, not stick around a little village for a ridiculous pig trial.

"Beatrice is right," David added firmly. "We really must get to Ghent without delay."

"I understand," Brother Matthias said with a nod. "I will carefully consider everything I've heard tonight in their absence."

"Thank you, Brother." Beatrice forced a smile. "But I wish you didn't have to go." She slowly shook her head and turned away, leaving Brother Matthias to contemplate her words.

With an apologetic glance at the monk, Elisabeth followed Beatrice inside, trudging over the earthen floor, her yawn betraying exhaustion. She surveyed the room, desperate for a place to lay her head.

A low-hanging ceiling crowned the entryway, with a quaint loft nestled above. In the center of the cottage was a hearth. Like the Flamel residence, the smoke escaped through a hole in the roof. Yet, this hearth differed—a brick enclosure cradled the flames. Safety came first here, in a home where young children played. Above the idle hearth, a black cooking pot swung gently; its weight supported by a long chain attached to the sturdy rafters.

On Elisabeth's left, a tall, narrow oak barrel stood, possibly a churn for butter. Nearby, a broom, its bristles frayed from a thousand sweeps, leaned against the wall. Hooks held a hat, a cloak, and an apron—symbols of daily life and practicality. Further in, a dining table with two benches promised shared meals and stories yet to unfold. Claiming the back wall, the kitchen area featured a long worktable beneath a shuttered window, while shelves, baskets, and small tables cradled dishes, produce, and the like, all creating a peaceful domestic scene.

On her right was a wooden box with the swaddled, sleeping twins, and a ladder leading up to the loft. Finally, tucked in a corner, Elisabeth spotted the one and only bed. Her eyes narrowed in confusion, staring at the long wooden board running down the center with blankets on either side.

Beatrice pulled the board off and slid it under the bed. She then handed David a worn woolen blanket from a large basket.

Elisabeth absentmindedly scratched her cheek while yawning again, waiting as everyone piled atop the lumpy mattress. Clearly, private guest rooms were unheard of. With a dejected sigh, she slipped off her shoes and joined them. Beatrice and Lance claimed opposite ends, forcing David and Elisabeth into the middle, under the itchy blanket. The straw and hay beneath them rustled loudly as they shifted, seeking comfort in the shared space.

Eventually, everyone settled.

Tucked in between Beatrice and David, Elisabeth exhaled, shut her eyes, and sank contentedly into the lumpy mattress—and then there was a tap at the door.

Elisabeth's eyes shot open.

The straw and hay crinkled loudly again as Lancelot crawled back out to answer it.

Stefan's head poked in. "Room for one more?"

With a heavy sigh, Lance revealed his frustration, momentarily breaking through his composed demeanor.

"Another fight with Marc?" Beatrice whispered in a soothing tone.

His shoulders drooped. "Yes."

"Well, there's always room for one more," she said. "Just be quiet so you don't wake the babies."

"You wake them, you take them," Lancelot countered, his words tinged with a hint of playful exasperation.

Stefan nodded in agreement.

After Lance gave a theatrical wave of his arm to enter the cottage, Stefan placed a coin on the table. Then, to make room in the bed, Beatrice scooted closer to the edge, Elisabeth scooted closer to Beatrice, and David scooted closer to Elisabeth.

Stefan eyed the edge but Lance shook his head. "My spot."

Stefan nodded and climbed in next to David, making enough room for Lancelot.

When all the crinkling and moving finally stopped, Elisabeth closed her eyes. Before she drifted off to sleep, she couldn't help smirking at the situation. Suddenly, the childhood nursery rhyme made sense to her.

There were five in the bed and the little one said, "roll over, roll over."

Chapter Four

"Cor meum." It was barely a whisper.

Elisabeth half-opened her eyes. A sleepy grin spread across her face while gazing at David.

With a slight head movement, he gestured toward the door.

Elisabeth's breath hitched and she raised her shoulders enough to look over at Stefan and Lance. They slept on their sides, facing away from each other, with the former softly snoring. She then glanced over her shoulder. Beatrice was sound asleep too.

"Now?" Elisabeth mouthed the word.

David nodded.

Her muscles tightened in readiness and she signaled for him to go first.

David pushed the scratchy blanket aside and crawled out of the crowded bed, ever-so-slowly, cringing each time the straw crinkled.

In silence, Elisabeth followed.

As they grabbed their shoes and tiptoed toward the door, a floorboard creaked beneath David's feet.

Elisabeth froze. Then, holding her breath, she turned her head, watching to see if anyone heard.

One of the babies stirred, but then settled.

David opened the door, just wide enough for them to slip through, trying to stop sunshine from spilling into the dark cottage.

Once outside, Elisabeth exhaled as they put their shoes on. Lacing hers up seemed to take an eternity, her fingers fumbling over the stubborn laces. Each twist and pull extended the process, turning a simple task into a drawn-out affair. A rooster crowed, as if mocking her efforts. Finally, Elisabeth bit down on a smile and grabbed David's hand, sprinting with him across the tiny yard as the rooster crowed again. "Oh, my gosh." She let out a quiet laugh. "I thought for sure—"

When the cottage door creaked open once more, both David and Elisabeth froze mid-stride, then turned, their eyes widening in surprise at the sight of Lancelot stepping outside with one of the babies cradled in his arms.

David's shoulders slumped in guilt, and Elisabeth couldn't help but release a heavy sigh of apology. "Sorry. We tried *so* hard not to wake any of you," she said, her voice tinged with regret.

Lancelot, however, shook his head, and with a reassuring smile, gently closed the door behind him. "No apology necessary." He adjusted the baby's linen nightshirt while approaching them in wooden shoes. "Hannibal-Joe is always up early, so I thought I'd show you how to get to Ghent."

"I'm afraid Beatrice will be disappointed." David hesitated, clearly bearing the weight of Beatrice's expectations, "but we haven't time to stay as witnesses to—"

"To the attempted murder?" Lancelot chuckled—his amusement evident. With a playful lift, he hoisted the baby over his head and onto his shoulders, eliciting a delighted giggle. "No sense delaying your journey." Taking hold of the baby's chubby hands, Lancelot led the way. "Besides, last night half of Lindenhart heard what happened, so that should count for something."

"That's true." Elisabeth plucked a blue daisy-like flower from the side of the road. Pausing, she savored the scent of herbs wafting from a nearby cottage. As they strolled through the village, a gentle breeze stirred the grass around them. Near the bridge, the sound of water trickling over stones reached her ears, accompanied by the sight of a bird frolicking in the stream.

David glanced up at the baby. "So, is Hannibal-Joe named after—?"

"Hannibal Barca," Lancelot confirmed with a proud smile, his eyes shining with admiration. "The greatest general and tactical genius in history. Led his war elephants over the Alps, defying all odds."

David nodded as they crossed the bridge, a wide grin spreading across his face. "Hannibal. Excellent name."

Elisabeth shot him an incredulous look.

Really?

Hannibal?

"You're familiar with Hannibal." David chuckled and raised an eyebrow. "And here I thought you were just a humble brewer."

Lance grinned. "Well, truth be told, I'm more of a carpenter by trade. But I have my moments of greatness, you know."

"A carpenter with the spirit of Hannibal Barca." David smirked. "I like that."

"I always wanted my first-born son to be named Hannibal." Lancelot's voice was tinged with a hint of wistfulness. He then swallowed hard, the lump in his throat unmistakable, before diverting his gaze to the stream below. "But Beatrice likes the name Joseph, so…" Suddenly engrossed with a leaf drifting along the sun-dappled surface of the water, he watched as it disappeared under the bridge. When he glanced back at David, there was a flicker of something in his eyes, a shadow of unspoken emotion. "Have you been to Ghent before?"

"Never."

As they strolled down the dirt road, Lancelot's easy, unhurried pace matched his relaxed demeanor. "Where're you heading? I know the city well."

David's brow wrinkled. "I'm to look for the dragon—"

"Dragon?" With a bark of laughter, Elisabeth extended her arm through the cascading branches of the majestic willow. "*What* dragon?"

"The one atop the belfry," Lancelot explained as they continued their walk along the dirt road covered with wooden planks. He glanced up at Hannibal-Joe, perched on his shoulders, and grinned mischievously, prompting giggles from his son.

David looked at Elisabeth and nodded. "The old man said there's a huge dragon perched atop the bell tower."

"Wait." Elisabeth's eyes narrowed as she plucked petals off the flower. "You don't seriously believe—"

"It's true," Lancelot interrupted, his voice rich with conviction. "Legend says it was captured by a Viking king in 1111 and later given to an emperor in Constantinople. The dragon somehow made its way to Ghent about a decade ago."

Elisabeth's head flinched back. "Whaaat…?"

Lance raised an eyebrow, feigning astonishment. "You've *really* not heard about the dragon that guards Ghent?" His words hung in the air, tantalizing and mysterious.

She tossed the stem away, captivated. "No," she admitted, her mind racing.

David, adjusting the rope sling on his hip, chimed in. "To be fair, the only dragons I know of are the ones that guarded the golden fleece and the Hydra that Hercules killed."

"Ah," Lance said, "but surely you've heard of *St. George's* dragon?" His gaze swept over them, inviting both into a world where myth and reality intertwined.

David shook his head. "Afraid not."

"Me neither," Elisabeth blurted out. "Why? What happened?"

Lancelot stepped back, extending Hannibal-Joe's little arms. "When my grandfather was a boy, St. George became the patron saint of England after slaying a dragon."

"Go on," Elisabeth urged, her voice brimming with wonder.

"In the village of Silene, an enormous dragon terrorized the inhabitants." Lance's tone deepened. "It demanded offerings—their finest livestock, their meager savings. But the dragon hungered for more. Instead of gold and livestock, it craved a *human* life."

Elisabeth leaned in, her eyes wide.

Lancelot's gaze held hers. "Year after year, the townsfolk reluctantly offered one of their own—a somber lottery to appease the insatiable dragon."

Elisabeth nudged David, her laughter mingling with awe. "You sure we should go to Ghent?"

He winked in response. "You've nothing to fear. Ghent's dragon is friendly."

Lancelot's bemused smile widened. "Indeed." His eyes sparkled as he spun his tale, and the air around him seemed to pulse with ancient magic. The dragon, once relegated to myth and legend, now danced on the edge of reality. "Listen closely," he urged, drawing them into his narrative. "One day, the tribute demanded by the dragon was none other than their beloved princess."

Elisabeth stepped closer, her interest sparked.

"As the townsfolk wept over their princess' fate, a brave knight, St. George, heard about the town's plight. On the evening before she was to be sacrificed, St. George rode to Dragon Hill to face the beast. The fighting was fierce, the clash of metal against scale echoing through the valley. But St. George's determination never wavered. With every strike of his blade, he drew closer to victory. And then, amidst the chaos, his sword found its mark, piercing the dragon's scales and reaching its beating heart. With a final, decisive thrust, he vanquished the beast, its mighty form crumbling to the ground. In the end, St. George's bravery not only saved the princess, but bestowed hope upon the entire town, a beacon of courage in their darkest hour."

Elisabeth flashed David a cheeky grin. "Hey, Romeo, notice *his* story has a happy ending?"

He snorted in amusement, but then his shoulders pushed back as he addressed Lancelot. "So, how big is the *Ghent* dragon? What's it look like?"

Lance pulled in a deep breath. "I'd say about twelve feet long. It has copper scales that shine in the sun."

Elisabeth, caught between skepticism and wonder, did a double take. They weren't seriously discussing a dragon.

Were they?

She pulled at her ear, lost in her own thoughts as David and Lancelot continued ahead.

Lancelot.

Just like *Sir* Lancelot in the tales of King Arthur's Court, The Knights of the Round Table, Merlin…

Arthurian legends definitely had dragons. In fact, there were countless tales of brave knights who slayed fire-breathing dragons in the medieval days. Well, here she was—smack dab in the medieval days. Elisabeth's breath hitched, realizing even David knew about dragons. How old were the stories? At least since Ancient Roman days, probably even older. There were dragons in Asian folklore too.

Where'd all the legends come from?

Her heart raced, knowing Pompeii was once nothing but a legend. In the 1700s, men beginning work on a summer palace for the King of Naples rediscovered the forgotten city buried twenty feet beneath them. Until then, it had been nothing but a myth. Like Atlantis.

"There is a measure of truth in all legends and stories. That is why they resonate with us and why we love them so," Balinus had said to her.

Elisabeth's eyes widened.

A dragon in Ghent? For real?

There must be a—

"Well, Hannibal's at the gate," Lancelot said, his tone light, drawing Elisabeth's attention back to the present with a gentle nudge of humor.

David confined his laughter to a snort, unable to contain his amusement. "Something tells me you've used that line before."

Lancelot's smile remained genuine, his sharp cheekbones becoming more pronounced as he grinned. "Never," he insisted with a twinkle in his eye.

As Elisabeth squinted in confusion at Lancelot's joke, they walked beyond the village's protective wall of sharpened logs. He stopped and gestured ahead with one hand, the other holding onto Hannibal-Joe, still perched on his shoulders. "All right, listen. I know a short-cut to Ghent. It's off the main road, but will cut some time off your journey."

David's posture perked up.

"You're going to follow this road around the lake until you come to a crossroad." Lancelot pointed in the direction they needed to go, guiding their gaze to the path ahead.

David and Elisabeth both followed his gesture, absorbing his instructions with interest.

"Then, you're going to make a right and then a left. Stay on that trail and you'll eventually reach the Scheldt," Lancelot explained, his finger tracing the imaginary path in the air.

"The Scheldt, is that a river?" David asked.

Lancelot nodded. "You can't miss it. Follow the river north and it'll take you all the way to Ghent. You'll have no problem finding the belfry once you arrive. Just look for the tallest tower."

"With the dragon on top," Elisabeth whispered, mostly to herself.

"Right," Lance said with another nod. His breath then hitched. "Oh—" He reached into his belt pouch and handed David a small, fabric-wrapped bundle. "Beatrice prepared some food for you in the night."

"Really?" Elisabeth pressed fingers to her smiling lips. "That was so thoughtful." Heat rushed to her cheeks and she stole a glance at David. Perhaps they *should* have stayed a bit longer to help her out as witnesses instead of sneaking away.

David cleared his throat and stepped forward, accepting the food, and offered Lancelot a firm handshake. "Thanks for everything."

"Anytime, Romeo. Anytime." He smiled at Elisabeth. "It was good to meet both of you."

A genuine grin formed on her face. "You too."

"Safe travels."

David quirked an eyebrow and extended his elbow to Elisabeth. "Shall we, *Juliet*?"

She giggled while slipping her arm through his. "Absolutely, Romeo."

Lancelot's eyes sparkled with amusement as he watched the pair. "Maintain a steady pace and you'll arrive by *nones*."

"Understood," David replied, glancing back. "My thanks, once more."

With a final nod, they parted ways, leaving behind the charming Lancelot and the warmth of his companionship.

As they walked away, a twinge of sadness tugged at Elisabeth's heart, knowing that they were leaving behind someone whose presence had brightened their journey.

Chapter Five

Lancelot's route to Ghent from the village was more trail than road. Elisabeth maneuvered around tree roots criss-crossing the path and then paused to take a deep breath, enjoying the smell of damp earth and pine needles. The sun-dappled leaves created dancing shadows on the forest floor, which seemed to keep time with the birdsong. She smiled, watching two playful squirrels scamper up the trunk of an ancient tree, before disappearing into the tall canopy.

"You've been quiet since we left," David said, interrupting her thoughts when they came upon a creek.

A simple wooden board created a crude bridge. "Have I?" Elisabeth tilted her head to the side. "I'm just thinking." Arms outstretched for balance, she gingerly crossed and then turned, waiting for David to follow.

He stepped onto the narrow plank, spanning the width of the creek, and then let out a nervous laugh when the weathered wood creaked underfoot and his balance teetered. "How'd you make this look so easy?"

Elisabeth covered her mouth, trying not to giggle, watching David's outstretched arms sway as he took one measured stride at a time, eventually reaching solid ground again.

"You did it," she said, playfully falling against him.

He wrapped his arms around her and raised an

eyebrow. "Now, what occupies your thoughts, *cor meum*?"

"Is…?" Elisabeth's eyes narrowed. "Is there *seriously* a dragon in Ghent?"

"According to Lancelot and the old man there is." He flashed a bemused grin and grabbed her hand, strolling along the forest path next to the creek. The water ran noisily around moss-covered rocks and boulders. "Have you never wanted to be an Argonaut?"

"I don't even know what that is."

"*Who* that is." He ducked under a waist-high fallen tree blocking the path and then turned. "You actually do. The Argonauts—"

Suddenly, Elisabeth's dress snagged on a rough branch as she followed. "Wait—" While untangling it, her stomach growled.

Loudly.

"Did you hear that?" The wind rustled through the leaves and David looked toward the clear blue sky, biting his lips to hide a smile. "Was that thunder?"

"Very funny," she replied with a shy grin, emerging on the other side of the fallen tree, rubbing her belly. "I'm starving."

When David wrapped his hands around Elisabeth's waist, pulling her close, her heart raced. She then burst into laugher as he suddenly lifted her onto the tree trunk.

Legs dangling over the side, she glanced down at her puddling skirts and swinging feet, waiting while David clambered onto the log, finding his balance as he settled next to her. He reached into his belt pouch and handed over the provisions Beatrice had prepared.

Elisabeth unwrapped the fabric and arranged the

food between them, turning the fallen tree into a makeshift picnic table.

David licked his lips and leaned in. "This looks good."

Elisabeth eyed a wedge of cheese, something that looked like beef jerky, and a generous scoop of walnuts. "So, *who* are the Argonauts?" she asked, popping a handful of nuts into her mouth.

"Well…" David unsheathed his dagger and sliced the cheese in half. "In the ancient city of Iolcus lived a young man named Jason."

"Thanks," she said, taking the cheese he offered.

"King Pelias was Jason's uncle—a usurper who came to power by seizing the throne from Jason's father. One day, an old woman approached Jason by the river. 'Help me cross,' David said in a high-pitched croaking voice, trying to sound like an old lady. 'Help me cross.'"

Elisabeth giggled while biting into the cheese.

David ripped a piece of jerky with his teeth before continuing. "Jason obliged and carried the old woman across the river, but after making it to the opposite bank, she revealed her true self—Juno."

Elisabeth's head tilted to the side. "Juno?"

"Queen of the gods."

Her brow wrinkled, thinking back to when they were at Marmore Falls with Balinus and Cato, before she'd been bitten by the viper asp. "Isn't Juno the one who turned Nera into a river because she fell in love with Velino, the shepherd?"

"That's her."

A slow smile spread across Elisabeth's face. "So, Juno's kind of a vindictive *you-know-what*."

"Definitely." David's eyes twinkled with mischief. "Juno told Jason to seek the Golden Fleece. If successful, he'd be restored to his rightful place on the throne."

"I wouldn't trust her if I was him," Elisabeth mumbled, helping herself to a piece of jerky.

David let out a small laugh. "Jason assembled a band of heroes to accompany him on his journey to find the Golden Fleece. They included Hercules—"

Elisabeth's posture perked up. "Hercules?"

He nodded. "Atalanta, The Dioscuri Twins, and Orpheus."

Her head jerked back. "*Our* Orpheus?"

David reached out, his hand cradling Elisabeth's cheek. "Yes, *our* Orpheus." As his thumb brushed against the curve of her jaw, his voice lowered. "These events took place *before* Orpheus met Eurydice."

Elisabeth melted into his touch, a silly grin on her face. "I think I've heard parts of this before, but don't remember who told me."

In that quiet moment, David leaned in. Elisabeth's eyes fluttered shut as his lips met hers.

"Because these heroes set sail on the Argo," David whispered between tender kisses, "they became known as the Argonauts." He pulled away slightly, only to return, each kiss soft and unhurried.

His fingers lingered on her waist and she pulled away, just a fraction, smiling as her gaze traced the curve of his lips.

"Under the leadership of Jason, they embarked on a legendary journey to Colchis to reclaim the Golden Fleece," he murmured before stealing another lingering kiss.

And then another.

The sudden rustle of leaves, flutter of wings, and distant trill, sent Elisabeth a gentle reminder of reality. She pulled back, but felt the connection with David remain—an invisible string stretching between them.

The red string.

David and Cato once told her an old Asian legend of how the gods tied an invisible red string to connect two people who are destined to be together. Place, circumstance, even *time* do not matter. This red string can stretch and tangle, but can never be broken.

She glanced down at the Hercules love knot on her wrist and her eyes suddenly prickled with tears, remembering the moment David gave it to her—before they'd both been sold as slaves.

"Give me your arm, cor meum."

Her limbs had felt too heavy to lift, but she'd placed her hand into his waiting palm, blinking back tears at the sight of the bracelet he'd made from her red hair ribbon and a piece of rope from his sling. Entangled together, they formed a beautiful ornamental knot.

"This is a Hercules Love Knot," he'd whispered into her ear while tying the bracelet around her wrist. *"It is the strongest knot you can tie and is a symbol of..."* He'd then looked at her with a quivering smile. *"Of the unbreakable bond you and I share."*

Her own voice had choked with tears. *"Aquarius..."* Who'd have thought her feminine hair ribbon, intertwined with rope from his primitive sling, could form something so beautiful and complementary to one another. *"They're perfect together."*

"We should get going, *cor meum*," David said,

breaking the daydream. Grabbing the remainder of the walnuts, he popped them into his mouth. "We've yet to make it to Ghent."

Elisabeth nodded, but then her brow furrowed. "Wait! Finish your story. Where's the dragon come in?"

"Why, it guarded the Golden Fleece, of course." He sheathed the dagger and hopped down from his seat on the toppled tree.

"Ah, of course."

David stepped in front of Elisabeth and stashed Beatrice's napkin into his leather belt pouch. "Just give me a moment to gather my belongings."

As she glanced over to see what he'd forgotten, David playfully scooped Elisabeth over his shoulder, causing her to squeal with laughter.

"All right, I have everything I need." He marched off as she broke into a fit of giggles while hanging half-upside down.

****

When David and Elisabeth stepped out from the protective canopy the forest had provided, the air itself changed, from cool shadows to warm sunlight. Here, the trail ended and joined with the main road, running alongside the river. Hand-in-hand, they traveled through wide-open countryside—the walls of Ghent visible in the distance.

Elisabeth's muscles tensed and she swatted at flies after they reached a bustling shanty town outside the city gates. Under the hot afternoon sun, the air smelled of dust and body odor. A dog barked and tarp roofs fluttered in the breeze. Her eyes widened, watching a shabbily dressed woman dump a bucket of dirty water out the door of a haphazardly constructed shack. The main road was filled with peasants and travelers alike, merchants and men on horseback, while a group of guards lingered near the city wall, talking amongst one another.

Elisabeth glanced down a narrow alley. Three children, faces smudged with dirt, played barefoot, their laughter echoing off thin walls. Huddled in a nearby doorway, a woman nursed a baby. When they walked by an old beggar with an outstretched hand, Elisabeth swallowed a lump in her throat. Neither she nor David had food, coins, or even the costly nutmegs she had once traded. Right now, everything rested on a promised apprenticeship with a bookmaker in Ghent.

When they reached the sentry at the gate, Elisabeth smoothed down her dress as David straightened his spine, but the guard paid them no attention. Under foot, cobblestone replaced the dirt road, and the city was a hive of activity.

Narrow streets wound through tightly packed half-timbered buildings, their upper floors often jutting out over the roads. Colorful signs swung above doorways, indicating workshops, taverns, and inns. The merchants, craftsmen, and laborers went about their business, their voices blending with the clatter of wooden carts and the occasional neighing of horses.

A slow smile spread across David's face as they walked alongside the picturesque river running through the city, passing barges that carried goods to and from far-away ports.

Merchants haggled on the docks and boats navigated the river. In the distance, the stone belfry rose like a sentinel above its square base. High atop it, metal glinted in the sunshine.

David's stance stiffened and his attention shifted to Elisabeth. "I believe we may find Ghent *quite* to our liking."

She swallowed and nodded while glancing up at the heavens. "Yeah, so far it's really nice."

He rubbed his chin, looking up at the sky as well. "What's wrong?"

"Nothing." Elisabeth fiddled with her bracelet, her gaze scanning the rooftops. Along with the belfry, the spires of two nearby cathedrals dominated the skyline, and other buildings featured stepped gables and carved finials. Dormer windows punctuated the roofs, which were mostly terracotta or straw. "Who are we looking for again?"

"Hendrik Lanchal." David's forehead wrinkled while observing Elisabeth. "Nicolas told me to find the bookshop with the swan over the door. It should be just beyond the belfry." He glanced up at the sky once more. "What are you searching for?"

"I don't see the dragon on the belfry." She then gasped and looked at David. "Do you think it sometimes flies to other rooftops?"

His head flinched back slightly. *"What?"*

Elisabeth's breath hitched. "Oh my gosh…" She licked her lips as her tummy fluttered. "Can you imagine if we actually get to see it *flying?*"

David's eyes widened. "The dragon?"

Elisabeth bit her fingernails. "As long as it doesn't have wings like a *bat*," she added as an afterthought.

"Cor meum…" David, stifling a laugh, pressed a fist against his lips. "By the gods, you're adorable." He shook his head in disbelief. "But let me clarify: there

really is a dragon in Ghent, but it's not *real*."

Elisabeth stopped walking as her brow furrowed in confusion. "What?"

He pointed up at the belfry. "Do you not see it up there? Look at the very top. On the pole. The sunlight is glistening off the copper right now."

She tilted her head to the side and squinted, trying to get a better look. Then, her mouth fell open, eying the metal dragon perched atop a spike—like an enormous weather-vane. Elisabeth's shoulders slumped. "That's it?"

David leaned in, barely containing his amusement. "Don't tell me you were *really* expecting—"

"Yes!" She kicked at the ground while laughter bubbled up. "I thought…" Heat surged to her cheeks. Unable to restrain it any longer, Elisabeth buried her face in both hands and burst into giggles. "Oh my gosh," she managed between wheezy breaths, "I'm so embarrassed." Her gaze lifted to David, eyes squinting. "You guys both said it was *real*," she playfully reminded him before letting out another peal of laughter.

With a wide grin, David pulled her into a side hug. "There seems to have been a misunderstanding."

She fell against him as they walked, forcing her lips into a pout. "I was all psyched up to see it too. I half-convinced myself I'd traveled back in time far enough to see one."

"Only *half* convinced yourself?" David chuckled as they strolled toward the belfry. "Why don't you help me find the shop with the swan over the door instead. It's around here somewhere." He gave her a playful nudge. "But it's not actually a *living* swan."

She exchanged a knowing smile with him. "I'm never going to live this down, am I?"

David's wink held a promise. "Never."

The sun cast a warm golden hue over the cobbled road as David and Elisabeth searched for Hendrik Lanchal's bookshop. The air was thick with the scent of wood smoke and freshly baked bread. They walked hand in hand, passing ground-level shops that spilled out onto the street. Windows dotted the upper floors, some with lead glass catching the light, others with wooden shutters thrown wide open.

A well-dressed portly man rushed past them; a leather satchel clutched in sausage-like fingers. Huddled against a nearby wall was a thin beggar, his bony hands extended, as if in prayer. Ahead, two young boys broke into a sprint, their wooden shoes clomping rhythmically against the cobblestone. Their race ended abruptly when one crashed into a woman stepping out of a shop.

Elisabeth tilted her head to the side, watching the boys' shoulders hunch as they were scolded rather harshly. The middle-aged woman, draped in silk, adjusted blonde hair peeking out from beneath her delicate veil and then stormed off in a huff.

Yet the boys remained undeterred. They exchanged glances, rolled their eyes, and shrugged off the reprimand.

Elisabeth's lips pressed together, suppressing a laugh, as they darted down a side alley.

David snorted in amusement. "You saw that too?"

She nodded.

"Reminds me of Cato and I as children when we angered Domina."

As they headed toward the belfry, Elisabeth noticed the buildings seemed to lean into one another. Heavy oak beams crisscrossed whitewashed plaster, creating a patchwork of squares and rectangles.

With a chuckle, David pointed slightly ahead. "I've discovered the house I'll purchase for us one day, love. When I finish my apprenticeship and become a master."

"Where?" She bounced on tippy toes, looking where he pointed.

Painted directly on the plaster of the building was a colorful scene of a knight battling a winged dragon.

Elisabeth responded with a good-natured poke. "Very funny."

"Although," David whispered, as if sharing a secret, "if I do become a master, I will inherit the old man's shop in Paris and we can reside above it there." He shook his head in disbelief and opened his mouth to say more, but no words came out.

Elisabeth tilted her head up. "As long as we're together, I don't care where we are." She playfully puckered her lips, inviting a kiss.

David leaned down, closing the gap between them. His kiss was a swift stolen moment, before the bells tolled the hour; their melody ringing through the streets of Ghent.

"We should continue our search," David said after pulling away.

Elisabeth nodded, fingertips brushing her lips as she tried to hold on to the memory. Suddenly, her eyes widened at the sight of a swan sign above the building to her right. "Aquarius, look!"

The three-story building's wooden façade leaned slightly left, its weathered sign above the door spelling out, "Lanchal & Son, Bookmakers." The upper half displayed traditional half-timbering, with dark brown wood contrasting against white plaster infill, exuding a quaint charm. Completing the picturesque scene, a steeply pitched roof topped with red-brown tiles and dormer windows added to the building's rustic appeal.

As Elisabeth stood on the cobblestone street, the leaded glass window to the right of the doorway was softly illuminated from within. Above, cream-colored shutters adorned each window, while vibrant blooms overflowed from the flower boxes beneath them.

She pointed above the entrance to the carved wooden swan. "That's it, isn't it?"

Painted alabaster white, its feathers seemed to glow. The woodcarver's skill was evident in every detail, from the curve of the beak to the ripples in the plumage. The wings of the swan were outstretched, giving the impression it guarded the knowledge within.

"It must be." David's words hung in the air, tinged with a mix of anticipation and uncertainty. With a nod, he led the way to the entrance.

The heavy oak door was ajar, inviting one inside. Elisabeth noticed a brass handle that seemed polished by countless hands. As she stepped across the threshold, a slow smile graced her lips, and the fragrance of ink, beeswax candles, and aged leather enveloped her senses.

The interior was quite different from Nicolas' shop in Paris. Here, the limestone floor was uneven, worn after years of footsteps. Bookcases, weathered and bowed, formed a dark labyrinth at the back of the shop. Each shelf sagged under the weight of heavy manuscripts and bookmaking supplies.

In the center of the room was a large oak workbench. The surface was covered with ink stains, knife marks, and countless imprints from feather quills. Tools lay scattered about; bone folders, brass clasps, and half-translated sheets.

Against the left wall, a crimson curtain concealed an obvious doorway—the entrance to a backroom or access to the upper floors, perhaps.

Next to the curtain, an artist's table awaited the illuminator's touch, positioned strategically for inspiration and creation. At the front door, two modest work desks sat beneath the window, inviting natural light to brighten the tasks at hand.

David's brows furrowed, a fleeting moment of hesitation crossing his face. Then, with a gentle exhale, he uttered a simple, "Hello?"

From the back of the ancient bookstore, where dust particles danced in the slanting sunlight, a tender voice replied. "Hello." A moment later, an elderly man with a slender frame and a simple earth-toned tunic, shuffled forward, his steps deliberate and measured. Silver-gray hair, thinning at the temples, fell in unruly waves around his face. His hands, gnarled and weathered, cradled a heavy book. The old man smiled, his eyes creasing at the corners as he added, "How can I help you?"

Chapter Six

The heart of the workshop beat with the scent of ink—a mixture of gall nuts and gum Arabic. Elisabeth's memory stirred, recalling the day David demonstrated how it was made. At the time, she was half-convinced he was making a love potion rather than ink.

"Master Lanchal?" David stood taller and squared his shoulders. "I'm David Perrier." The words hung in the air. "Your new apprentice?"

"Ah, yes." The old man's eyes softened, a spark of recognition flickering briefly. "Flamel's nephew. And you must be…?" His gaze shifted to Elisabeth who stood beside David, her knuckles white from clasping her hands together.

"I'm Elisabeth, sir." The room seemed to hold its breath, as if the walls leaned in to catch her words. David's promising future hinged on this apprenticeship—a path to becoming a master bookmaker and (someday) inheriting the Parisian bookshop.

The plan?

Return to Paris once Cato was no longer a threat.

Was that even possible?

They'd eluded Cato's men so far, yet now, standing before Hendrik Lanchal, the stakes soared.

Lanchal put the leather-bound book on the worn worktable, a wry smile playing on his lips. "Running away from an arranged marriage, correct?" His eyes twinkled with mischief. "A daring escape, I presume?"

Elisabeth felt her cheeks flush, wondering how much of the story he'd been told. "Yes, quite."

The old man leaned in. "Your secret is safe with me." His attention then shifted when the crimson curtain swayed, fixing upon a man who emerged from its folds, his ink-stained hands holding a heavy stack of books.

"Grandfather, I—"

"Gerrit," Lanchal interrupted, gesturing toward the newcomers, "meet David Perrier, our new apprentice." His eyes twinkled as he added, "And Elisabeth, David's resourceful bride who'll be helping out around here. This is my grandson, Gerrit Lanchal."

The younger Lanchal blinked, surprised by the sudden introduction, but placed his books on the worktable and extended a slightly trembling hand to David.

Seemingly in his early twenties, Gerrit had a polished appearance, his clothing a testament to his tastes: a knee-length tunic of fine light brown wool cinched at the waist with a leather belt, paired with dyed linen leggings and a sleeveless, bright green surcoat. His tousled chestnut hair framed a furrowed brow, and his pale, unblemished skin and large, shadowed eyes hinted at countless hours spent by candlelight, poring over faded parchment and ink.

As Gerrit leaned forward, his shoulders tense with nervous anticipation, he offered a polite nod to Elisabeth, their gazes briefly locking before he looked away. "Grandfather, if you'll excuse me…" His voice carried a respectful tone, tinged with eagerness to return to his craft.

Lanchal placed a reassuring hand on his shoulder. "Of course, my boy."

For a fleeting moment, a subtle unease passed between Gerrit and the couple, like a hesitant puppy unsure of its place. With a polite nod, he excused himself and retreated to a quiet corner where his tools awaited.

"Your uncle," Master Lanchal said, turning to David again, "is a fine craftsman." He gestured toward the shelves, where heavy books were piled. "You'll carry his legacy just as Gerrit will carry mine."

David cleared his throat. "I hope to honor it, sir."

Lanchal's smile deepened, lines etching his weathered face. "You must be famished. I'll have Theresa prepare you something to eat. Why don't you gather up your things and—" His gaze shifted to the empty space where bags or bundles might have been and then he looked back at David and Elisabeth with a knowing expression. "Ah, you travel light. A rare sight indeed."

David cleared his throat and nodded.

Lanchal pushed the curtain aside, revealing the wall of an oak paneled hallway. "Sometimes," the old man said in a soothing tone, "the weight we carry is not in our hands but in our hearts." He gestured for them to follow. "Come with me."

As they stepped into the dimly lit hallway, the air was thick with the comforting smokiness of wood and the warm, yeasty scent of bread. Elisabeth's eyes widened in surprise as she glanced to her left, where a nondescript door led back onto the bustling street. She hadn't even noticed it while looking at the bookshop's façade from outside. Clearly, it was an entrance to the house that bypassed the bookshop. But it was the rightward turn that intrigued her.

Beyond a flight of stairs heading to the second storey, they entered what Perenelle would have called "the great hall." The space radiated old-world charm. Half-timbered walls were lined with tapestries depicting forgotten battles and mythical creatures, their colors muted by time. Underfoot, the rough-hewn limestone continued.

Elisabeth's gaze was drawn up to the rafters, where oak beams criss-crossed the ceiling. Directly below the vast space was the central hearth. Despite having multiple floors, the heart of the house remained open, allowing smoke to spiral upward from the cooking fire. An iron cauldron hung over the embers from a tripod, simmering as smoke escaped through a vent in the roof.

A sturdy wooden table was pushed against one wall, its surface marked by years of shared meals and late-night conversations. Elisabeth imagined bowls of hearty stew and goblets of ale often graced its worn top. A broom leaned casually against another wall, flanked by shelves holding pots and mixing bowls. On the worktable was a medley of fresh vegetables waiting to be added to the next meal.

The large, rectangular space was lined with benches adorned with brightly colored cushions. The back of the house mirrored the Flamel's simple design, with rooms stacked atop one another. The rear section featured a low ceiling, creating a cozy atmosphere. To the right, a staircase led to an upper doorway, while to the left, a walled-off room occupied the corner. Next to the small room was a sturdy wooden door, its weathered appearance suggesting it was the back entrance to the house.

At that moment, an older woman emerged from the corner room, clutching a bunch of onions. Her apron was dusted with flour, and behind her, shelves lined with jars and sacks of provisions clearly marked the space as a pantry. From where she stood, Elisabeth could see the pantry's shelves were neatly organized, showcasing a variety of ingredients and supplies essential for the household.

"Theresa," Lanchal said, "may I introduce two new members of our household? This is David, my new apprentice, and this young lady is his bride, Elisabeth, who will be helping with various tasks around the house."

"It's a pleasure to meet you both," she said with a smile, her voice carrying the assurance of someone who'd spent years in the heart of this household.

Soft lines etched Theresa's face. She wore a plain linen dress and an apron tied around her waist, while a simple kerchief concealed most of her gray hair. Warm brown eyes lit up with a spark of mischief as she confidently gripped the onions—and then launched them into a surprise juggling act.

Caught completely off guard, Elisabeth and David burst into laughter.

"And this is Theresa, our resident juggler," Lanchal said, his laughter mingling with theirs.

The onions flew in a perfect arc—until one escaped her swift hands and bounced off Lanchal's head, rolling to a stop at David's feet.

Lanchal winced, then chuckled while rubbing the sore spot. Meanwhile, David picked up the wayward onion and playfully bowed as he presented it to Theresa.

The woman dipped her head in a dignified nod, her apron sending a cloud of flour puffing into the air. She gracefully accepted the onion and placed it on the worktable amongst the others.

"Theresa, would you be so kind as to provide David and Elisabeth something to tide them over until supper?"

The woman didn't miss a beat. With a quick turn, she reached for the bread basket and selected two buns. "Here you are, my dears." She handed one to each of them. "A little something to keep your spirits high and your feet light."

"Thank you," they both said, exchanging a brief, appreciative glance with the woman.

Elisabeth's fingers curled around the bun, the heat from the freshly baked bread a small comfort in the whirlwind of the day. She hesitated for a moment, allowing herself to savor the aroma before taking a bite.

"Come, David," Lanchal said with an inviting wave of his hand. "Let us return to the bookshop. There are many things I wish to show you."

David nodded, a mixture of anticipation and respect in his eyes as he followed the old man.

Theresa turned to Elisabeth, her arm sweeping through the air in a grand gesture. "And you, my dear, shall have the honor of my company. Now, let's put those hands to work, shall we? We've got a supper to prepare."

Elisabeth nodded, quickly savoring the last morsel of the bun. She then made her way to the worktable while dabbing away any crumbs from her lips. "Thank you for welcoming us into your home, Madame Lanchal."

Theresa let out a hearty chuckle. "Oh, sweet child," she said, wiping both hands on her apron, "I'm the keeper of this house, not its lady. Call me Theresa."

Elisabeth felt her cheeks flushing, but the woman's laughter was kind, devoid of any sting.

"And how are your cooking skills?" Theresa asked with an encouraging tilt of her head.

Elisabeth cleared her throat, thinking back to her lame attempt at trying to skin a rabbit for Isabeau's stew. "Severely lacking," she confessed. "But I'm eager to learn and hope to improve." Her hands shook ever so slightly, and she clasped them together in an attempt to steady herself, determined not to mess things up for David here.

Theresa's eyes softened, and in a motherly fashion, she reached for a spare apron hanging by the broom, offering it with a smile. "This will protect your lovely dress," she said, helping to tie it in place.

"Thanks." Elisabeth's voice brimmed with appreciation as she smoothed down the apron.

"Well…" Hands on her hips, Theresa surveyed the ingredients before them. "The first rule of cooking is to always keep your wits about you. The second rule"— she paused for dramatic effect—"is to forget the first rule because it's all nonsense anyway."

Elisabeth chuckled, her nerves easing at Theresa's playful demeanor.

"First, we tackle the cabbage." Theresa handed Elisabeth a sharp knife. "It can be a bit tough so watch your fingers."

Elisabeth chopped, and Theresa nodded in approval

before moving on to the herbs. "Now, these herbs *must* be treated with respect. Whisper sweet nothings to them…it helps with the flavor," she advised with a straight face.

Elisabeth raised an eyebrow but then playfully leaned in. "Aren't you the best little herb I ever did see?" she purred, causing Theresa to let out a hearty laugh.

"And the most important part," the woman said, holding up a turnip, "is the turnip juggle. Watch closely." With surprising agility, she tossed the turnip into the air, catching it behind her back. "Your turn." She tossed the turnip to Elisabeth.

Catching it awkwardly, Elisabeth attempted to mimic Theresa's move, only to have the turnip bounce off the table and roll across the floor. They both burst into laughter as the older woman retrieved the runaway vegetable.

"Ah, well." Theresa shrugged. "Perhaps juggling's not for supper tonight. Let's stick to cooking, shall we?"

As Elisabeth looked up, her eyes met those of a woman in the hallway, roughly the same age as her own mother. Chestnut braids were neatly coiled under a delicate linen headscarf, light enough to catch the gentlest breeze. Her gown was tailored snugly around the torso, with buttons adorning the sleeves and a belt cinched at the waist, accentuating a well-proportioned figure. The fabric, a rich blue, complimented the intelligent sparkle of gently-wrinkled eyes.

"Theresa, always the entertainer." With an affectionate chuckle, the woman stepped through the doorway. Her basket was brimming with freshly picked leeks, hearty cabbages, and ripe plums.

Theresa looked up from her task and greeted the woman with a broad smile. "Johanna, you've returned just in time. Elisabeth, this is Johanna Lanchal, the finest illuminator you'll find this side of the Scheldt."

Johanna blushed and waved an ink-stained hand dismissively. "Oh, Theresa, you flatter me too much," she said. "A pleasure to meet you, Elisabeth. I just had the opportunity to make David's acquaintance. Welcome to our home. I trust it will be to your liking."

Elisabeth cleared her throat. "Thank you, Madame Lanchal."

Johanna offered a gentle correction with a smile. "Oh, please, just Johanna will do. I am but the daughter-in-law to Master Lanchal, and Gerrit's mother." Her tone held a note of pride as she mentioned her son.

"Oh!" Elisabeth's eyes widened. "We met Gerrit earlier," she said, realizing the woman before her was not the matriarch of the house, but rather the supportive figure behind the heir.

Acknowledging Elisabeth's understanding with a gentle nod, Johanna then turned her attention to the basket she carried, overflowing with summer produce. She placed it on the worktable. "I shall leave these with you and excuse myself to the bookshop. Manuscripts won't illuminate themselves," she said with a small laugh before withdrawing from the great hall.

As the sound of Johanna's footsteps faded, Theresa leaned closer to Elisabeth. "Both Master Lanchal and Johanna have known the sting of loss," she confided with a whisper. "He lost his dear wife and then his son, who was Johanna's husband. Now, they find a quiet comfort in each other, sharing a bond of grief that words need not express."

Elisabeth's posture stooped. "That's so sad." Her gaze then lingered on the doorway where Johanna had been.

With a subtle shift in her stance, Theresa handed Elisabeth a wooden spoon. "Now, go stir some love into the pot, dear."

With a grin, Elisabeth took the spoon and approached the simmering pot over the fire.

"Stir clockwise," Theresa instructed, "unless you want to reverse time, and trust me, Master Lanchal won't want to relive the onion juggling incident."

With a laugh, Elisabeth stirred the pot clockwise, the rich aroma wafting through the air. After a moment, Theresa nodded toward a ladle. "Now, give it a taste. If you suddenly speak in rhyme, we've added too much thyme."

Elisabeth sampled the stew, her taste buds dancing with the flavors. "It's perfect."

Theresa beamed. "Of course it is. It's seasoned with humor—a spice that never grows stale."

Elisabeth watched as the woman navigated the work space, a domain she clearly ruled with a wooden spoon and a sharp wit.

"You know," Theresa said while walking toward the cooking fire, "they say too many cooks spoil the broth, but they never say anything about too many jesters. Hand me the carrots?"

Elisabeth couldn't help but smile as she passed a bowl of chopped carrots to Theresa. "Is that why the stew tastes so *funny*?"

Theresa chuckled, giving the pot a lively stir.

"Exactly! It's my secret ingredient: a dash of humor and a pinch of mischief. Keeps the spirits high and the bellyaches away—well, most of the time."

As they moved in tandem, seasoning and tasting, the great hall was filled, not just with the aroma of cooking, but also with laughter.

"Well, it's time to tackle the beast," Theresa said with a mischievous sparkle in her eye.

Elisabeth's brows furrowed in confusion. "The beast?"

Theresa gestured toward the hefty oak table placed up against the wall, out of the way. "It's time for its daily dance to the center of the room."

With a shared chuckle, they heaved the table into place, the older woman groaning in mock protest. "You'd think it'd learn to walk on its own by now."

Elisabeth played along, panting in exaggeration. She then widened her eyes in feigned amazement when it was in position. "So, this is the fabled beast."

Theresa nodded. "Indeed. It's a wild creature, known to devour entire feasts in a single night. But fear not—it's easily tamed with linens and cutlery." With a dramatic swoop, Theresa unfurled a tablecloth, sending it sailing through the air. It landed gracefully across the table's back, draping it like a cloak. "First, we disguise our beast," she said with a wink.

Elisabeth couldn't help but smile as she set out the spoons, half-expecting a candelabra to start singing at any moment.

Theresa leaned in, her voice conspiratorial. "Beware, my dear. *That* particular spoon has a secret."

Elisabeth raised an eyebrow. "A secret?"

Theresa leaned even closer; her eyes wide. "It's a

shape-shifting spoon. At night, when the moon is just right, it transforms into a tiny dragon."

Elisabeth let out a belly laugh. "A dragon? Really."

"Oh, yes." Theresa's tone was dead serious. "Legend has it that it once flew out of a nobleman's soup bowl and terrorized the entire kitchen staff. They had to chase it with ladles and rolling pins."

As Elisabeth placed the spoon down, it started to tilt. "Behave," she scolded playfully.

Theresa then brought out a set of wooden cups, each carved with intricate designs. "These," she said with a chuckle, "were once raised high in a toast by a cheerful merchant at a feast here. He crowned himself king and wore it as his crown all night long."

The room echoed with their laughter and the clinking of hearty tableware. By the time they finished, the table was no longer a beast, but a stage set for an evening of joyous conversation, each piece of tableware playing its part. As the final preparations for dinner were underway, benches were dragged to the table and the savory scent of stew wafted through the air, mingling with the aroma of freshly baked bread.

Elisabeth was placing the last of the wooden cups on the table when Master Lanchal entered, a stack of books tucked under his arm. He paused to take in the scene, his eyes lighting up with approval at the sight of the well-laid table. "Ah, lovely as always," he said while setting the books aside.

Gerrit hurried in, his youthful steps a stark contrast to his grandfather's measured pace. With a nervous energy, he rushed to assist Theresa with the heavy pitchers, his movements similar to a nervous puppy bounding into a room. Then, he approached Elisabeth with an awkward yet sincere smile. "You, uh, seem to have a knack for this already." He nodded toward the neatly arranged cups. "And, um, working with David has been rather enjoyable too."

A wide grin spread across Elisabeth's face. "Thank you. That really means a lot."

As Johanna entered with a grace that seemed to calm the room, Elisabeth caught a fleeting glance between her and Theresa, sharing a silent conversation that only years of friendship could produce.

And then, there was David. As he stepped through the threshold, his gaze sought Elisabeth, locking onto hers in a moment brimming with unspoken affection. In response, her heartbeat quickened and a smile unfurled across her face.

Theresa clapped her hands together. "All right, everyone, take your places. The stew won't serve itself, and I daresay our stomachs won't fill on laughter alone—though we'll certainly try."

With that, the family gathered around the table, each person finding their seat as the room filled with the sounds of shifting benches and the anticipation of a hearty meal. Elisabeth took her place next to David, their shoulders brushing lightly. The candles were lit, casting a soft glow over the faces of those present, and for a moment, all the day's drudgeries seemed to melt away.

Master Lanchal, sitting at the head of the table, had a mischievous twinkle in his eye. "Elisabeth, I trust you haven't let Theresa's tall tales scare you off?"

"Not yet, sir. Although she claims the spoons are enchanted and the pots whisper secrets."

The table erupted in laughter as Theresa feigned a

scandalized look. "My dear, those pots have seen more history than any book in Master Lanchal's library!"

Johanna, her hands still marked with the day's work, chimed in. "And what of the knives? Don't they sing as well?"

"Apparently, only when they're happy," Elisabeth said while trying—and failing—to suppress her laughter.

Gerrit cleared his throat and raised his wooden cup. "To enchanted spoons and singing knives—may they always grace our table," he said quickly, his words rushed as his gaze darted around the room.

Master Lanchal nodded in agreement, hoisting his cup high. "And to our new friends, who've already brought much life and joy into our home."

As the laughter dwindled and the gentle thud of wooden cups being placed back on the surface subsided, Elisabeth saw Theresa catch David's eye from across the table. With a hearty laugh and a twinkle in her eye, she addressed the room. "And let's not overlook young David here, who's clearly been distracting the hens in the yard with his dashing looks. Why, I dare say, if he weren't so busy learning the bookmaker's trade, he could give the local troubadours a run for their money."

Everyone burst into laughter once more, with David blushing a shade that matched the wine in their cups. He raised his with a sheepish grin. "I fear my heart is already signed and sealed, much like the books we bind." He cast a fond glance at Elisabeth before taking a drink.

Elisabeth nudged him. "Am I the hen in this situation?" she asked, raising an eyebrow playfully.

The table erupted in laughter again, and asthe family dug into the feast, their conversation weaved between the serious and the silly. Master Lanchal chuckled as he shared a particular request from a customer for a book containing the "*Secretum Secretorum*," a text rumored to hold the wisdom of Aristotle and sought after by many scholars. Gerrit spoke excitedly of his latest concoction of ink, a vibrant hue derived from the crushed petals of the purple iris, which he insisted held the secret to an ink that would last for centuries.

Theresa, not to be outdone, regaled them with the tale of a spoon that refused to stir any stew unless it was serenaded first. Elisabeth and David shared their own stories, each more embellished than the last, as the room filled with the warmth of shared tales and hearty laughter.

When the merriment settled for a moment, Master Lanchal wiped his hands on a cloth and turned to David. "Tomorrow, we'll head to the guild and have you registered properly."

David nodded, eyes shining with gratitude, and Elisabeth quietly exhaled.

By the meal's end, the table had indeed become a stage—a stage where a family's happiness took the spotlight. But, as the embers of the cooking fire died down to a soft glow, Elisabeth's smile faded. A shiver of foreboding crept through her, silent and insidious. In her heart, a grim certainty took root: Cato and his men were out there, their shadows inching closer with the passing of each day.

It wasn't a question of *if* they would find her and David, but a question of *when*.

Chapter Seven

Theresa, with a twinkle of mischief in her eyes, plunged both hands into the sudsy water of the sturdy wooden basin. "You know," she said, her voice laced with laughter, "they say cleanliness is next to godliness, but I've yet to have any angels offer to help me wash dishes."

Elisabeth couldn't help but chuckle. "I'm pretty sure they don't bother with such earthly tasks, although you do make this chore seem *divine*."

Theresa, with a playful grin, splashed a bit of water in Elisabeth's direction. "Oh, I'm certain they're just envious of my heavenly dishwashing skills."

Elisabeth's laughter subsided into a genuine smile. "Honestly, you make everything so fun, even dishwashing."

Theresa paused, her hands still in the water, and looked at Elisabeth with a tenderness that reflected years of laughter and wisdom. "In this old heart of mine, there's always room for more joy. And *you*, my dear, have just made it beat a little happier." She reached out, flicking a bit of foam at Elisabeth's nose, her laughter echoing in the room, as comforting and lively as the summer night outside.

As they scrubbed and rinsed, Theresa entertained Elisabeth with tales from the bookshop's daily life. The others had long ago drifted back to the bookshop, their eagerness to continue showing David the workings of their craft almost tangible. Elisabeth sensed it wasn't just a place of business, but a repository of memories and laughter, where every quill had a story and every ink stain told a tale.

"You should have seen Gerrit as a small boy." Theresa cocked her head to the side. "He once asked his grandfather about invisible ink. Master Lanchal, with a straight face, told him it was so good at being invisible that even he couldn't find where he put it."

Time flew by as the pair turned the mundane task into a comedy show, their laughter mingling with the clinking of clean dishes being stacked away.

As the evening waned, David's weary form shuffled into the great hall. Elisabeth, catching sight of him, stopped working and let out a sympathetic sigh. "Oh, you look exhausted."

Theresa dried her hands on her apron, casting a mock-stern glance at the young couple. "All right, you two, no more dawdling down here with me—I'm known to saw logs louder than a woodcutter at night, so you'll get no sleep in here with me. See that staircase?" She made a sweeping gesture toward it. "March yourselves all the way up, past the second floor, until the stairs won't let you climb any higher. There, you'll find the attic room, boasting a bed that's been whispering about its own fluffiness all day, and windows that have been bragging about their nightly show of stars. Off with you now, shoo!"

Elisabeth's smile broadened as she placed her apron on its hook before turning to Theresa. "Thank you, for everything."

David nodded. "Indeed, thank you, Theresa." His

smile was weary but filled with gratitude.

"Take this lamp with you," the woman said as she handed it to them.

David took the lead, lantern in hand, guiding Elisabeth up the staircase. Their steps were in unison, his confident stride paving the way as they ascended. At the top, Elisabeth paused, casting one last glance back at Theresa, whose silhouette was framed by the faint glow of the great hall. With a final wave, she turned to follow David, who had already stepped through the doorway, leading them both up another narrow staircase.

The oak steps, aged and sturdy, creaked under their weight. The summer night's breeze whispered through the open windows, carrying with it the muted sounds of Ghent as it settled into slumber.

Upon reaching their attic room, they were greeted by a space that was modest yet full of character. The rafters above formed dark silhouettes against the whitewashed walls, and a simple bed with a straw mattress sat invitingly against one wall, an oak chest at its foot.

A small table with a sturdy chair was tucked into a cozy spot beneath a dormer window. David approached the table, the lantern in his hand casting a circle of light in the dim room. With a gentle touch, he placed the lantern down, the flame steadying and brightening to fill the space with a comforting amber glow. The shutters were flung wide open, inviting the cool night air to mingle with the warmth inside, creating a serene atmosphere.

But—Elisabeth's hands twisted, her fingers tangling together as she stared at the single bed, a silent reminder of the charade they were playing. She swallowed hard, throat dry, as she shifted her weight from one foot to the other. Their marriage wasn't real, not yet anyway. She loved David deeply but wanted to take things slow, enjoying sweet kisses without feeling pressured to rush into anything more. Her heartbeat quickened, and she smoothed down her dress while stealing a glance at David. As if high school wasn't hard enough, juggling time travel and having a boyfriend she'd met in ancient Rome added an extra layer of complexity to her life. Though their future together was certain, for now, she couldn't shake the nervous flutter in her chest.

David, stoic as ever, seemed to sense her unease. He gave her a reassuring smile and, without a word, settled onto the hardwood floor, making a pillow of his arm.

Elisabeth's heart swelled with affection. His silent understanding was exactly what she needed, and it made her love him even more. She bit her lip to keep from smiling as she stood over him. "Don't be ridiculous. You take the bed."

However, David's response was not in words. With a roguish grin, he gently pulled Elisabeth down onto him. They tumbled into a playful tussle, dissolving into tickles and hushed laughter. His eyes twinkled with mischief as his lips found hers, peppering her face with light kisses. Each kiss ignited further laughter, sending ripples of joy through Elisabeth's heart.

"I have an idea," she whispered between his teasing kisses, her voice a melody of giggles. As she attempted to get up, David's embrace tightened, his arms a gentle prison from which she found herself unwilling to escape.

"What's your idea?" he murmured against her lips, his smile audible in the dim light.

"A contest for the bed. We each toss a rock toward the bedpost. The closest, without touching, wins the bed for the night." She knew very well that David's aim was amazing.

He chuckled and sat up, retrieving two small rocks from his pouch. "As you wish, *cor meum*."

Elisabeth took a turn, her rock landing a hair's breadth from the post.

David, with feigned clumsiness, let his stone drop far from the mark. "Oh dear." His grin betrayed his cheeky deceit. "It seems you've won."

Elisabeth tried to suppress her smile while groaning. "You're impossible."

David leaned closer, brushing a kiss against her forehead. "I just want you to sleep comfortably."

"I know, but…" Elisabeth's gaze drifted to the oak chest at the foot of the bed, a thought popping into her mind. "Wait here." She approached the chest, her fingers tracing the intricate carvings before lifting the heavy lid. Inside, a trove of blankets lay neatly folded, their colors muted in the lamplight. As she unfolded a blanket, the delicate scent of lavender wafted up, infusing the air and calming the room.

With a wide grin, Elisabeth gathered an armful of the thick woolen blankets and turned to David, who watched her with a curious look on his face. "I'll make you a bed fit for a king."

She spread the blankets on the floor, layer upon layer, until a makeshift bed took shape beside the straw mattress. It was a humble arrangement, but one that carried the promise of comfort. "There." She stepped back to admire her handiwork. "Now neither of us will have to sleep on the floor."

David rose to his feet, gratitude shining in his smile. He removed his shoes and doublet, revealing a simple linen shirt. Then, he settled onto the improvised bed, sinking comfortably into its cozy embrace.

Elisabeth watched him for a moment, satisfaction washing over her. Then, with a playful grin, she whispered, "Seems I've bested the sling master himself."

David's eyes, heavy from the long day, met Elisabeth's with a tender weariness. "Indeed, you've bested me, love. But let it be known, I'll willingly lose a thousand contests if it means seeing you smile."

Elisabeth's heart skipped a beat. "You are ridiculously adorable, you know that?" She stepped toward the table, unlaced her shoes, and extinguished the lantern. Her fingers trembled as she removed her dress, intending to use the cotton chemise under it as a nightgown. The lilac fabric slid down her shoulders, pooling at her feet, before she quickly picked it up, draping it over the back of a chair. Then, with a sprightly leap, she vaulted over David's reclined form on the floor, giggling as she nestled into the bed. The straw mattress rustled beneath her weight and she pulled the covers up to her chin.

The room was silent save for the soft breathing of David and the distant call of the night. As she closed her eyes, Elisabeth felt a profound peace wash over her.

Chapter Eight

Elisabeth hurried through the corridors of her high school in Mahone Bay. The fluorescent lights hummed overhead, casting a clinical glow on the rows of lockers. She was a chameleon here—a student like any other; her backpack heavy with textbooks. But beneath the façade of normalcy lay a secret deeper than any teenage gossip.

Safe from Cato, and settled into a comfortable pattern with David in Ghent, Elisabeth resumed her practice of time-traveling on alternate days, taking the elixir weekly to stop herself from aging twice as fast.

In the familiar routine of high school, she raced to keep up with algebra equations and historical dates. Amidst bustling hallways and the ever-present buzz of activity, Elisabeth couldn't shake the feeling of being pulled toward another era—a world of cobblestone streets and thatched-roof cottages. Where she found comfort in a love that transcended centuries.

Yet, with each passing day, the tension mounted, threatening to unravel the delicate balance she maintained. Christmas at home had come and gone, leaving behind memories of festive cheer and family gatherings. As the groundhog promised an early spring, Elisabeth wondered how long she could sustain this precarious dance before one timeline inevitably overtook the other.

Her friend, Anna, with sun-kissed hair and eyes that sparkled, was a vibrant presence in the hallway—a blend of Nova Scotian charm and curiosity. Her excitement was contagious, and as she leaned against the locker, Elisabeth couldn't help but smile.

"Can you believe prom will be here before we know it?" Anna said. "It's like waiting for our own little fairytale to arrive."

Elisabeth switched her chemistry manual for a history textbook, her mind momentarily shifting to satin gowns. "I know," she sighed wistfully. "The place will be transformed into a starry wonderland, and everyone will be dancing under those twinkling lights."

Although she tried not to dwell on it, Elisabeth's heart ached with longing to attend prom with David.

Well, with *Aquarius* to be more precise.

Attending prom with him wasn't just a fleeting desire; it was a relentless tempest raging within her chest. Whenever she imagined herself in a satin gown, the soft fabric whispering against her skin, it only amplified the emptiness she felt.

In her daydreams, they'd dance together under the twinkling lights, swept away by the music and each other. She imagined his eyes, reflecting the stars above, while his hand rested on the small of her back, leading her through the dance as the world around them faded away.

Prom, the pinnacle of teenage dreams, taunted her with its promise of escape—a portal to a reality where she could be with him *here*, if only for a fleeting moment, like the little dancing couple in the cuckoo clock. Yet, it remained an impossible dream, a cruel reminder of what she longed for but couldn't have.

So, as a distraction, Elisabeth threw herself into the prom committee, ensuring every detail was perfect for others. With her hands full planning and organizing, she hoped to drown out the ache and loneliness that threatened to consume her that night.

Anna nudged playfully. "So, who's your dream prom date? Anyone special?"

Elisabeth hesitated, her gaze darting down the hallway. "Well, there's someone…" Her voice trailed off, knowing she couldn't reveal the truth.

Anna's lips parted slightly. "Spill it, Chickie. Wait—Is it Luke from history class? I think he likes you."

Elisabeth felt her cheeks heating. "No, it's…it's complicated." Her tone carried a hint of resignation, and she shrugged, trying to downplay the significance of her words. "It doesn't matter though. He can't come."

Anna's head jerked back. "Who? You gotta tell me who."

Elisabeth replied with a sheepish smile, her fingers tracing the edges of the history book cradled in her arms. "I have to run. See you later." With a wave, she hurried off to class, leaving her friend with curiosity piqued and a mischievous grin on her face.

"Oh, come on, E-beth!" Anna yelled playfully. "You can't just drop a bomb like that and take off!"

But Elisabeth was already disappearing around the corner, her secret safe for now amidst the busy school corridors.

In the classroom, she sat amongst her peers, notebook open, pen poised. The teacher's voice blurred into a soothing monotone as she scribbled notes, her fingers tapping rhythmically on the desk. Friends chatted in hushed tones, exchanged texts and shared secrets—the familiar routine of teenage life in the twenty-first century.

****

"Elisabeth, dear, listen close," Theresa said the next morning, back in Ghent. "I'm sending you on your very first quest to fetch our clothes from the washerwoman."

"A quest?" Elisabeth perked up at the call to adventure. "All right. Where do I go?"

"Ah, my valiant explorer..." Theresa's eyes twinkled with mischief. "Make your way toward the belfry. You know, that towering fortress that looms over us all?"

"Yes." Elisabeth clamped her lips together to keep from laughing. "The one with the dragon."

"Correct. Head east along the main street. You'll pass the mill—where the miller is always more flour than man."

Elisabeth chuckled at the image, nodding along with Theresa's instructions.

"After the mill, follow the river's flow and seek out the ancient willow tree. Its branches reach out like welcoming arms, ready to guide you on your noble quest."

Elisabeth smiled and nodded, her imagination soaring with each word.

"Just a stone's throw from the willow, there's a quaint cottage with blue shutters. That's your destination, and the washerwoman awaits, ready to reunite you with our linens." Theresa concluded her directions with a bemused smile. "Remember, the old willow's your guiding star. Now off you trot, and don't let those market distractions lead you astray."

"Consider it done," Elisabeth said with a mock salute, her spirit lifted by the call to adventure. "Off I trot."

As Elisabeth embarked on her quest, the towering belfry watched over the town like a vigilant guardian, while she amused herself with thoughts of the dragon perched atop. Following Theresa's directions, she turned eastward along the main street, noting the shift in the crowd's energy. While the market to her right buzzed with activity, the path toward the mill beckoned with quiet intrigue.

Passing the weathered water wheel, a smile graced Elisabeth's lips at the thought of the miller, always more flour than man. Continuing along the river's gentle curve, she soon reached the ancient willow tree, its branches outstretched in welcome. With each step, anticipation swelled within her, fueled by the journey.

Approaching the tree, she couldn't help but feel a sense of wonder at its towering presence. Its twisted branches reached out, luring her closer with a silent invitation. As she walked beneath its shade, a thought occurred to her — this would be the perfect spot for a romantic afternoon.

The sccluded setting, the gentle rustle of leaves in the breeze, and the babbling of the nearby river all combined to create an atmosphere of tranquility and intimacy. Elisabeth imagined spreading out a blanket beneath the branches, sharing a picnic with David as they laughed and talked, surrounded by nothing but the beauty of nature and each other's company.

With a smile playing at the corners of her lips, she

made a mental note to suggest the idea to him later. But for now, there was a mission to complete. The washerwoman's cottage awaited her a stone's throw away.

Finally, just as Theresa had described, Elisabeth spotted the quaint cottage with blue shutters nestled beyond the willow. A sense of accomplishment washed over her as she approached, knowing that her noble quest was nearing its end. A satisfied grin spread across her face and she knocked on the door, her heart light at the thought of returning to the Lanchal household with the freshly laundered items.

Chapter Nine

"Theresa!" Elisabeth gasped as they stepped out of the house one morning, her voice rising above the rhythmic thud of a blacksmith's hammer after biting into a fruit-filled pastry. "This is amazing!"

With a wide smile, the older woman handed Elisabeth one of the empty water pails. "Do you want to know my secret?"

Elisabeth smiled and nodded, awaiting the inevitably nonsensical ingredient.

"A sprinkle of laughter, of course."

Elisabeth snorted in amusement. "Of course. I should have guessed you'd say that."

"Why do you think they're so flaky? It's the giggles trapped between the layers." Theresa's laughter blended seamlessly with the bells tolling the hour.

Elisabeth wiped crumbs from her lips, feeling inexplicably lighter.

So far, she adored Ghent. The city embraced her— a tapestry of chatter, bustling activity, and the distant clang of artisans' tools. But it was the Lanchal family who truly welcomed her and David, including Gerrit, who went out of his way to make them feel at home.

One recent evening, Elisabeth found herself seated at the Lanchal's table, engrossed in lively conversation with Gerrit. His usual nervous demeanor melted away, and she found herself drawn to his company more and more with each passing day.

As the conversation ebbed, Gerrit reached beneath the table and produced a small bundle tied with a simple strip of cloth. "I came across this and thought of you." He cleared his throat and averted his gaze.

Elisabeth accepted the offering, her curiosity piqued. As she untied the cloth, the soft fragrance of lavender and chamomile wafted up from a finely crafted herbal sachet. She smiled, the gentle aroma filling her senses.

"It's exquisite! Thank you."

Gerrit's cheeks flushed at her words. "It's nothing." A hint of pride colored his tone. "It's supposed to ward off bad dreams."

Touched by his thoughtfulness, a genuine smile spread across Elisabeth's face. The delicate scent lingered in the attic bedroom, a silent testament to Gerrit's kindness and the blossoming friendship they shared.

As Theresa led the way down the nearby alley, Elisabeth's thoughts lingered on the heartwarming exchange with Gerrit. She couldn't help but grin, the memory of his considerate gesture still fresh in her mind. Yet, with each step forward, the present-day began to gently reclaim her attention.

The bustling street faded, replaced by a hidden oasis. Stone walls surrounded a courtyard, adorned with potted plants and herbs. Their leaves reached toward the sun, as if yearning for its heat. In the heart of the courtyard stood a well; it stone rim polished smooth by countless hands, and a pulley system allowing everyone to draw from its depths.

But—Elisabeth quickly learned the well was more

than a water source; it was the gathering place for shared stories and gossip.

Without fail, her face lit up with a wide smile as soon as she saw the old oak tree. Its twisted branches stretched wide, casting intricate shadows on the cobblestones below. Under its leafy canopy, neighbors gathered, their conversations blending with the rustle of leaves. "I look forward to seeing that tree every day."

Theresa leaned closer. "You know," she whispered, "that oak has seen more gossip than the belfry itself. If those branches could talk, they'd spill the juiciest secrets—like how Master Brewer's braies got stuck up there last summer."

Elisabeth grinned, knowing that braies were basically medieval underwear. She nudged Theresa's shoulder playfully. "That oak tree must have some wild stories."

As if in agreement, the breeze caused colorful linens, strung between neighboring houses, to sway and pirouette. It seemed laundry day had arrived for those who didn't hire a washerwoman, and the air carried the sweet fragrance of sun-dried fabrics, a comforting reminder of everyday life.

Theresa's eyes lingered on the fluttering sheets. "Do you see that blue one?"

Elisabeth followed her gaze. The sheet in question billowed like a captured cloud, its edges worn from countless washings. "Yes, it's been hanging there every day. Has it been forgotten?"

Theresa leaned in closer, squinting in amusement. "Well, at first, it was shrouded in mystery. Some speculated it was a makeshift awning, while others thought it was just another forgotten laundry line. But oh, my dear, it's far more scandalous than that."

Elisabeth's posture perked up, a slow smile forming on her lips.

"It turns out, almost every moonlit night, Gerrit and Marguerite Van Den Heuvel, a weaver's daughter, sneak off to this secluded spot."

Elisabeth's head jerked back. "*Our* Gerrit?"

Theresa nodded solemnly. "Yes, indeed. They whisper sweet nothings, their laughter mingling with the gentle rustle of the sheet as they hide behind it. Gerrit, bless him, reads love sonnets, while Marguerite giggles and pretends to swoon, her heart dancing to the rhythm of Gerrit's words."

Elisabeth suppressed a smile, thoroughly entertained by the gossip as they made their way toward the well.

"Then, one starry evening…" Theresa leaned in further, her voice barely above a whisper, "Gerrit and Marguerite were mid-sonnet when old Finn, the night watchman, materialized like a grumpy ghost. His lantern illuminated their faces, revealing their wide-eyed surprise. In a flurry of movement, they quickly shuffled apart, flushed cheeks betraying their innocent affection."

Unable to contain her amusement, Elisabeth chuckled. "And what did old Finn do?"

"Ah, well," Theresa said with a conspiratorial wink. "He cleared his throat, the sound echoing through the alley like a distant thunderclap. 'Young love, eh?' he grumbled. 'Remember, curfew starts at sundown.' And off he shuffled, shaking his head."

Elisabeth burst into laughter, stealing another glance at the blue sheet. "How'd you find out?" she asked between giggles.

An impish grin spread across Theresa's face. "An eavesdropping pigeon told me," she confessed with a wink. "But don't worry, Gerrit doesn't know I know." With practiced ease, she took hold of a worn rope attached to the pulley, lowering the empty pail into the depths below.

As Elisabeth and Theresa made their way back home, buckets of water sloshed with each step. Their laughter still lingered from the earlier conversation.

When they rounded the corner, they came face to face with Gerrit, who was rushing out the front door of the house. His eyes widened in surprise as he caught sight of them, their cheeks, no doubt, flushed from laughter and the exertion of carrying heavy pails.

Elisabeth exchanged a quick glance with Theresa, both trying to suppress giggles at the unexpected encounter.

Sensing their amusement, Gerrit couldn't help but chuckle nervously himself. "Well, well, what have we here?" Without missing a beat, Theresa stepped forward. "Ah, Gerrit, perfect timing." She gestured to the heavy pails. "Would you be a dear and lend us a hand? These pails are rather heavy."

Elisabeth nodded in agreement, her lips twitching with suppressed laughter. "Yes, it would be much appreciated."

Gerrit grinned, stepping forward to relieve Theresa and Elisabeth of their burden. "Of course." He hoisted the pails effortlessly. "Consider it my good deed of the day."

The trio made their way back inside the house, the echoes of their laughter lingering from the impromptu encounter. As Gerrit placed the pails down with a contented grin, Theresa shot Elisabeth a knowing glance, the amusement they shared twinkling in the older woman's eyes.

Gerrit's awkward demeanor lightened as he turned to Elisabeth, a shy smile forming on his lips. "I must admit, I'm glad you and David are here." Then, with an endearing touch of goofiness, he added, "When I was young, I always wanted a brother and sister to share our own little adventures in the old bookshop. But with more danger and less ancient scrolls."

Elisabeth couldn't help but chuckle at his playful remark. "You've certainly made our stay here more interesting, Gerrit. I never imagined Ghent would be so entertaining."

Gerrit grinned in response, his nerves seemingly forgotten in the comfort of their friendship.

At that moment, Lanchal emerged from the hallway, his steps echoing on the stone floor. With gnarled hands clasped behind his back, he approached, his brow furrowed in concentration. He glanced around the great hall before his gaze settled on Theresa. "My dear," he called out, "can I borrow Elisabeth for the time being? We could use her assistance."

"Of course, Master Lanchal," Theresa said with a smile. "Elisabeth will be happy to assist you."

Elisabeth's heart skipped a beat, her eagerness to spend time with David evident in the way she hurried toward the old man. "What do you need?"

With a nod of gratitude, Lanchal gestured for Elisabeth to follow. "I thought you could assist in sorting and stacking the parchment and vellum sheets. It's a simple task, but an important one. We need to keep our materials organized, and your help will make a big difference."

As Elisabeth stepped into the bookshop, she noticed Johanna seated at her desk, immersed in the delicate art of illuminations. The shop was filled with the soft scratching of quills against parchment.

Johanna glanced up; her smile radiant despite the concentration in her eyes. "Good morning."

"Good morning," Elisabeth said with a grin.

Just then, from the back of the shop, David appeared, a smile spreading across his face as he caught sight of Elisabeth. "Ready to tackle a mountain of parchment?"

She nodded. "Absolutely."

"This way." He made a subtle gesture with his head toward a concealed corner at the back of the shop. Elisabeth's grin widened, and with another nod, she followed him to the secluded area, nestled behind the bookshelves, anticipation bubbling within her as they prepared to work together.

A cluttered table dominated the space, its surface covered in a chaotic jumble of parchment and vellum sheets. The papers were strewn about, some crumpled and creased, others folded or rolled into unruly bundles. Ink stains marred the edges of some sheets, evidence of previous endeavors in bookmaking.

Quills and inkwells stood amidst the disarray, their presence adding to the sense of disorder. Scrolls and loose pages spilled over the edges of the table, threatening to cascade onto the floor at any moment.

Elisabeth sighed as she surveyed the mess. "Oh man, this is going to take a while."

David shot her a mischievous glance, wiggling his

eyebrows. "Hopefully."

She returned his playful glare. "Behave," she whispered, trying not to laugh.

David pulled in a deep breath. "You know, I think Lanchal is impressed with my work," he whispered back. "This will be my very own space when it's all cleared off."

Elisabeth felt a lightness in her chest. "I *knew* you'd impress him."

David's eyes met hers, gratitude shining through. "Thank you for believing in me."

Elisabeth's heartbeat quickened. "You've earned every bit of it."

Together, they set to work—hands moving with precision as they sorted and stacked the parchment and vellum sheets. In between tasks, they exchanged knowing glances and contorted their faces into absurd expressions, trying desperately to stifle their laughter.

"I'll be back shortly," Lanchal announced. "Don't miss me too much," he added, earning a chuckle from Johanna as he disappeared from view, his voice resonating through the shop as he slipped through the crimson curtain and into the house.

When they reached the halfway point of their task, Elisabeth nudged David. "Remember this?" With exaggerated seriousness, she picked up a particularly large sheet of parchment and held it up like a shield, scanning the ceiling and towering bookshelves for an imaginary foe. The corners of her mouth twitched with suppressed giggles as she whispered, "Here comes the Ghent dragon."

David stifled a laugh, his eyes sparkling with amusement. With theatrical flair, he seized a rolled-up parchment tube, waving it like a knight's sword, ready to engage in mock combat with Elisabeth's imaginary dragon.

Suddenly, the sound of footsteps approaching interrupted their antics. Elisabeth and David quickly composed themselves, their hushed laughter fading as they refocused on their work.

"Nice to see you both enjoying yourselves." Johanna's tone carried a hint of nostalgia. As she reached for a vial from a nearby shelf, Elisabeth couldn't help but notice a wistful look in her eyes. It was as if overhearing the playful banter had stirred memories of her own past, perhaps reminiscent of moments shared with her late husband.

Elisabeth's gaze shifted toward David, heart fluttering with affection as she looked at him. In that moment, amid the gentle chaos of the bookshop, she couldn't help but feel a deep sense of contentment, appreciating the simple joy of working alongside him.

Upon completing their task, they moved toward the shelves positioned behind the spacious oak workbench. There, they arranged the newly organized parchment and vellum, ensuring each sheet was neatly displayed.

Meanwhile, both Gerrit and Lanchal returned, slipping back into their routine with focused determination.

However, the rhythm was soon interrupted by the arrival of a young woman. Long blonde hair framed her face, catching the sunlight like spun gold as her gaze darted around, searching for something—or someone.

Draped in a flowing sky-blue dress that seemed tailored for summer, its lightweight fabric billowed gently with her uneasy movements. The soft blue complemented her fair complexion, and the dress was adorned with delicate floral patterns embroidered in shades of gold and green, adding a touch of elegance to her ensemble.

Elisabeth's head tilted to the side, noting the anxious look on the young woman's face, her demeanor giving away the nervousness within.

Johanna, engrossed in her illuminating work, looked up and greeted the newcomer with a smile. "Hello, dear. How lovely to see you today."

The young woman's nerves seemed to ease slightly at Johanna's friendly greeting. "Hello, Madame Lanchal."

Elisabeth then observed Gerrit's already nervous disposition escalate as it mirrored the young woman's unease. He mustered a hesitant "hello," his gaze darting anxiously between her and his work, betraying an amplified sense of concern and curiosity.

Lanchal approached the counter, smiling. "Good day, Marguerite. How may I be of service today?" He chuckled, his eyes twinkling with amusement. "Another illuminated Book of Hours for one of your sisters, perhaps?"

Elisabeth's head jerked back. *Marguerite? Gerrit's secret love?* As her eyes widened with intrigue, she caught David's puzzled yet entertained expression as he observed her creeping closer, pretending to dust. With a mischievous grin, she subtly waved her hand, silently promising to fill him in on the gossip later.

Marguerite hesitated for a moment before responding. "Um, no, Master Lanchal." Her voice was shaky. "I-I heard about a book, a rare tome on ancient herbal remedies. I was hoping you might have it in your collection."

Lanchal nodded, his fingers tapping against the wooden surface of the counter. "Ah, yes, I believe I know the book you speak of. A fascinating read indeed. Let me check our inventory for you."

As the old man vanished into a distant corner of the shop, Elisabeth couldn't help but notice Gerrit's struggle to appear nonchalant. His gaze darted anxiously between Marguerite and his work, while his hands fidgeted with items on his desk. Meanwhile, Marguerite looked everywhere but at Gerrit, her watery eyes betraying a struggle to hold back tears.

After a few moments, Lanchal returned to the counter, a small frown creasing his brow. "I'm afraid we don't have the book you're looking for in stock at the moment, my dear. It seems to have been quite popular lately."

As Marguerite's shoulders slumped and disappointment clouded her features, Elisabeth's eyes narrowed, curiosity sharpening her gaze. She shifted position, pretending to straighten a nearby stack of books, but her attention remained fixed on Marguerite's every move: the way her breath caught in her throat, her fingers curling into tight fists as if trying to hold back the flood of emotions threatening to overwhelm her.

"Oh, I see. Thank you anyway," Marguerite uttered to Lanchal, her voice barely above a whisper, each word laden with a heavy weight of resignation. But when she turned to leave, Elisabeth caught a subtle exchange between her and Gerrit. Marguerite's hand brushed against her hair—a seemingly innocent gesture, yet Elisabeth caught its significance.

A flicker of understanding passed between the two, a silent agreement conveyed through their shared gaze and subtle movements. It was a signal—a secret code exchanged in plain sight, unnoticed by anyone else in the room. Marguerite then took a few steps toward the door and disappeared outside.

Lanchal returned to his work. He hummed a tune to himself, his focus on the leather-bound book he was repairing. Meanwhile, Johanna remained seated at the desk, engrossed in illuminating her work, her attention consumed by the delicate strokes of the brush.

Elisabeth's gaze shifted back to Gerrit. Her heartbeat slowed as she watched him fumble with items on his desk. Brows furrowed in concentration, his movements lacked their usual precision, indicating his preoccupation with Marguerite.

Despite a desire to ease his evident distress, Elisabeth forced herself to focus on her own tasks as she straightened books, wiped shelves, and organized parchment. Yet—her mind kept drifting back to the tantalizing secret romance unfolding before her, her curiosity burning brighter with each passing moment.

Chapter Ten

With a swift excuse about assisting Theresa with dinner, Elisabeth hurried from the bookshop, back into the house. The urgency in her steps matched the curiosity swirling within her. As she entered the great hall, her mind buzzed.

"Theresa," she whispered, "you won't believe what just happened."

Theresa looked up from the worktable, her eyes narrowing. "What is it? What happened?"

Taking a deep breath, Elisabeth recounted the events of Marguerite's visit, Gerrit's distracted state, and the tense atmosphere she had sensed in the shop.

Theresa listened intently; her brows furrowed with concern. "I wonder what it could be," she said once Elisabeth had finished, her voice tinged with sympathy. "I just pray dear Gerrit doesn't end up with a broken heart," she added with a heavy sigh.

Elisabeth nodded, her thoughts already swirling with speculation. She reached for the apron hanging near the broom, tying it around her waist with brisk movements. Gripping the knife, she couldn't help but wonder aloud, "Do you think something happened between them?"

Theresa sighed, wiping both hands on her apron. "Love can be a tempest. Secrets, misunderstandings— they can tear even the strongest bonds apart."

As they chopped vegetables side by side, the kitchen filled with the comforting scent of onions and herbs. Elisabeth stole a glance at Theresa, her mind still occupied with thoughts of Gerrit and Marguerite. Despite Theresa's calm demeanor, she sensed a hint of concern in the way the older woman avoided meeting her gaze.

"I feel like we should do something," Elisabeth said, her voice laced with curiosity as she sliced through an onion with precision.

Theresa bit down on a smile, a subtle acknowledgment of Elisabeth's nosy speculation. "Sometimes, the best course of action is patience. Let the storm rage, but keep a lantern burning in the window."

Elisabeth nodded, a pang of protectiveness stirring within her. Despite his awkwardness, or perhaps because of it, Gerrit's eager innocence endeared him to her heart. Like a loyal puppy, he exuded an irresistible charm that stirred within her a desire to shield him from any discomfort or unease he might face.

"We'll be here to catch him if he falls," Theresa said.

As they continued their preparations for supper, Elisabeth let out a spontaneous laugh. "You know, I can't believe how invested I've become in Gerrit's secret romance. It's like something out of a book, but it's happening right here in this very house."

The late afternoon sun cast a long shadow across the room, its golden rays filtering through the small window. The cozy aroma of the meal preparation lingered in the air as Theresa exchanged a knowing glance with Elisabeth while adding some herbs to the pot. "Indeed, it is. Life has a way of weaving its own intricate stories, doesn't it?"

Elisabeth nodded.

"And sometimes, we find ourselves entangled in them without even realizing it."

As the bells of the Ghent belfry resonated through the streets, the dining table stood ready; its surface adorned with pewter plates shining softly in the candlelight. The rustic wooden cups awaited the family members, their grain worn smooth with age. Flickering flames danced upon the pewter, casting intricate shadows on the rough-hewn tablecloth. As everyone gathered around, Theresa and Elisabeth exchanged a knowing glance, their thoughts still lingering on the secret romance that had captivated their attention.

Gerrit sat in silence, his usual jovial demeanor replaced by a somber expression. Elisabeth couldn't help but notice the worry etched into his features, and her heart ached with empathy. It was clear he carried the weight of something deeper than the usual concerns of the day.

Theresa leaned in closer to him. "You know, Gerrit," she whispered, "your presence always adds a touch of magic to any room." She paused, her smile warm. "And tonight, it's like you've brought stardust with you." As she placed the roasted chicken on the table, she added, "Let's enjoy this meal, shall we?"

Gerrit's eyes softened as he met Theresa's gaze. The weight on his shoulders seemed to ease, if only for a moment, and he replied with a small smile.

David, clearly sensing the tension in the air, attempted to steer the conversation toward lighter topics. "Master Lanchal, have you heard the news about the upcoming faire? They say there'll be performers from all over the region."

Lanchal nodded in acknowledgment but remained silent, his attention drifting to his grandson. Elisabeth caught David's puzzled expression and responded with a reassuring smile, subtly shaking her head to convey that she'd fill him in on the situation later. Meanwhile, Johanna poured cups of water, her anxious glances toward Gerrit revealing her concern.

"Well, you won't believe what happened to me at the market today," Theresa exclaimed, still aiming to brighten the atmosphere. "I spotted what I thought were the juiciest apples I've ever seen. But when I took a big bite, imagine my surprise when it turned out to be an onion! Oh, the look on the vendor's face was priceless!"

They all chuckled, appreciating the momentary reprieve, yet their glances gravitated back to Gerrit, their hearts heavy with evident concern for him.

As the meal progressed, the façade of cheerfulness continued to crack, revealing the undercurrent of worry that ran through the family. Gerrit's forced smiles and distracted mannerisms only served to deepen the unease.

As Elisabeth's attention shifted to Johanna, she could almost see the wheels turning in her mind. Johanna leaned forward, about to speak, but then settled back into her seat, seemingly deciding that confronting her son in front of others might only worsen matters.

Master Lanchal cleared his throat and addressed his grandson directly. "Is something troubling you, my boy?" His tone was gentle but concerned.

Gerrit hesitated for a moment before shaking his

head. However, his wrinkled brow spoke volumes. He shifted in his seat, and then mustered a faint smile and cleared his throat. "Will you all excuse me?" he asked, rising from the bench. "I have some work I need to finish."

With a nod of acknowledgment from those gathered, Gerrit left the table.

****

When bedtime arrived, Elisabeth grabbed a lantern and climbed the wooden stairs to the attic room, her steps gentle against the worn treads. The glow of the light cast dancing shadows against the walls, enveloping the cozy space as she removed her gown and settled into the bed in her white chemise.

A few minutes later, David's footsteps echoed on the stairs. Elisabeth sat up, her heart quickening as she waited for him. When he entered the room, he dropped a coil of rope into a corner.

"What's that for?"

"In case of a fire. An attic is not the safest place."

She gave a half-hearted shrug. "True."

As he slipped off his shoes, his expression shifted to one of wonder. "By the gods, *cor meum!* What's going on? What's wrong with Gerrit?" Concern and intrigue mingled in his voice as he moved closer to her.

Elisabeth's eyes widened; her gaze fixed on his. "Remember that blonde girl, Marguerite?"

David nodded, his attention now entirely captured. "The one who came into the shop today?"

Elisabeth leaned in closer, her body shifting eagerly on the bed. "That's Gerrit's secret love. They meet *clandestinely*," she revealed, drawing out each syllable for dramatic effect. "Every moonlit night in the

112

courtyard by the well."

David sat on the edge of the bed, his hand seeking hers. "Gerrit," he said as their fingers entwined, "must be heading there to meet her now."

Elisabeth's head jerked back. "Seriously?"

"I just saw him leaving the house."

"I'm following him." With a throaty laugh, she threw off the blanket and sprang out of bed, her bare feet padding against the floorboards.

David's eyebrows shot up in amusement. "Oh, no you're not," he said, laughter bubbling in his voice as he stood.

"I am." Elisabeth's tone brimmed with a potent mix of determination and excitement as she slipped back into her gown. "I'm not going to eavesdrop or anything. I'm just curious whether they're having a secret rendezvous or if it's something else. They both looked so anxious." Her mind raced with possibilities. "If it looks like it's bad news, maybe there's something I can do to help." Her shoulders straightened with a fresh sense of purpose.

"Help with what? What are you talking about?" David's expression shifted from amusement to worry. "Elisabeth, this is a bad idea. Don't you remember what happened when you *helped* Isabeau and Giovanni?"

Elisabeth's heart fluttered as she closed the distance between them, her lips meeting his in a quick kiss. "I'm going now," she whispered, a mischievous undertone in her voice.

"Well, it's dark out. You're certainly not going alone," David replied with a resigned chuckle, his voice conveying playful surrender as he put his shoes back on.

Elisabeth, lantern in hand, tiptoed toward the door, her movements fluid and silent as she glanced back at David, gesturing for him to follow.

Together, they crept out of the attic chamber and descended the stairs, their steps cautious to avoid alerting anyone else in the house. The flickering light of the lantern now cast eerie shadows along the walls, adding to the covert nature of their adventure.

As they reached the stairs in the great hall, its vast expanse was dimly illuminated by the dying embers in the firepit. Theresa was nowhere to be seen. Elisabeth motioned for David to stay close as they made their way down the staircase, her heart pounding with excitement and the thrill of the unknown.

"Quick, behind here," she whispered, pointing toward a nearby chest. They darted behind it while straining to hear any sign of Theresa's approach.

Elisabeth lowered the lantern she was carrying, dimming its light to cast the area in shadows and conceal their presence.

Moments later, footsteps echoed down the hallway. Elisabeth watched nervously as Theresa passed by, vanishing into the pantry. Seizing the chance, they emerged from their hiding spot and dashed onward, barely containing their laughter as they fled.

Approaching the front door, its hinges creaked as Elisabeth pulled it open. A gentle breeze greeted them, carrying the scent of moonlit air. As they ventured into the night, the darkness enveloped them, the glow of the lantern guiding the way. With a silent understanding, they turned around and placed the lantern back at the doorstep, ensuring it wouldn't betray their presence to Gerrit.

David moved closer to Elisabeth, his hand reaching out protectively for hers. With fingers entwined, they headed toward the courtyard, footsteps echoing on the cobblestone road. She bit down on a smile, knowing each step brought her closer to the truth she sought. Her heart pounded while David remained steadfast by her side, a reassuring presence in the dark.

As they neared the small square, Elisabeth sucked in a quick breath. The twisted old oak tree stood sentinel, its gnarled branches framing a secret meeting. There, behind the moonlit sheet—still hanging from the line—the courtyard transformed into a silhouette theatre. The sheet fluttered gently, and the two figures behind it leaned closer, their outlines almost merging into one, yet maintaining a respectful distance.

The woman's silhouette was delicate, like a paper-cutout princess. Her head tilted toward the man's; lips poised as if whispering sweet confessions.

And the man? Leaning toward the woman, his shadow seemed to shrink slightly, as if uncertain of himself in her presence. His hand reached out, fingers trembling with hesitation. And yet, despite his nerves, there was a quiet determination in his silhouette, a resolve to overcome his fears and express his love for the woman who had captured his heart.

Elisabeth gestured for David to stay low as they crept closer, their movements careful and deliberate.

But—just as they reached the edge of the courtyard, Elisabeth's foot caught on a loose cobblestone, sending her stumbling forward with an undignified yelp.

David caught her before she fell, pulling her into his arms. Their eyes locked for a moment before

Elisabeth broke into a sheepish grin. "Smooth move, huh?" she said, trying to stifle her laughter.

David grinned, pressing a finger to her lips to silence her. "Shh, they might hear us," he teased, his voice low and warm against her ear.

They shared a brief, stolen moment, hearts beating in time with the rhythm of the night. Then, refocusing on the silhouettes ahead, Elisabeth and David crept closer, breaths held, crouching behind the gnarled oak tree, attention fixed on the unfolding scene.

As Marguerite's weeping voice reached Elisabeth's ears, her eyes widened, and a sudden tightness gripped her chest. "Something's wrong." Her heart raced with a sense of foreboding.

David's posture slumped. "We really shouldn't be eavesdropping," he whispered, his fingers tightening around the rough bark of the tree. But curiosity held him in place, and he strained to listen.

Marguerite's words sliced through the night air, revealing the devastating truth. "I overheard my father." Her voice trembled with emotion. "He has arranged my hand in marriage—to Adrian van der Wollen."

In response, Gerrit's stunned silence spoke volumes.

Marguerite's tears flowed freely, each sob a testament to the depth of her despair.

Elisabeth felt a pang of sympathy, her own heart heavy with sorrow.

When David exchanged a solemn glance with her, she sensed the weight of their shared understanding. They knew they had to leave, yet the pain in the young woman's voice held them rooted to the spot.

Marguerite shook her head in denial. "I can't marry

him," she said anxiously; her words heavy with unspoken longing.

Elisabeth's eyes welled with tears as Marguerite poured out her heart, the raw anguish in her voice unmistakable; a testament to love forsaken in the name of duty. Memories of her own defiance against Cato's arranged marriage to Guglielmo Tartare flooded back.

"I-I care for you deeply, Marguerite," Gerrit confessed, his voice strained with emotion.

Elisabeth couldn't help but feel the weight and agony of his words.

His shoulders then slumped forward. "But there are...there are paths dictated by tradition—incontestable, unyielding."

But there are paths dictated by tradition?

Incontestable?

Unyielding?

Elisabeth's jaw dropped, her eyes wide in disbelief as she turned to David, whose expression mirrored her astonishment.

Gerrit's shadow drooped, his head bowed, swaying slightly as if caught in a storm. "Honor demands that I step aside. I-I cannot stand in the way of your father's wishes," he uttered. "I must honor the traditions that bind our families, even at-at the cost of my own happiness."

"And what of *my* happiness?" Marguerite's desperate plea echoed in the night.

With a firm grip, David clasped Elisabeth's hand as tears cascaded down her cheeks. "Come on," he said, his voice a low grumble. "Now."

Elisabeth sniffled and stole one final glance behind, her heart aching for the two figures entwined in their shared anguish. With a nod, she yielded to David's lead and away from the haunting silhouettes.

As they returned to the house, the air held the lingering scent of wood smoke. Theresa, worn out from a hard day's work, lay sprawled on a pallet in a far corner of the great hall, snoring with the gusto of a seasoned traveler, dreaming, most likely of tiny dragons and singing spoons.

Elisabeth followed David up the narrow, creaky stairs. The wood groaned under their weight, echoing through the otherwise silent space.

They reached their attic sanctuary, where moonlight spilled through the open window. Elisabeth stood in the middle of the room, and David joined her, a silent pillar of support.

"Perhaps I have no honor, or integrity, but I'd be damned before I stepped aside," David whispered, his voice a tender vow. "I'd fight for you."

Their fingertips brushed against one another with the lightness of a butterfly's kiss before he pulled her close, shielding her from the world's ache.

Elisabeth nestled against his chest, her head finding the perfect resting place. "I know."

David traced the contours of her fingers with his own, and then, in that intimate moment, he lowered his head, meeting her lips in a gentle kiss.

Elisabeth's wistful sigh hung in the air. Her gaze then drifted to the window, where the stars twinkled like distant diamonds, casting a soft glow upon the world outside. "I wish you could be my prom date."

David's brows furrowed with curiosity, his eyes searching hers for answers as he stepped back. "What's that?" he asked, his voice a tender invitation.

Elisabeth's heart fluttered. "Never mind. It's impossible really."

His expression softened, and she knew he heard more than just words. The attic room seemed smaller now, cocooning them in shared longing. He reached out, taking her hand in his—a gesture of reassurance.

Their intertwined fingers whispered of promises unspoken.

In that tranquil moment, where hearts dared to hope, they leaned in for another kiss—a promise sealed with moonlight and the sweet taste of possibility.

Chapter Eleven

As Elisabeth stepped out of the house, the rhythmic clatter of Theresa's wooden shoes against the cobblestones accompanied them. The air carried the scent of damp earth and recently butchered meat, hinting at the activities that lay ahead. Amidst the bustling streets, they made their way through the crowds of people, each immersed in their own tasks. Elisabeth glanced up at the sky, assessing the clouds, wondering whether rain threatened to disrupt their day.

Their first destination was the vibrant market at the heart of Ghent, where merchants and traders gathered to make deals, and fortunes changed hands constantly. Surrounded by towering guild halls, the colorful and imposing buildings stood as symbols of tradition and authority, casting their shadow over the lively square below.

Theresa's seasoned presence steadied Elisabeth in the busy bazar as they wandered about, vendors proudly showcasing their goods. Wooden carts and makeshift stalls brimmed with fruits and vegetables, filling the air with the earthy scent of freshly dug carrots, the sweet aroma of ripe pears, and the peppery tang of radishes. Amid the chatter of buyers and sellers, the sound of clinking coins added to the lively atmosphere, while distant laughter and the occasional shout of a vendor echoed through the square.

Theresa moved with expertise, selecting the finest produce. Her fingertips tested the firmness of a parsnip and traced the curve of a green pea pod.

Beside her, Elisabeth wandered along wide-eyed, her senses overwhelmed. The vibrant range of colors—the lush greens, deep purples, and vivid crimson—captivated her. As the market burst with activity, she observed a baker's young apprentice haggling for flour, his voice cutting through the noise, while nearby, a weaver unfurled bolts of dyed wool.

Theresa's eyes twinkled with mischief, the rhythmic clatter of her wooden shoes against the cobblestones adding to the atmosphere. "Elisabeth," she said with a grin, "let me share a secret—a tale that unfolded right here in this very square."

Elisabeth leaned in, unable to resist Theresa's stories.

"It was a day much like today," she began, her tone growing more theatrical. "The clouds hung low, casting a gray hue over the market square, and the air was thick with the scent of freshly baked bread and ripe cheeses. Now, old Zeger—the cheese vendor—was known for his colossal wheel of gouda. It was a thing of legend, my dear."

Elisabeth nodded as she admired a collection of hand-painted pottery, her imagination running wild with visions of the oversized cheese. "What happened to Zeger's prized cheese?"

When Theresa burst into laughter, Elisabeth's lips stretched into a grin. "Imagine this: Zeger had positioned the wheel precariously close to the edge of his stall. Perhaps he sought to impress the passersby, or maybe the wheel had ambitions of its own."

Elisabeth leaned in closer, hanging on Theresa's every word. "What happened next?"

"A gust of wind swept through the square." Theresa's eyes widened with mock horror. "And before anyone could react, the wheel of gouda teetered—whoosh!—it rolled off the stall like a rogue cart wheel." Theresa's hands gestured wildly as she recounted the chaos. "Down the cobblestone street it went, gathering speed. Zeger chased after the cheese, arms flailing, shouting at it to stop."

Elisabeth doubled over with laughter, unable to contain her amusement. "Did he catch it?"

Theresa shook her head, her own laughter infectious. "Not a chance! The wheel of gouda zigzagged through the market, knocking over baskets of apples, scattering chickens, and narrowly missing the mayor. People leaped out of its path, and the whole square erupted into chaos."

"And then?" Elisabeth urged, eager for more

"Well," Theresa said, wiping tears of laughter away, "the cheese eventually rolled into a nearby stall. But not just any stall—it was the spice merchant's!"

Elisabeth's eyes widened in anticipation. "No! Not the spice merchant!"

"Yes! The wheel of gouda crashed right into a display of saffron, sending golden threads flying. And there stood the spice merchant, utterly flabbergasted."

Elisabeth burst into laughter. "Oh my gosh, what did he do?"

Theresa grinned mischievously. "He scooped up the fallen saffron, held it up high, and declared, 'Behold, the rarest cheese seasoning: gouda-infused saffron! Adds flavor and lightness to any dish!"

Elisabeth's laughter lingered, echoing through the market as she moved about the crowd, pausing to examine some hand-woven baskets.

But then—an inexplicable sense of foreboding washed over her.

It felt as if unseen eyes followed her every step; a silent observer lurking in the shadows of the guild hall façades. She glanced over her shoulder, yet the bustling market offered no comfort.

Elisabeth bit at her nails, a nervous habit betraying her growing unease.

What if Cato's men found her?

What if *Guglielmo Tartare* found her? The man commanded a powerful mercenary army and certainly had the means. She'd faked her own death to avoid marrying him, breaking the power alliance he had arranged with Cato.

The fear gnawed at the edges of her mind, threatening to consume her. Nevertheless, as quickly as the thought arose, Elisabeth pushed it away, chiding herself for entertaining such irrational fears.

"No," she murmured under her breath, her voice barely audible amidst the noise of the market.

There's no way they could have found us.

We've been careful.

She repeated the words in her head like a mantra, each repetition bolstering her resolve.

There was no reason for henchmen to be lurking in the shadows of Ghent's bustling marketplace.

No reason at all.

With a deep breath, Elisabeth forced herself to focus on the task at hand. There were errands to run, groceries to buy, and no amount of unfounded paranoia was going to stand in their way. And so, with a determined step, she followed Theresa back into the throng of merchants and traders, pushing her fears aside for the time being.

"Speaking of gouda," Theresa started again, her eyes squinting in amusement. "Last year, Gerrit approached another cheese vendor with all the grace of a startled rabbit. Instead of asking for extra cheese, he complimented the vendor's hat—a fine choice, mind you, but not quite the dairy-related conversation starter one would expect. Eventually, Gerrit found himself laden with more cheese than he could carry, and the vendor, convinced he was a cheese connoisseur, treated him like royalty, offering him the rarest varieties and insisting on his expert opinion."

Elisabeth laughed, her worries momentarily forgotten as she savored Theresa's humorous anecdote about Gerrit's mishap.

After purchasing their produce, they ventured to a nearby market stall, where Theresa bought herbs and spices to replenish their dwindling supply. The fragrance of dried lavender and rosemary filled the air as they browsed the selection, selecting ingredients for their next culinary masterpiece.

Leaving the bustling market square behind, they backtracked along a different road. The river now flowed at their right, its gentle murmur a companion on their journey. At Elisabeth's side, a basket swung, signaling their final mission—to procure the finest cuts of meat from the butcher's hall.

The wooden building stood weathered and sturdy, its timeworn beams bearing witness to countless transactions. Inside, a portly man caught their attention, his blood-stained apron betraying his profession as he greeted them with a smile. "Good morrow, Theresa," he called out, wiping both hands clean on his apron. "What brings you to the market today?"

"Fresh beef, Arthur. Master Lanchal fancies a hearty dish."

Arthur acknowledged with a nod, a spark of recognition in his eyes. "Ah, Lanchal has good taste. Follow me."

As they walked amongst the hanging carcasses— beef, lamb, and pork—Elisabeth caught a whiff of something foul. She wrinkled her nose. "What's that smell?" she whispered to Theresa.

Theresa pointed to a table piled high with what looked like guts. "That, my dear," she said, hesitantly, "is offal—the edible insides of animals. Hearts, livers, kidneys, and other bits that defy both logic and good taste."

Elisabeth's lip curled, her mind drifting back to a day years ago in Scotland when Malcolm introduced her to haggis. "Ah, I see," she replied, her voice dripping with the enthusiasm of a damp rag. "A delicacy, right?"

Theresa chuckled. "Delicacy for some, abomination for others."

After careful consideration, Arthur proudly presented his selection—a marbled slab of beef, promising tenderness. "This one," he declared, gesturing toward the meat. "Tell Lanchal it's from a young heifer, fed on sweet clover."

Theresa nodded in approval, exchanging a handful of silver coins for the neatly wrapped parcel. The butcher had bound the meat with twine, and Theresa's fingertips grazed the rough edges of the package as she thanked him.

On their journey back home, Elisabeth noticed two young women crossing a bridge. Uncertainty crept into her mind as she squinted, trying to discern the features of one of the distant silhouettes. She turned to Theresa; her voice hesitant. "Isn't that Marguerite?"

Theresa followed Elisabeth's gaze, her eyes scanning the figures dressed in soft, flowy gowns made of fine fabrics. After a moment of observation, she nodded in confirmation. "Yes, that looks like Marguerite and her sister, Katherina. Their house is just over there." Theresa gestured across the bridge, toward a stately timber-framed dwelling with a tiled roof, its windows adorned with planters of blooming flowers. Above the door hung a sign bearing the family name, marking them as prominent and respected weavers in the city.

Elisabeth's heart weighed heavy. "Theresa, there's something I need to tell you. Last night, while David and I slipped out...for a bit of, uh, fresh air...we stumbled upon Gerrit and Marguerite. They were...they were having a private conversation."

Theresa's gaze softened, sensing Elisabeth's apprehension. "Go on, my dear."

"We didn't mean to eavesdrop." Elisabeth cleared her throat. "But we heard everything. Marguerite's father has promised her hand in marriage to another man, and Gerrit...he said he has to do the honorable thing and step aside—but I think he's just too insecure to fight for her."

A flicker of concern passed across Theresa's features as she absorbed Elisabeth's words. "I see," she mumbled. "Love and duty often find themselves at odds in matters of the heart. It's a difficult path to navigate for all involved."

Elisabeth nodded in reply, her heart heavy.

But then—as Marguerite and Katherina strolled along the street on the opposite side of the river, Elisabeth tilted her head. They moved with a certain grace and elegance that reminded her of the heroines from the classic stories she had read in books and watched in movies.

Suddenly, an idea began to take shape.

Her fingers tapped lightly against her lips as she contemplated the possibilities, inspired by the way Marguerite's dress billowed romantically in the breeze.

Elisabeth's brows furrowed, already anticipating David's skeptical expression and his inevitable attempts to dissuade her from meddling in others' affairs.

"*Elisabeth, no*," he'd say. "*No more of your great ideas.*"

Yet, defiance swelled within her and a wide grin spread across her face.

This time, she couldn't shake the feeling that it was a *really* good idea.

Chapter Twelve

Evening settled in as Elisabeth made her way down the dimly lit hallway, snacking on a handful of salted nuts. All day, her mind had buzzed non-stop while planning out the details of her matchmaking scheme. Entering the bookshop, she was embraced by the glow of flickering candles and lanterns, casting dancing shadows on the floor and worktops.

The shop was empty, except for David, whom she found nestled in the secluded alcove at the back. On his desk, a lantern bathed the area in a gentle ambiance. Amongst shelves loaded with books, David seemed engrossed in his task, coating a freshly bound tome with protective varnish.

At the sound of her arrival, he looked up, a smile spreading across his face. Setting the work aside, he rose to greet her, his expression tender as he reached for her hands. "What brings you here at this hour?" he asked, pressing a sweet kiss to her forehead.

"You're working late and I miss you," she replied with a grin. "And, ah, perhaps searching for a pen and parchment?" Elisabeth stepped away, swaying back and forth, feigning innocence.

David lowered his chin and quirked an eyebrow. "What are you up to?"

A sudden pang of thirst, triggered by the salted nuts, caught her off guard. "Nothing," she said, her voice nonchalant while reaching for a cup on his desk. "Just a little secret project." Anticipating a refreshing sip, she lifted the tumbler to her lips, only to find it empty. With a disappointed sigh, she placed it back and resumed her search for parchment and ink.

David chuckled. "A secret project? In here?" His eyes narrowed. "What are you plotting, *cor meum*?"

Elisabeth took a step back, hands clasped behind her as she rocked on her heels. "If I told you, it wouldn't be a secret anymore, would it?" Her smile widened, and she spun around, skirt twirling as she inspected the shelves. "Now, where's the parchment and ink again?"

With a resigned sigh, David pointed to a cabinet near the front of the shop. "You'll find what you need there," he said, his tone light yet laced with concern.

Elisabeth retrieved the parchment and ink, tucking them away with a quill. "Thank you, my dear darling," she called out with a giggle, her voice carrying a note of triumph. "Your assistance is invaluable, as always," she added theatrically, flashing David a mischievous grin before making her exit.

As she prepared to leave, David caught her by the wrist, his grip gentle but firm. "Promise me this doesn't have anything to do with a certain couple." His eyes searched hers for reassurance.

"Trust me." She flashed him a bemused smile. "This is a *really* good idea."

David let out a heavy sigh. "Your *really good ideas* have a habit of turning into disasters," he reminded her, his tone serious.

Elisabeth's resolve wavered for a moment, but then she gave him a playful swat. "Oh, come on. I knew you'd be like this. I have a great plan to help Gerrit and Marguerite."

David's posture slumped. "There's no talking you out of anything once you've made up your mind, is there?" he asked, his tone resigned.

"Nope." With a grin, she rose onto her tiptoes, tilting her head to meet his lips in a kiss before slipping away through the crimson curtain.

As Elisabeth passed through the great hall, she caught sight of her water cup, sitting on the worktable where she had left it. Without hesitation, she grabbed it and took eager gulps, quenching the intense thirst caused by the salted nuts.

But the moment was fleeting; the rich, robust flavor of wine, not water, took Elisabeth by surprise. Pausing mid-swallow, her eyes widened with the realization that it wasn't her cup. A small cough escaped as the now *empty* tumbler was placed back down. Heat rushed to her cheeks. "Wine?" she whispered, confining laughter to a snort as she climbed the stairs.

Upon reaching the landing, flickering light at the bottom of the stairs caught her eye. With a playful grin, Elisabeth raced back down to grab the candle, the dancing flame casting whimsical shadows on the walls as she climbed back up again.

Finally, Elisabeth entered the attic bedroom and settled at the table. Brows furrowed, she arranged the parchment and ink before her. The candle's soft glow filled the workspace, creating an inviting ambiance. With a steady grip on the quill, she held it over the blank page, eager to begin her secret endeavor.

Glancing up at the moonlight that spilled through

the open window, her mind buzzed with ideas, each one more brilliant than the last—or so it seemed in her slightly tipsy state. A small chuckle escaped her lips and she pondered whether the wine might grant her an extra dose of eloquence.

With a wobbly hand, Elisabeth dipped the quill into the inkwell, nearly tipping it over in the process. She giggled at her clumsiness, then steadied herself and focused on the task at hand. As she wrote, the strokes wavered on the page, mirroring her slightly unsteady thoughts. But with each word formed, she felt a sense of triumph—or was it just the wine talking?

Elisabeth held the parchment up and looked at the words before her. With exaggerated seriousness, she cleared her throat and began to read aloud.

"My Dearest Marguerite," she whispered, her tone melodramatic. "As I sit inside the bookshop, surrounded by the scent of velum and ink…" Her voice trailed off as she stifled a hiccup, then resumed with renewed determination.

"Since the day our paths first crossed," she continued, her words slurring slightly, "you have been the beacon of light guiding my every step, the sonnet that stirs my soul…" Elisabeth paused, then shook her head and soldiered on.

"Yet, I find myself at a crossroads, torn between the demands of duty and the yearnings of my heart." Her expression grew increasingly solemn. "For though it pains me to admit it, I cannot live without you, Marguerite. To see you bound to another, to watch as your laughter fades and your smile dims—it is a fate I cannot bear to witness…" She paused for dramatic effect, then found herself overwhelmed with emotion.

Tears welled up in her eyes, blurring the words on the parchment before her.

Elisabeth took a deep breath and composed the next part of the letter.

And so, despite my honor and integrity, I must confess the truth—I cannot live without you by my side. I cannot bear the thought of you marrying another man, of spending my days haunted by the memory of what could have been. Meet me at the ancient willow tree near the River Leie—

Elisabeth paused, her mind retracing Theresa's instructions to the washerwoman. With a determined nod, she resumed writing.

To reach there, head toward the belfry, then pass the mill, following the river's flow until you find the ancient willow. I will be waiting there for you on Sunday at sext.

With a final flourish, she signed Gerrit's name at the bottom of the letter and leaned back with a satisfied grin. "There," she declared to the empty room. "That should do the trick." As Elisabeth reread the letter a final time, a grin spread across her face. "Oh, Gerrit, you old romantic," she chuckled to herself.

After carefully folding the letter, Elisabeth reached for the nearby candle and dripped wax onto the parchment to seal it before blowing out the flame. With the letter sealed, she tucked it under her pillow, her steps wobbly from the wine. Curling up on the bed, still fully dressed, she drifted off into a tipsy slumber.

Chapter Thirteen

"School can wait," Elisabeth mumbled. She tucked the love letter into her bodice and descended the attic stairs, feeling slightly dehydrated from the mishap the previous night. She'd only had wine once before, at Aurelius' villa, and the outcome was much the same.

As she reached the great hall, Theresa, busy wiping off the worktable with a wet cloth, looked up. A playful grin spread across her face. "Ah, good morning, sleepyhead."

Elisabeth managed a smile and joined Theresa, fully aware of the tasks awaiting. Reaching for an apron, she couldn't help but chuckle at her own expense. "Theresa," she said with a grimace, "last night, I accidentally drank a huge tumbler of wine someone left on the table." She braced herself for a scolding or at least a disapproving look.

Theresa burst into laughter, the sound echoing through the house. "Oh, Elisabeth," she exclaimed between giggles, "I was wondering where it went! It was for the stew." With a playful wink, she added, "I hope it was at least good wine."

Relieved by Theresa's lighthearted reaction, Elisabeth joined in the laughter. "Well," she admitted, "I can't say for sure. But I certainly slept well." As she spoke, she reached for a pitcher of water on a side table, pouring herself a cup to quench her thirst.

Elisabeth and Theresa stood side by side in the kitchen, sleeves rolled up and aprons cinched tight around their waists. With determined expressions, they set out to make bread, armed with a recipe supposedly passed down through generations.

As they mixed the ingredients together, their contagious laughter started. Flour danced in the air like a delicate snowfall, accompanying the scrape of wooden spoons against the bowl. Elisabeth wrestled with the dough, sticky tendrils clinging to her fingers. Each knead seemed to cause a miniature snowstorm, with flour swirling everywhere.

"Looks like you're making bread and a mess in equal parts," Theresa teased. Taking over, she attempted her hand at the dough, but her efforts were met with the same stubborn resistance. Sticky strands defied any attempts at shaping, leaving both women coated in a floury mess. Theresa chuckled, eventually throwing her hands up in surrender. "Well, it seems we're not making bread today."

Their laughter rang out as they surveyed the area, flour covering the table like a blanket of snow. Theresa glanced at Elisabeth. "Why don't you head over to the baker and buy two loaves. I think we've done enough baking for one day."

Elisabeth, with a bemused smile, nodded as she wiped her hands on her apron, leaving behind streaks of flour. "Good idea."

Theresa rummaged through a drawer, retrieving a coin. "Here." She pressed it into Elisabeth's hand and then stepped closer, her expression softening. With a motherly gesture, she reached up and wiped a streak of flour from Elisabeth's cheek.

Elisabeth giggled at the affectionate gesture. "Thanks." Her smile widened as she hung her apron up. "I'll be back."

With a final wave, Elisabeth hurried down the hallway and out the front door, retrieving the love letter from her bodice and clutching it in her hand. This was the perfect opportunity to deliver it to Marguerite, and she wasn't going to let it slip away.

On the bustling street, she moved with a fast-paced stride, adrenaline surging through her veins. The morning air was crisp, carrying the scent of freshly baked bread and the distant clanging of metal from the blacksmith's forge. She weaved through the crowds of people, from the belfry toward the vibrant noise surrounding the Butcher's Hall. With each step, her heart beat a little faster, the weight of the love letter reminding her of the mission at hand.

Approaching the bridge, Elisabeth stopped mid-stride, her brows furrowed in confusion. Where there had been a clear path to cross the river to Marguerite's house, now stood a gap.

The bridge had seemingly vanished.

Her gaze followed the direction of the gap, and she was met with the sight of a boat approaching, its course unimpeded by the missing bridge.

As the boat drew nearer, Elisabeth's confusion gave way to fascination. Wide-eyed, she watched a medieval marvel unfold before her. It was then she realized what it was—a swing bridge, much like one she had seen back home in Nova Scotia. The bridge, instead of remaining stationary, had pivoted on its axis, swinging open to allow passage for the approaching vessel. In modern times, such bridges were operated with the push of a button, but here, she witnessed the manual labor involved.

After the boat passed, her attention was drawn to a man positioned on the bridge, diligently working a long pole. He ran in circles around a sturdy mechanism fixed in the floor, his motions turning the bridge to swing into place again, allowing pedestrians to continue about their business on both sides of the river.

After she crossed and approached the Van Den Heuvel's shop, her pulse raced. This was it—the moment of truth. Up close, she noticed intricate wooden carvings adorning the entrance, and colorful tapestries displayed in the windows.

But—as she reached for the door handle—she hesitated a moment. What if Marguerite's reaction wasn't what she hoped for? What if this matchmaking scheme backfired spectacularly? What if Marguerite couldn't read, despite her interest in books? Elisabeth quickly dismissed the thought. Being the daughter of a wealthy merchant in Ghent, it was almost certain that she had been taught to read and write. A girl of her standing would be educated in order to manage a household and possibly assist in running her future husband's business someday.

The love letter would be completely useless otherwise.

Pushing aside her uneasiness, Elisabeth squared her shoulders and stepped inside, determined to see her plan through to the end. After all, what was life without a little adventure and a touch of romance?

Stepping inside the weaver's workshop, Elisabeth found herself enveloped in an atmosphere of luxury and craftsmanship. The interior was spacious, with high ceilings and intricate wooden beams. The walls were lined with shelves displaying bolts of richly dyed fabrics and intricate tapestries, showcasing the family's wealth and expertise in weaving.

Large looms dominated the center of the room, their rhythmic clacking filling the air as skilled artisans worked diligently to create intricate patterns. Soft, colorful yarns adorned baskets and spindles, adding a cozy touch to the surroundings.

The scent of freshly woven fabric mingled with the faint aroma of herbs and spices, creating a sensory experience that spoke of elegance and refinement.

A blonde girl of about fourteen stepped forward with a smile. "Can I help you?" She wore a light, airy summer gown that billowed with each movement. Her smile and poised demeanor suggested she was likely one of Marguerite's sisters.

Elisabeth glanced around, her fingers tightening around the letter tucked against her chest. She bit her lip while considering the options. "I'm looking for Marguerite," she finally admitted, her gaze shifting between the girl and the letter.

The girl seemed to sense Elisabeth's hesitation and offered a reassuring smile. "She's not here at the moment, but I can make sure she gets your message." She extended a hand to take the letter.

Elisabeth's shoulders tensed, torn between her desire to deliver the letter personally and the pressing need to return to Theresa. Time was ticking, and she needed to hurry back with the loaves of bread. "Can you *please* make sure Marguerite gets this?" Her hands quivered while reluctantly handing over the letter.

The girl nodded, her expression kind and

sympathetic. "Of course. I'll make sure she receives it," she promised, her reassuring tone easing some of the apprehension.

"Thank you," Elisabeth said before making her exit, wondering just how many sisters Marguerite had.

After leaving, her footsteps echoed through the narrow streets as she hurried to the bakery. With determination driving her forward, she purchased two loaves of bread and rushed back home.

The door creaked open as she returned, and her gaze immediately fell upon Gerrit shuffling down the hallway toward her. "Ah, Elisabeth." His smile was warm, but his eyes lacked their usual spark. "Back from an adventure, I see. Did Theresa send you out to tame any dragons today?" His attempt at humor didn't quite mask the sadness in his voice, and her heart sank a little. "I hear our belfry dragon didn't quite live up to your expectations."

Elisabeth groaned theatrically. "I can't believe David told you about that."

Gerrit snorted in amusement.

"Alas, no dragons today, I'm afraid," she said, her tone playful but with a hint of mystery. "But who knows what adventures tomorrow may bring?" she called over her shoulder while heading into the great hall, as Gerrit slipped through the crimson curtain.

Theresa looked up, a welcoming smile lighting up her face. "Back already?"

Elisabeth nodded, her heart still racing from the exhilaration of her mission accomplished. "Yes, I've brought the bread," she announced, holding up the loaves for Theresa to see.

Elisabeth set the bread aside and then turned her

attention to sweeping the floor, the straw bristles of the broom swishing rhythmically across the stone. With each sweep, she found herself lost in a whirlwind of thoughts, her mind consumed by the uncertainty of whether Marguerite would indeed receive the letter.

As Master Lanchal strolled into the great hall, Elisabeth's gaze darted past him, catching sight of David standing just behind. A smile played at the corners of her lips as their eyes briefly locked, an unspoken excitement passing between them.

"Elisabeth, I have an important task for David, and I thought you'd like to accompany him," Lanchal announced while plucking at his clothing.

Her brows furrowed in confusion. "Accompany him?"

The old man nodded while grinning. "Yes, indeed. There's a completed manuscript that needs to be delivered to one of our clients across the city. Since it's such a splendid day, I thought it might be nice for you two to enjoy each other's company along the way. Besides, David has barely stepped out of the workshop, so this will be a refreshing change of pace. It's essential to find joy in both our work *and* our relationships."

Elisabeth's initial confusion transformed into excitement, her eyes lighting up as she shot David a playful glance. A wide smile danced across her face. "Thank you, sir. We'll make sure the manuscript is delivered safely."

David returned her gaze with a grin, his eyes twinkling with amusement. "Shall we?" He extended his elbow as she stepped closer.

Elisabeth nodded, heart fluttering in her chest. "Absolutely." They shared a brief, affectionate glance before she linked her arm with his.

Lanchal chuckled at their playful banter.

As they stepped outside and strolled along the streets, the sounds of the city filled the air, mingling with the buzz of conversation and the occasional clatter of hooves on the cobblestone. Merchants called out their wares from colorful stalls lining the street, while the tantalizing aroma of freshly brewed ale wafted from nearby taverns, mingling with the earthy scent of horses and the faint hint of spices.

Elisabeth's eyes widened, noticing a familiar sight—a broom pole sticking out over the door of an ale house, just like she'd seen at Beatrice's cottage. It stirred fond memories of their evening spent in the little village of Lindenhart.

Elisabeth leaned in closer, biting down on a smile. "Aquarius," she whispered conspiratorially, "there's something I need to tell you." She paused, locking eyes with him. "Last night, the parchment I needed…?"

David's brows furrowed in curiosity. "Yes…?"

An enormous grin spread across her face. "Well, it was to write a love letter to Marguerite, pretending it was from Gerrit so that—"

His eyes widened in disbelief. "You didn't deliver it, did you?"

"Yeah, I did." She giggled and gave him a playful nudge. "This morning."

David's reaction was immediate, his steps faltering as he pulled her to a stop beside him. "*Cor meum…*" His tone was firm. "This is…quite the plan you've concocted."

Elisabeth grabbed his hand, bouncing from foot to foot, unfazed by his skepticism. "I know!" she admitted with a huge smile. "I'm going to arrange a romantic picnic, just the two of them." She drew in a deep, satisfied breath. "Gerrit's just shy and needs a little push so he can muster the courage to confront Marguerite's father before it's too late."

David reluctantly listened as she spoke, his brows furrowing, as if he couldn't help but be intrigued by her plot.

"Every moment we delay is a moment lost in their chance for happiness together. And this picnic—it's not just a romantic meal in the open air—it's a chance for them to remember why they fell in love in the first place." She squeezed David's hand, her gaze imploring him to understand. "I know it might seem like a long shot, but sometimes all it takes is a little push in the right direction. Trust me, I've got a strong feeling this will motivate Gerrit to stand up and fight for their love."

David cleared his throat. "I admire your spirit," he said, reaching out to tuck a loose strand of hair behind her ear. "But, as you already know, meddling in others' affairs can be a risky business."

"Well," she said with a mischievous grin, "you and I are together because our future selves meddled in *our* affairs," she teased. "I guess I just can't help myself." She looked at David, eager to see his reaction, her heart fluttering with anticipation.

He said nothing, but his expression mellowed and he leaned in, planting a tender kiss on her forehead.

With a gentle tug, she urged him to resume walking, before letting out a nervous giggle. "The thing is, I could really use your help with the next part."

"No. Absolutely not." Although he shook his head,

Elisabeth could tell he was trying not to laugh.

She looked at him with a flirty pout. "Oh, come on."

David shook his head again, though his lips curved into an affectionate grin. "No. I'd rather not be involved in this scheme of yours. I'd prefer to be kept in the dark about it, if you don't mind."

Elisabeth's pout eased into a gentle smile as David wrapped his arm around her shoulders, pulling her into a side hug. Despite his refusal to be involved in her matchmaking plot, a wave of comfort enveloped her, and she leaned into his embrace. "All right," she conceded with a chuckle, tilting her head up to meet his gaze. "I won't drag you into my *really* awesome plan."

David swallowed his laughter. "Good."

Elisabeth groaned while biting down on a smile.

He grabbed her hand again; his affection evident in the gentle squeeze of her fingers. "Let's forget about matchmaking schemes for now and just enjoy the afternoon together, hmm?"

Elisabeth smiled, letting David lead her further down the busy street.

"See that?" He nodded toward an imposing building, his tone filled with a mix of pride and nostalgia. "That's the Bookbinders' Guild Hall. I think it's even nicer than the one in Paris."

Elisabeth's gaze shifted to the grand structure, her eyes tracing the intricate details of its exterior. Weathered stone walls stood tall and imposing, adorned with ornate carvings and elaborate arches. "It's incredible," she said, her voice filled with genuine awe. "To think of all the hard work and dedication you've put into everything." She looked at him and let out a satisfied breath. "I'm so proud of you."

David's cheeks flushed. "Thank you," he whispered.

As they continued their stroll through the bustling streets of the city, Elisabeth cast a final glance back at the guild hall. Suddenly, she couldn't shake the subtle chill that settled over her, an unspoken weight pressing down on her chest, the feeling of an approaching storm lingering in the air.

Beside her, David's grip tightened on her hand, a fleeting shadow crossing his features before he masked it with a smile.

But she noticed it—a flicker of concern in his eyes, as if he sensed an impending threat lurking just beyond the edges of their happiness too.

Chapter Fourteen

After school, Elisabeth sat on the sofa amidst the elegant furnishings of Sissi Waters' living room, meticulously reviewing prom committee notes. As she delved into the details, Felis made an appearance.

With a dignified air, the marmalade cat sauntered across the room, his fluffy tail flicking as he settled onto a window ledge to observe the falling snow. His paw stretched toward the glass, trying to touch the delicate flakes. Outside, the wintry wonderland provided a stark contrast to the comfortable living room. Elisabeth let out a satisfied sigh and refocused on the intricate details of organizing a prom, her commitment to the event sparking a brand-new passion within her.

When Mrs. Waters entered the room, carrying a vase of roses, Elisabeth glanced up, momentarily distracted from her work. "Ever consider a career in event planning?" she asked the old woman. "Seems like it could be rather fulfilling."

Sissi chuckled, placing the vase on a side table. "What are you working on?"

"Prom."

Mrs. Waters flinched slightly at the mention. "Ah, prom."

Elisabeth's eyes narrowed, watching Sissi's frail hands tremble while fidgeting with the roses. "I love the planning part, but I'm not sure if I'm going to go."

"It's a milestone event, one you *definitely* shouldn't miss, my dear."

Elisabeth's shoulders slumped. "I know, but what's the point if Aquarius won't be there? David's nowhere to be found, either."

Sissi crossed the room and sat beside her. "Elisabeth," she said, her voice firm, "*we* are not one of those girls who can't enjoy themselves without their boyfriend by their side. Prom is about creating memories with friends, celebrating the end of an era, and looking forward to the future. It's not just about who you go with, but about enjoying the experience itself."

Elisabeth felt heat rush to her cheeks. "Yeah, I know." She sighed. "You're right."

"It's important to remember that while Aquarius is perfect for you in countless ways, it's also crucial to maintain your individuality and independence. You're young, with a world of possibilities ahead. Remember to nurture your other friendships, pursue your passions, and continue to grow as an individual." She paused, her gaze drifting toward the majestic sugar maple outside the window, its branches dusted with snow. "Consider the branches of that tree—they may stretch in different directions, but their roots remain entwined." Sissi looked back at Elisabeth. "You can nurture your personal growth while still cherishing the enduring bond that connects you and Aquarius."

Elisabeth nodded while listening.

"Of course, that's just my humble advice." The old woman's voice was quiet. "But as words of wisdom to my younger self, as you navigate the complexities of living dual timelines, remember the importance of *balance*. I've told you before—don't be so consumed by one timeline that you neglect the other." Sissi reached over and gently clasped Elisabeth's fingers. Despite the marks of age, her hand radiated warmth and tenderness, carrying with it a lifetime of experience and insight. "Each timeline holds its own significance. Its own joys and challenges. Embrace the richness of both worlds, but never forget to tend to the needs of each." Sissi's touch lingered for a moment longer before she withdrew her hand, her smile quivering. "Loving yourself is a lifelong journey."

Elisabeth tilted her head to the side. "Is this your way of saying that I should be my own prom date? I shouldn't rely solely on Aquarius to make me happy by taking me there?"

Sissi nodded, but seemed to be holding back tears. "Your happiness should never hinge solely on someone else. Embrace your own light, and others will be drawn to it."

Glancing at Mrs. Waters, Elisabeth's heart felt full. Here was a version of her older self who had weathered the storms of time with grace and wisdom, offering invaluable guidance to her younger counterpart. With a gentle smile, she squeezed Sissi's hand. "Thank you."

As the conversation wound down, Elisabeth packed her belongings, remembering that it was "elixir day." She needed to take the elixir of life once a week to slow the aging process while time-traveling. Suddenly, her posture perked up. The thought of the vial in her bedroom sparked an idea. Pausing briefly, a quiet resolve stirred within her. Inspiration struck, revealing a possible path forward—a contingency for emergencies.

Meanwhile, Mrs. Waters remained seated nearby, emanating a calm reassurance. Her observant gaze hinted at a depth of insight and understanding that seemed to transcend the passage of time.

Chapter Fifteen

Sunday arrived, the day Elisabeth's plan to play cupid and reunite Gerrit with Marguerite would finally come to fruition, bringing with it a mixture of excitement, nerves, and a touch of mischief.

In the great hall, she found Theresa bustling about near the pantry, the sunlight filtering in through the lone window. Its golden rays cast a gentle glow over the stone floors, lending a cozy ambiance to the room.

"Theresa…" Elisabeth bounced from foot to foot. "I want to surprise David with a picnic by the river this afternoon. Can I borrow a few items to make it *extra* special?"

The woman turned from her task, a twinkle in her eyes as she observed Elisabeth. "A picnic?" A playful smirk tugged at her lips. "Well, that certainly sounds like fun. I'll help you prepare for your little riverside rendezvous."

"Thank you!" With a grin, Elisabeth rushed into the pantry to gather the necessary supplies. Spotting a woven picnic basket tucked away in the corner, her smile widened. It was perfect for the surprise outing.

With Theresa's assistance, they selected an arrangement of tasty treats: crusty bread, savory meats, assorted cheeses, and ripe fruits from the market. The tantalizing aromas that filled the air only added to the sense of excitement.

As they packed the food into the basket, Elisabeth let out a deep, satisfied sigh. Everything was falling into place for her matchmaking plan—the beautiful weather, Theresa's support, and the innocent guise of a picnic adventure.

Theresa handed Elisabeth a folded blanket. "The boys are in the workshop, buried under piles of scrolls and books as usual. As for Master Lanchal and Johanna, they're visiting a family friend near St. James', so it's the perfect time to drag David away for a surprise picnic. I'm glad you're taking him out for a while. I wish poor Gerrit would go out and get some fresh air and sunshine too."

Elisabeth smiled as she took the blanket. "I'll see what I can do about Gerrit," she promised, bouncing onto her tiptoes. "Maybe he can join us for a bit."

Theresa let out a sigh of gratitude. "If anyone can convince him, it's you. You've got a knack for these things. Good luck."

With a final nod to Theresa, she made her way down the hallway toward the bookshop. Taking a deep breath, she braced herself for the moment ahead, ready to spring her plan into action.

"Hello, gentlemen," Elisabeth sang out as she slipped through the crimson curtain, drawing the attention of David and Gerrit, who were working together at the main table. "Can I steal my *husband* away for the afternoon?" She directed her words and a meaningful look at David, her eyes widening just a fraction and head tilting slightly to convey an unspoken request for his cooperation. Maintaining a joyful demeanor, she glanced at Gerrit before returning her gaze to David, silently urging him to play along with her plan. "Today is the *perfect* day for a picnic by the river."

Gerrit, oblivious to the subtle exchange, looked between them with mild curiosity.

Elisabeth held her breath, awaiting David's response. She had anticipated this moment, knowing his reluctance to be drawn into her scheme.

A flicker of realization crossed David's features, and he let out a resigned chuckle. With a knowing smile, he shook his head. "A picnic? What's the occasion?" he teased, his tone carrying a hint of amusement, but also a subtle warning.

Elisabeth flashed him a coy smile. "The beautiful weather on this sunny day, of course." Gerrit nodded toward David. "Go spend the day with your lovely wife. It's Sunday, after all. Don't waste it away in here with me." Despite an attempt at cheerfulness, there was a hint of sadness in his eyes.

"Why don't you come too?" Elisabeth said.

David bit down on a smile. "You might as well join us. Elisabeth's not one to take no for an answer." He chuckled softly, a look of surrender in his eyes as he closed a book and prepared to leave.

Elisabeth grinned. "Resistance is futile. You're coming with us, whether you like it or not."

Gerrit hesitated, uncertainty evident in the furrow of his brow. "I don't know…I don't want to intrude on a *romantic* outing."

Elisabeth waved off his concerns with a dismissive gesture. "Oh, don't be silly. It's not a romantic outing! You're more than welcome to join us."

David shot Gerrit a wide-eyed look. "Please, don't leave me alone with her," he joked, earning a playful glare from Elisabeth.

Gerrit seemed torn between the warmth of the sun outside and the comfort of his familiar workshop. "I *really* don't want to intrude," he said, glancing at David.

David clapped Gerrit on the shoulder. "Nonsense. We enjoy your company."

After a moment of contemplation, he relented, a small smile playing on his lips. "All right, all right. I suppose it won't hurt to take a break for a little while."

"Perfect," Elisabeth said with a satisfied grin. "You won't regret it, I promise."

With David graciously grabbing the picnic basket from Elisabeth, they made their way outside, the anticipation of the afternoon adventure palpable in the air. She linked her arm with David's as the three strolled through the winding streets of Ghent. The vibrant colors of the buildings contrasted with the blue sky overhead, creating a picturesque scene that seemed straight out of a painting.

As they walked by the towering belfry, Elisabeth glanced toward the nearby Cloth Hall, its stalls silent and empty due to the Sunday rest. A figure in the distance caught her eye—a tall silhouette that seemed eerily familiar. For a moment, she thought it was Crooked Nose, his presence and stride sending a shiver down her spine.

But as she blinked, the figure dissolved into the quiet streets, leaving her to dismiss it as a trick of the light or a figment of her imagination. She shook her head, refocusing on the conversation at hand, determined not to let her thoughts run wild.

They soon reached the mill, its wheel turning

peacefully in the water, creating a rhythmic creaking sound. As they continued their stroll along the riverbank, Elisabeth's pulse raced, anticipation growing with each step. The warmth of the sun on her skin heightened her joy, while the serene surroundings further fueled her sense of eagerness.

With every glance at Gerrit's solemn expression, Elisabeth couldn't help but feel a surge of hope. She imagined the surprise and delight on his face when he saw Marguerite, and her heart swelled with excitement. It was a moment she'd been eagerly awaiting. As they drew closer to their destination, she smoothed down her dress, trying to appear relaxed. In reality, butterflies were doing loopy-loops in her tummy.

"Did David ever tell you how we ended up in Ghent?" she asked, trying to keep her tone casual.

She sensed a gentle nudge from David, his subtle warning glance reminding her of the delicate balance they maintained in keeping their own secret safe.

Gerrit tilted his head to the side. "No."

Elisabeth hesitated for a moment, her gaze meeting David's before returning to Gerrit. "We weren't always the picture of happiness you see today," she admitted with a wistful smile. "My wealthy father had arranged my marriage to another man." She paused, allowing the weight of her words to sink in before continuing. "But we made a choice to follow our hearts, no matter the consequences."

Gerrit's head jerked back. "Really?"

"Really," David said, casting a fond glance at Elisabeth. Their looks held a silent acknowledgment of the journey they had undertaken together. "And let me tell you, Gerrit," he added, his tone turning lighter, "it was the best decision I ever made."

Elisabeth's heart fluttered when he said that.

With a deep sigh, David offered Gerrit a thoughtful smile. "You know, sometimes the greatest adventures begin with a single act of bravery. It's like they say, your best life often lies just beyond the threshold of fear."

With a nod of understanding, Gerrit seemed to absorb David's wisdom.

In that moment, Elisabeth sensed a shift in his perspective, a spark of hope igniting within him. She hoped David's words would serve as a subtle encouragement for Gerrit to follow his heart, even in the face of uncertainty. She hoped he would hear the unspoken message—that love was worth the risk, worth pursuing, no matter the obstacles in its path. Elisabeth had learned that in the darkest of times, hope was often the guiding light.

As they approached the shady spot beneath the ancient willow tree, Elisabeth's pulse quickened. The scene before her seemed alive with possibility. The gentle rustle of the willow's leaves and the dappled sunlight filtering through the branches created a tranquil environment, inviting them to linger and embrace the moment. Colorful buildings framed the landscape, standing as silent witnesses to the beauty of Ghent.

With a wide smile, Elisabeth turned to David and Gerrit. "Isn't this perfect? I have a feeling today is going to be a day we'll never forget."

David raised an eyebrow, smirking at her with amused skepticism.

After spreading out the blanket on the grassy patch

beneath the tree, the trio settled down, taking in the surroundings. Elisabeth positioned herself where she could watch the road, the fluttery feeling in her tummy building as she awaited Marguerite's arrival. The birdsong provided a soothing backdrop to their gathering, with melodies ranging from the chirping of sparrows to the warbling of blackbirds. As they savored the moment, her gaze wandered over to the river where two elegant swans glided gracefully across the water. "Oh, l love swans."

"You know," Gerrit said with a playful sparkle in his eye, "they're called *lan chals* here. It means long necks."

Elisabeth's brows squished together. "*Lan chals?*" She then gasped. "Lanchal! That's why there's a swan over the door of the bookshop!"

Gerrit chuckled when Elisabeth made the connection. "Exactly." His grin stretched from ear to ear. "Lanchal and Son."

David snorted in amusement, clearly entertained by the discovery as well.

As Gerrit's revelation sunk in, the distant chimes of the bells echoed through the air, signaling *sext*, twelve o'clock in the afternoon. Elisabeth's attention shifted from the river to the road ahead as she fidgeted with the picnic blanket. Her eyes fixed on the winding path, anticipating Marguerite's arrival, but the heat rising from the ground created a shimmering effect that made it hard to see clearly.

Suddenly, she caught sight of a figure approaching in the distance. Certain it was Marguerite, even though the glare off the water from the high noon sun obscured her identity, she grabbed David's hand, her heart racing with anticipation.

"Oh! I just remembered I was supposed to pick up something from the washerwoman. David, come with me for a moment," she said with a throaty laugh. "I need you to help me carry it." With a playful tug, she pulled David to his feet. Then, still holding his hand, she began to backpedal, her giggles dancing in the tranquil air. Without waiting for a response, she led him away with light and playful steps. "We won't be long, Gerrit! Just a quick errand, and we'll be right back. Enjoy the food in the meantime!"

Leaving Gerrit unsuspecting, Elisabeth dragged David a short distance away, over a small hill. They hurried to a spot where the terrain dipped, creating a natural vantage point. From here, they could observe Gerrit under the tree without being seen, and still hear him clearly. A large bush provided further cover, allowing Elisabeth to monitor both Gerrit and the approaching figure. Crouching behind the bush, her heart pounded with anticipation.

The sun cast dappled shadows around them, adding to the sense of secrecy. Meanwhile, David's playful gaze shifted between Elisabeth and their unsuspecting targets. With a mischievous look in his eye, he leaned closer, his breath tickling her ear. "You know," he whispered with a grin, "if this fails, I'm denying any involvement."

Elisabeth suppressed a giggle while elbowing him. "Fine. But it's not going to fail. Nothing's going to go wrong with my plan because it's brilliant."

As the person drew nearer, Elisabeth squinted before her smile faded. "False alarm." She let out a heavy sigh. "It's not Marguerite yet. It's a man."

But her gaze fixed on the man striding purposefully toward them, his form imposing even from a distance. As he drew nearer, she noted his attire—the lightweight linen tunic flowing gently with each step, a testament to both comfort and status in the summer heat.

Elisabeth's heart pounded in her chest, a sudden feeling of nervousness overwhelming her. David cleared his throat, a sign of his own unease. As they watched the approaching figure, Elisabeth couldn't help but bite her nails, uncertainty gnawing at her with each passing moment.

Cato?

The man's leather shoes pounded against the cobblestones, and a hat with a distinctive elongated tail, draped elegantly over one shoulder, shielded his face from the sun's glare and cast a shadow over his features. Yet, even from afar, his presence commanded attention, his stature conveying authority and determination.

Elisabeth's hands trembled as the man drew nearer. For a fleeting moment, dread gripped her heart, fearing it might really be Cato. But as he came into clearer view, the subtle differences in his features and demeanor became apparent. It wasn't him. Relief washed over her, and she released a breath she hadn't realized she'd been holding. Her gaze flickered past the stranger, still awaiting Marguerite's arrival.

"She's late," Elisabeth whispered with a shaky laugh. "And where's that man going?" She glanced behind at the cottage with the blue shutters. "To see the washerwoman?"

David chuckled. "You didn't play matchmaker for the washerwoman too, did you?"

Elisabeth bit down on a smile as she nudged him. "Don't temp me."

Their hushed laughter mingled with the rustle of leaves around them. But as the man came closer, David tilted his head to the side. "Wait—where's he going?"

Elisabeth's brows furrowed in confusion as she watched the man's determined stride. "Is he heading toward *Gerrit*?" she asked, her voice tinged with concern.

"GERRIT LANCHAL?" the man roared angrily.

Gerrit's head jerked back and he stood, extending a trembling hand. "Master Van den Heuvel…"

Van den Heuvel?

As in Marguerite Van den Heuvel?

Elisabeth's chest caved in. "Oh crap," she muttered.

"What in God's name is the meaning of this?" Marguerite's father thundered, his voice no-doubt echoing across the river. His nostrils flared with barely contained fury as he brandished the love letter in the air, the parchment fluttering slightly in the breeze.

Chapter Sixteen

David rubbed the back of his neck while Elisabeth whimpered. Both watched Gerrit standing before Marguerite's father, eyes wide with shock and fear. His extended hand dropped limply to his side, brows furrowing in confusion.

"I-I don't understand, sir." Gerrit's voice trembled with genuine confusion.

As the man's anger hung heavy in the air, Elisabeth's heart pounded with dread. Horrified, she listened to Gerrit vehemently deny any knowledge of the letter.

Van den Heuvel's face hardened with disbelief, his gaze narrowing as he regarded Gerrit with suspicion. "Do not play the fool with me," he growled. "This letter was delivered to my daughter, bearing your name."

Gerrit shook his head frantically, panic rising. "I swear, sir, I have no idea what you're talking about. What letter?"

Marguerite's father held up the parchment, his expression grim. "'My Dearest Marguerite, since the day our paths first crossed, you have been the beacon of light guiding my every step, the sonnet that stirs my soul…'" His voice dripped with sarcasm and anger.

While Van den Heuvel continued reading the impassioned letter, David shot Elisabeth a wide-eyed look, a mixture of frustration and bewilderment flashing across his face. Despite his obvious irritation, Elisabeth sensed he was hiding a twinge of amusement at the ridiculousness of the situation. She buried her face in her hands, unable to meet his gaze.

"'Yet, I find myself at a crossroads, torn between the demands of duty and the yearnings of my heart. For though it pains me to admit it, I cannot live without you, Marguerite.'"

Elisabeth peeked through her fingers, glancing up again as Van den Heuvel's voice droned on, the weight of her own words hitting with renewed intensity.

"'To see you bound to another, to watch as your laughter fades and your smile dims—it is a fate I cannot bear to witness…'"

David's jaw tensed as he struggled to contain his emotions, a hint of a smirk tugging at the corners of his lips despite his irritation. He pressed a fist against his mouth, trying not to laugh outright, before composing himself. "Elisabeth, you've really done it this time," he whispered, his voice teetering between exasperation and reluctant affection.

Van den Heuvel's voice thundered through the air. "You dare to write such words to my daughter without seeking my permission first? Have you no respect for our traditions or for me as her father? This—this blatant disregard for our customs is an insult to my authority and to our family's honor!"

Elisabeth's heart pounded; palms sweaty as she watched the confrontation unfold. She swallowed hard, her mind racing. This was not how she had imagined it would go. Her stomach churned with anxiety, but she knew she had to act quickly. Paralyzed by indecision, she hesitated, fear and uncertainty holding her back for a crucial moment.

The imposing man took a step closer to Gerrit, eyes blazing with anger. "Do you think you can simply sneak around behind my back, filling her head with foolish notions of love? The entire town knows of your secret meetings, where you read sonnets to her under the moonlight. Your impudence threatens to bring shame upon us all! What gives you the right to pursue her in secret, without even the courtesy of speaking to me first?" Marguerite's father paused; his breath heavy with emotion. "If you truly cared for her, you would have approached me like a man, not skulked about like a thief in the night. Now, explain yourself, Gerrit Lanchal, and make me understand why I shouldn't banish you from seeing Marguerite ever again!"

Before Gerrit could respond, Elisabeth emerged from behind the bush, her legs trembling as she ran toward Van den Heuvel. "Wait!" she called out. "Please, sir, he's telling the truth. Gerrit had nothing to do with it. This is all a huge misunderstanding."

Van den Heuvel shuffled back a step. "Who are you?"

Elisabeth took a deep breath, trying to steady her racing heart. "My name is Elisabeth. I'm a friend of Gerrit's. I wrote the letter, pretending to be him."

Van den Heuvel's eyes widened in shock. "You did what?"

Gerrit, equally stunned, took a hesitant step forward. His face pale as he stammered slightly. "Elisabeth...you...you wrote that?"

Feeling overwhelmed by the situation, Elisabeth glanced around anxiously. Just then, David appeared behind her, his presence offering silent support. She looked at him gratefully, finding comfort in his reassuring presence amidst the chaos. Gathering her courage, she turned her attention back to Van den Heuvel. "I'm sorry, sir…" Her voice trembled. "I only wanted to help. Marguerite and Gerrit love each other, but he's too shy to tell you." She stole a glance at Gerrit, her posture stooping as she leaned in to whisper, "It's true. The entire town knows."

Gerrit's eyes widened in shock, his cheeks reddening further at the realization. He shifted uncomfortably, unable to meet anyone's gaze.

Van den Heuvel's anger wavered, replaced by a flicker of understanding. He glanced at Gerrit, then back at Elisabeth. "*You* wrote this letter?"

"Sir, please forgive me, but after learning about Marguerite's betrothal—"

"Marguerite's betrothal?" Van den Heuvel's shock deepened visibly, his brows furrowing as his mind raced to make sense of the situation.

"To Adrian van der Wollen," Gerrit responded, his voice still soft but with a brand-new steadiness. Though his natural shyness lingered, there was a hint of bravery in his tone as he faced Marguerite's father. "A man who will *never* love her even half as much as I do," he added, his words carrying a touch of conviction despite his timidity.

As Gerrit spoke, Elisabeth watched a realization dawn on Van den Heuvel's face. A chuckle escaped him, starting as a rumble deep in his chest before erupting into full-bodied laughter. Elisabeth couldn't help but smile as she witnessed the tension of the moment dissolving with each peal of laughter. It was as if a weight had been lifted off his shoulders, replaced by amusement at the absurdity of the situation.

"I think there's been a misunderstanding," the man finally said. His voice still carried an undertone of authority that made the air tense. "Gerrit, my boy…" He turned to face him with a stern yet encouraging gaze, "this misinformation has shed light on something important. I'm not sure where you heard about Marguerite's betrothal, but it's incorrect. My daughter *Katherina* is the one betrothed to Adrian Van der Wollen, not Marguerite. Now, I understand your affection for Marguerite, and I must say, you come from a respectable family. If you really love her, it's time for you to step forward. Marguerite needs a man who will provide for her, who will stand by her side through thick and thin. I've been waiting for you to come and see me about her. Don't let fear hold you back any longer. Be the man she deserves," he said, his tone firm, emphasizing the gravity of the situation.

As Elisabeth observed Gerrit's reaction to Van den Heuvel's words, she could see the turmoil playing out on his face. His eyes widened with a mixture of overwhelming relief and a new sense of purpose.

"Thank you, sir." Gerrit's voice trembled slightly. "I…I'll do what's right. For Marguerite," he vowed, his gaze steady while making his promise.

Elisabeth felt a surge of pride for her friend as he gathered his courage to face the challenges ahead.

Meanwhile, Van den Heuvel cleared his throat, his expression softening. "Well, Lanchal," he said with a small smile, "at least we know you have a heart as brave as a lion, even if your roar is yet to be heard." With a gentle pat on Gerrit's shoulder, he then bid them farewell. "It seems you youngsters have things well in hand," he added with a chuckle, giving them a nod of approval. "I'll leave you to your picnic then. Just remember, Gerrit," he added with a meaningful look, "don't keep my daughter waiting too long."

With those parting words, Van den Heuvel turned and made his way back to the road.

As Elisabeth and Gerrit shared a moment of relieved laughter, David stepped closer, shaking his head in amusement. "Only *you* could turn a simple matchmaking attempt into such a delightful mess," David said, his tone laced with affectionate teasing. He exchanged a knowing glance with her as he settled onto the picnic blanket, reaching for a piece of crusty bread.

Elisabeth flashed him a bemused grin and parked herself beside him. "Isn't that part of my charm?" she countered, giving him a gentle swat. "Besides, where's the fun in a predictable love story?"

Gerrit chuckled, a warm smile lighting up his face. "You two have certainly made life more interesting."

Elisabeth bowed her head, her eyes lifting to meet his. "I'm *really* sorry, Gerrit. This matchmaking plan didn't go as expected. I never imagined it would become so…complicated."

David couldn't resist adding his own playful jab. "Yes, because nobody warned you *repeatedly* not to get involved," he said, wide-eyed, earning another playful swat from her.

"It's all right." Gerrit bit down on a smile. "Sometimes the greatest adventures are the ones that take us by surprise. It certainly worked out for the best in the end, didn't it?" He paused, taking a moment to look around at the romantic setting. "Well, I should probably let you two enjoy the rest of your picnic in peace. I have a feeling there might be some more unexpected adventures waiting for me elsewhere. Who knows, maybe even involving a certain *someone*." With a nod of farewell, Gerrit turned to leave, his steps carrying him away from the idyllic scene.

David turned to Elisabeth with a raised eyebrow, a hint of disbelief in his gaze. "I'm going to start calling you Pandora from now on."

Elisabeth squinted in confusion. "Pandora?"

"The first woman the gods ever made."

Elisabeth's head jerked back. "Pandora?"

"A woman of unparalleled beauty, gifted by the gods themselves," David said with a mischievous wink.

Elisabeth flicked her hair over her shoulder in an exaggerated motion, mimicking the graceful gesture of a great beauty. "Oh, that definitely sounds just like me," she teased.

David's chuckle faded into a tender smile as he leaned in, his lips gently capturing hers in a sweet, stolen kiss. Under the sheltering branches of the willow tree, with the tranquil waters of the river gently flowing beside them, his hands rested on her waist, drawing her closer on the soft picnic blanket they sat on. The dappled sunlight filtering through the leaves created a magical ambiance, casting a soft, romantic glow over their embrace.

"Jupiter gave Pandora a jar and warned to never open it," he whispered against her lips.

Elisabeth pulled back, a subtle smirk playing at the corners of her mouth. "She opened it, didn't she?"

"Of course." David's voice softened as he continued the tale. "Despite being *repeatedly* warned not to open the jar, curiosity got the better of her, and she couldn't resist taking a peek inside."

Elisabeth smiled as she listened, the pieces of the puzzle slowly clicking into place. "What did Pandora find inside?"

"Well, she found all the sorrows and troubles of the world, swirling within the confines of the jar. But amidst the chaos, something remarkable happened." He paused and quirked an eyebrow. "All the evils escaped, leaving only one thing behind."

She leaned in, her curiosity evident. "What was it?"

David's fingers trailed along the back of Elisabeth's hand, his touch sending a pleasant shiver up her spine. "Hope," he whispered, his voice barely audible. "In the end, *hope* was the only thing that remained. It's a bit like you, really."

Elisabeth's eyes widened in amused surprise. "How?"

"Well," David said, leaning back, "you're always coming up with these 'great ideas', even when warned not to get involved. Just like Pandora was warned not to open the jar."

Elisabeth laughed, her voice carrying a hint of recognition. "Are you saying my ideas bring trouble?"

David's head jerked back. "You swallowed poison to fake your own death!"

Her lips curved into a playful smile. "Yeah, but you can't argue with results, can you? Besides, I knew you had the elixir."

He chuckled, shaking his head in amazement. "Don't *ever* attempt something like *that* again, *cor meum*. Your ideas stir things up, but it seems they always lead to something good in the end. Just like

Pandora's jar still held hope."

She playfully poked him. "Are you implying I'm a mix of trouble and hope?"

David grinned, brushing a stray lock of hair from her face. "I wouldn't have it any other way, even if it means dealing with a little chaos now and then."

Elisabeth inched closer, her lips brushing his ear as she whispered, "Well, just be warned, I'll probably have lots more of my 'great ideas'."

David smiled as he gently took her hands in his, intertwining their fingers. "You know, Pandora's husband, Epimetheus, loved her deeply. Despite the trials they faced, his affection for her never wavered. He understood her complexities, her curiosity, and accepted her for who she was, imperfections and all."

As he spoke, Elisabeth's lips parted slightly and her heartbeat quickened, hanging onto his every word.

"Their love endured, serving as a reminder that even in the face of challenges, true love remains steadfast."

"It's a bit like us, isn't it?" she whispered with a shy smile, their fingers gently tracing each other's palms, savoring the intimate connection.

In response, David drew nearer, their lips meeting in another tender kiss.

"Should we head back now?" Elisabeth eventually suggested, breaking the tranquil moment with a gentle prompt.

David's gaze held hers for a moment longer, filled with unspoken affection, before he nodded in agreement. "Sure."

As they wrapped up the picnic and gathered their belongings, her heart swelled with gratitude for the day's unexpected turn of events. With each item carefully stowed away, a sense of contentment washed over her, and they began their journey home.

Along the way, Elisabeth couldn't help but marvel at their surroundings—the towering spires of the churches, the gentle flow of the river, the friendly faces passing by. "I *really* like Ghent," she said, her voice filled with genuine affection.

David glanced at her with a smile. "It's hard not to." His own admiration for the city was clear in his tone. "There's just something about this place that feels like home."

Upon reaching the belfry, Elisabeth stared up at its towering spire. "We should climb to the top someday. Theresa says the view is breathtaking."

David snorted in amusement. "But what of the dragon perched atop it?"

Elisabeth nudged him. "Just remember, this will be our meeting place if we ever get separated for some reason. It's a silly habit, I know, but when I was little, whenever my parents took me somewhere new, we'd always looked for the tallest building or monument and agreed to meet there if we got separated."

David drew nearer as he looked at her. "I recall you mentioning that in Paris, outside of Notre Dame." He paused. "But I have no intention of ever losing you, *cor meum.* I'll always protect you."

Elisabeth gave him a shy smile and lowered her gaze. Her hand sought his, their fingers entwining in a silent pledge of trust and affection.

As they returned to the house, they slipped through the crimson curtain into the bookshop, drawn by the sound of laughter from within.

"Perfect timing," Johanna said to Elisabeth. "Why don't you come sit for a miniature portrait?"

Her eyes brightened at the invitation. "Really?"

Johanna nodded. "Absolutely. I've been wanting to capture your likeness for some time now." She gathered a wooden easel and a small piece of parchment, arranging them in a well-lit corner of the bookshop. As Johanna set up, Elisabeth noticed David giving her a subtle, grateful nod. This silent acknowledgment made her wonder if he had secretly requested the portrait.

Elisabeth settled into a chair while Johanna picked a selection of colored inks and fine brushes from her collection. Nearby, Master Lanchal worked at his desk, meticulously binding a book. "Our Johanna is truly a remarkable artist. Her talent knows no bounds."

Elisabeth chuckled. "I've heard the same praise from Theresa," she said, causing Johanna to blush. "It seems your talents are quite legendary around here."

David stood nearby, watching with a content smile. He leaned against a shelf, his eyes following Johanna's skilled movements as she painted Elisabeth's features with delicate strokes of colored ink. Occasionally, he offered a word of encouragement, his presence a comforting backdrop to the creative process.

The atmosphere was filled with quiet concentration and the rustle of parchment. Everyone chatted happily, the conversation light and full of shared stories and laughter. Johanna captured Elisabeth's likeness with each stroke, bringing her image to life on the tiny piece of parchment.

After a while, Johanna paused, her expression filled with satisfaction. She offered the painting to David. "What do you think?"

David's eyes sparkled with gratitude as he carefully accepted the miniature portrait, ensuring he didn't smudge the still-drying paint. Elisabeth watched closely, noting the way he examined it with tender admiration. "It's…it's beautiful." His voice trembled with emotion as if he might cry. He then blinked, trying to compose himself. "Thank you."

Johanna offered a comforting pat on his back, her gesture motherly and reassuring.

Elisabeth moved closer to get a better look at the portrait. Her cheeks flushed as she gazed at the tiny picture of herself. "You're too flattering," she admitted with a modest smile. "What an incredible job."

David waited patiently until he was sure the painting was dry. Then he pulled a tiny leather pouch from beneath his shirt, where it hung on a new string around his neck. With a wink, he gently tucked the portrait into the pouch, treating it as though it were a precious locket. "Mind if I keep you close to my heart?"

Elisabeth's pulse quickened as she met his gaze, feeling a surge of warmth at his request. "Of course not," she said with a shy smile.

"David, is it possible you could help me with a task?" Lanchal asked. "It won't take long, but there's something important I need to finish."

"Certainly, I'd be happy to help."

Elisabeth excused herself from the shop, giving David's hand a gentle squeeze. "I'll see you later," she whispered, their eyes meeting briefly in a moment of shared understanding.

He nodded, a reassuring smile on his lips. "I'll be here."

With a last glance at David, Elisabeth grabbed the picnic basket and walked into the house. Inside, she found Theresa sweeping the floor.

The older woman looked up with a grin. "You're back. How was the picnic? Did you manage to evade the predictable ants?"

Elisabeth set the basket down. "It was wonderful. And, thankfully, no ants."

Theresa chuckled. "Could you do me a favor and fetch some water from the well? We're running low."

"Of course."

She grabbed a pail and left the house, the distant sound of hooves clattering against the cobblestone echoing in her ears. As she hurried down the street, the rhythmic clip-clop of the horse's hooves became more distinct, punctuating the stillness of the late afternoon.

Glancing over her shoulder, the hairs on the back of Elisabeth's neck stood on end. Gripping the bucket tighter, she quickened the pace, knuckles turning white with tension.

"Relax," she whispered to herself, trying to quell the rising panic. She'd felt this way several times before and each time, it turned out to be nothing. Surely, this was just her imagination running wild again.

Approaching the courtyard, the sun painted long shadows across the square. Despite the comforting golden light, a chill ran down her spine, an instinctual warning that she was not alone.

Elisabeth glanced over her shoulder again, heart pounding with the unshakable sensation of being hunted. Gripping the bucket, she quickened her steps, each one a desperate attempt to outrun the invisible threat that lingered just beyond her sight.

As she reached the well, the sound of hooves grew louder, the steady rhythm now accompanied by the creaking of leather and the snorting of a horse. This time, it wasn't her imagination running wild.

Panic surged through her.

She spun around, eyes wide with fear.

Out of the shadows, Crooked Nose emerged.

The water bucket slipped from Elisabeth's trembling hands, clattering to the ground as her grip faltered.

Chapter Seventeen

"My lady," Facio hissed from atop his horse, his gaze scanning their surroundings to ensure they were not overheard. "You and your husband need to leave Ghent now." The tall, imposing figure with his crooked nose and weathered attire towered over her. His dark hair streaked with gray gave him a rugged appearance that underscored the firmness of his voice.

Elisabeth's heart pounded in her chest.

"The guild records," Facio explained, his sharp glances around the courtyard heightening the tension in the air, "registering David as an apprentice—it left a trail straight to your doorstep."

She swallowed hard, trying to steady her breathing. "I need to get David and leave now."

Facio leaned in closer, his voice dropping to a whisper. "Your father is here. Tartare knows you're alive. They intend to proceed as planned."

A chill ran down her spine as the gravity of his words sank in. This could only mean one thing: they were going to kill David and force her into marriage to secure their alliance. The thought of it made her blood run cold. Unlike Cato's men, who she had come to know after they saved Rosamund, her horse, Tartare's were far scarier—cold, calculating, and relentless.

Facio nodded, the dark horse shifting impatiently beneath him as he spoke. "I rode ahead, trying to buy

172

you more time. But you must hurry."

"Thank you." Elisabeth's voice was filled with gratitude despite the fear gripping her.

As she turned to rush back to the house, the sound of Facio's horse's hooves echoed in the empty courtyard, a grim reminder of the dire situation.

Heart pounding in her ears, Elisabeth fled, terror propelling her forward. Each step was a race against time, the weight of impending doom pressing on her. She darted down the street, the clip-clop of hooves fading into the distance.

Cato was here.

In Ghent.

Reaching the bookshop, she burst through the door, breathless and wild-eyed. "David!" she cried, her voice strained as she ran to the back of the shop to his little nook. "We need to go. *Now*. Cato's here. They found us."

David's hands trembled, dropping the tools he held as her words sunk in. Panic swept across his features and he grabbed Elisabeth's hand, pulling her toward the front of the shop.

As Elisabeth's heart pounded in her chest, the distant sound of approaching hooves grew louder, echoing through the streets like a grim omen. Cato and Tartare were closing in.

Lanchal and Johanna exchanged worried glances, their concern evident. "What's happening?" Lanchal asked, his brow furrowed.

At that moment, Gerrit walked through the front door, his eyes wide. "Come see the lavish carriage pulling up outside." He let out a low whistle, his voice tinged with disbelief. "The craftsmanship and brazen display of wealth are unbelievable. Who could it possibly be?"

David's demeanor shifted suddenly, his posture straightening and his eyes hardening with resolve. The gentle bookmaker he'd become seemed to melt away, revealing the former gladiator who had vowed to protect Elisabeth at any cost. "It's Elisabeth's *extremely* powerful father." He reached for his rope sling and grabbed a rock from his belt pouch, securing it to the end of the rope with a few swift knots, his fingers moving with practiced ease. "We eloped to escape her arranged marriage, but now the man wants me dead so he can proceed with his plans."

That was the short version.

A stunned silence enveloped the room. Lanchal's eyes widened in shock, his mouth agape. Johanna gasped, both hands flying to her mouth, while Gerrit's face turned pale, his gaze darting nervously toward the entrance.

Realizing the imminent danger, Master Lanchal straightened his own frail frame. "Hide at the back. I'll handle this," he said, his words surprisingly steady. "I'll tell your father you're not here. Go, quickly."

David shook his head, his expression unyielding. "No. We need to leave. I'm sorry," he said, regret heavy in his voice. "We never meant for any of this to involve you." With a swift glance at Elisabeth, he motioned for her to follow as he moved toward the crimson curtain, every movement conveying a sense of urgency and purpose.

Just then, the door opened, and Cato strode into the shop with an air of calm authority, followed by two men Elisabeth assumed were Tartare's. His presence filled the room, casting a shadow over everyone present.

Her shoulders tightened as she met his steely gaze. Their former friend, with his now gray hair and handsome yet sinister features, exuded an aura of controlled danger.

"Ah, my prodigal daughter." His voice cut through the tense atmosphere. "I've come to take you home."

Elisabeth's breath caught in her throat as the words hung heavy in the air.

"Seize Monsieur Perrier," Cato commanded, his tone cold and unforgiving. "Though vows may be binding in the eyes of the Church, he is to be charged with abduction, theft, and the grave crime of disrupting a contract of noble accord."

Cato had no interest in David, except as a pawn. It was Elisabeth's ability to time-travel that he found useful. He envisioned himself as one of the gods of old, wielding power and influence beyond imagination. With Elisabeth's access to modern technology and knowledge, he saw an opportunity to become an unstoppable force. To Cato, this was not merely about personal gain; it was about reshaping the world and bending it to his will. He was determined to exploit her ability, believing that together, they could conquer any foe and rewrite the very fabric of history.

As Tartare's mercenaries advanced, David's hand shot out, the weighted rope whirling through the air with precision. The end looped around the ankles of the first man, yanking him off his feet with a heavy thud. The second mercenary lunged forward, but David was ready. With another rock from his belt pouch, he hurled it with pinpoint accuracy, striking the man in the forehead and sending him crashing to the ground.

Cato's expression became rigid, but David and Elisabeth didn't wait. They dashed toward the crimson curtain. As they passed, Cato made a sudden dive, his hand swiping through the air, narrowly missing Elisabeth's arm.

"Go, go!" David yelled, his grip tight on Elisabeth's hand as they barreled through the drape and into the house. Behind them, Cato's furious roar boomed, spurring them to move even faster as the thunderous footfalls of his men stormed into both the shop and the house, their voices mingling with Cato's enraged commands.

Elisabeth and David didn't look back. They sprinted down the narrow hallway, their footsteps echoing off the stone floor.

As they dashed through the great hall, Theresa emerged from the pantry, stepping into the center of the room. Her eyes wide with alarm as the clamor reverberated through the house, indicating that something significant was happening.

With quickened strides, David and Elisabeth maneuvered around her, leaving the woman stunned in their wake.

At that moment, more of Tartare's men crashed through the back door, their presence announced by the splintering of wood and urgent shouts.

"Upstairs!" David called to Elisabeth.

Uncertainty clouded her mind, but his grip on her hand remained strong. The tension in his muscles and the firmness in his movements gave her strength as they pushed forward. Without hesitation, they raced up the wooden stairs, each step echoing beneath their pounding feet. Desperation fueled their flight, hearts racing and breaths coming in sharp gasps.

The dimly lit attic loomed above them, a fleeting promise of safety amidst the chaos below.

Reaching their room, David locked the door behind them. "We need to block it." He scanned the cramped space, searching for something to secure their makeshift refuge. Spotting the coiled rope tucked away in a corner, he grinned with a hint of cockiness, eyes sparkling with mischief. "Knew I'd need this one day." With a wink at Elisabeth, he grabbed the rope, looping it cross-body, draping it over his shoulder and across his chest.

Elisabeth grabbed the trunk, their eyes meeting in silent understanding, and together they pushed it against the door. The muffled sounds of pursuit grew closer, but for the moment, they had a brief respite.

David glanced at Elisabeth; his posture strong. "There's only one way out, love."

She swallowed the lump in her throat and nodded.

With no time to lose, they hurried to the dormer window. David flung the shutters open and climbed onto the table, testing the strength of the clay roof tiles as he eased himself out. The tiles held under his weight, and he carefully positioned himself on the roof of the three-storied house, then reached back to help Elisabeth climb through. Positioned at the rear of the half-timbered building, their path to freedom lay across the steeply pitched rooftops of neighboring houses, away from Cato and his men.

They carefully slid down to the eaves, where the roof met the wall. The warm summer air provided little solace as David moved first, edging toward the neighbor's roof. His boots scraped against the tiles, and Elisabeth followed, her heart pounding. The other houses blurred into a mosaic of beige and brown as they focused on their escape.

"Easy now." David's hand gripped Elisabeth's while stepping onto the lower section of the adjacent roof. After steadying themselves, they crept along the sharply pitched edge, moving toward the third house's rooftop. His voice, steady and reassuring, was a comforting presence amidst her rising panic.

They reached the third roof and David motioned for Elisabeth to follow his lead. With cautious steps, they pressed on, movements quick yet deliberate, navigating the uneven surface.

David pointed across a daunting gap toward the next building. "We need to get onto *that* roof. It'll bring us down in the little courtyard. I'll jump first. Ready?"

"No," Elisabeth whimpered, fingers tightening around David's hand, clinging to him for dear life. A wave of dizziness hit as she stared at the hard cobblestone in the narrow alley below.

David gently lifted her chin, redirecting her gaze to meet his. "Trust me. You can do this. I won't let anything happen to you."

She nodded, taking a deep breath, trying to stop shaking. Despite the ground appearing distant and foreboding from the three-story height, she reminded herself it couldn't be more than a four-foot jump between the rooftops. The steep pitch of the opposite roof, however, made the leap even more frightening. They needed to land precisely on the eaves where the roof met the wall, or risk sliding off the tiles.

David gave her hand a reassuring squeeze before

letting go. He took a few steps back, then sprinted toward the edge and leaped across the gap.

After landing on the opposite roof, he stumbled slightly, grabbing a sturdy wooden beam for support. Steadying himself, David turned and extended his other arm toward Elisabeth, fingers outstretched, ready to catch her. His eyes met hers, conveying both reassurance and insistence as he motioned for her to jump.

"Your turn, love," he called out in a hushed yet audible whisper, his voice calm despite the danger that surrounded them. "Jump to me. I swear, I will catch you."

As Elisabeth prepared to leap across the gap, a sudden commotion erupted from behind, sending a jolt of fear through her veins. David's expression tightened with determination, his focus shifting between Elisabeth and the approaching men. "Don't look back. Look at me," he instructed, firmness lacing his words. "You need to jump *now, cor meum*."

Elisabeth gritted her teeth, wrestling with the rising tide of panic threatening to overtake her. Time was running out. With David's silent encouragement spurring her on, she took a step back, muscles tensing in anticipation. She drew in a deep breath, summoning every ounce of courage, and then sprinted to the edge and jumped to the next rooftop, propelled by a burst of adrenaline and unwavering trust in David.

As she landed beside him, pulse still racing from the exhilarating leap, a rush of relief washed over her. Before she could even register her foot slipping off the narrow ridge, David's arm wrapped around her waist, pulling her back from the edge. He anchored Elisabeth against him, steadying her instantly.

"Gotcha," he said, keeping her close. She felt the steady rise and fall of his chest against her, grounding her amidst the chaos.

The men chasing them abruptly changed their minds, retreating toward the attic window. Elisabeth couldn't help but snort in amusement at their sudden reversal. Undoubtedly, they planned to rush down the stairs and out the front door, determined to cut off their escape from the street instead.

The sun dipped lower, casting ominous shadows over the medieval city. Elisabeth followed David along the narrow roof ledge, fear and determination warring inside her with each precarious step.

Don't look down.

Don't look down.

Elisabeth wiped sweaty palms on her skirt when they reached the far side of the roof. She peered over the edge at the courtyard far below, where the infamous sheet still billowed like a captured cloud. Her heart raced, but there was no time to dwell on fear.

"Listen to me." David's voice was firm. "We're going to use the rope to get down, but you need to move quickly." He unslung the coil of rope from across his body, laying it down as he spoke.

Elisabeth nodded, breath catching in her throat while trying to calm her nerves.

With swift movements, David looped the rope around Elisabeth's waist and shoulders, his hands moving with efficiency. "I'm making you a harness. It'll keep you safe, I promise." With each knot and twist, he crafted a secure support.

David then tied the end of the rope to a roof

bracket, giving it a firm tug to ensure its stability. As he finished, his eyes met Elisabeth's with firm confidence. "Sit back, let the rope slide through your hands. I'll guide you and then follow. Trust me, you can do this."

Elisabeth stood at the edge, her fingers gripping the rope. She took a deep breath and lowered herself over the side.

Following David's instructions, Elisabeth sat back into the makeshift harness, extending her legs out in front. With a steady hand, she released her hold on the edge of the roof, allowing herself to slide down the rope. As she descended, she kept her feet pressed against the uneven wall, using it to control speed and maintain balance.

With David's guidance from above, Elisabeth's descent was rapid, her movements smooth and controlled. Despite her pounding heart, she remained calm, trusting David and the strength of the harness. In mere seconds, she reached the ground, her swift descent a testament to her composure.

Releasing the rope, she stepped away from the building, legs shaking with relief. She glanced over her shoulder, then looked up to see David already positioning himself at the edge, holding the rope just as he had instructed her.

David descended at breakneck speed, his movements sure and steady. In no time, he joined Elisabeth on the ground, a proud smile on his face as he grabbed her hand and ran—their escape hurried by the sight of Tartare's men on horseback, who spotted them and gave chase. The sound of pounding hooves echoed behind, driving them to push their pace even harder.

As they twisted through the labyrinthine streets,

they dodged the occasional passerby and navigated around closed shopfronts, putting more and more distance between themselves and their pursuers.

"This way!" Without hesitation, Elisabeth pulled David down a side street toward the bustling riverfront. Though he was the faster runner, it was her quick thinking that propelled them forward.

They narrowly avoided colliding with a family out for an evening stroll, the children laughing and playing. Ducking under the arms of a baker carrying a tray of freshly baked bread, Elisabeth caught the tempting aroma wafting through the air. A startled man dropped a crate of vegetables, scattering produce across the cobblestones and briefly delaying their pursuers.

With a fleeting glance to her right, Elisabeth spotted a boat approaching and trusted her instincts as they dashed toward the swing bridge. They had to reach it before it swung fully open.

David and Elisabeth burst forward, leaping onto the bridge just in time as the structure began to move. The bridge swayed beneath their feet as they sprinted across, the operator focused on his task and unaware of their presence.

As they approached the edge and prepared for their final jump, the operator finally glimpsed them, shouting, "Hey!"

Elisabeth's heart pounded with adrenaline, every step feeling like a leap of faith. With one final, daring jump, they leaped off the bridge and landed safely on the other side of the river.

Now with a substantial lead, Elisabeth and David pressed on toward the city wall. The streets were alive with activity as city folk savored the late summer ambiance. Elisabeth struggled to steady her breathing after the prolonged sprint, each inhalation shallow and quick. Her heart raced, but she forced herself to remain composed. As they neared the gate, David's grip on her hand tightened, their pace easing into a brisk walk to blend with the flow of travelers and avoid drawing attention.

They maneuvered through the bustling crowd, dodging children playing nearby. Elisabeth stared ahead, scanning the faces for any hint of recognition or suspicion. The distant toll of a bell marked the passing hour and signaled the imminent closing of the city gates for the night. A quick glance at David confirmed the gravity of their predicament: they had to blend into the crowd, becoming anonymous figures to evade any sharp-eyed guards just ahead. The pressure mounted. Reaching the gates before they sealed shut was their only chance to avoid being trapped inside with Cato and Tartare's men.

Finally, they passed through the imposing entrance. Elisabeth felt a surge of excitement rush through her veins. Each scrutinizing stare seemed like a spotlight, threatening exposure. Despite this, she maintained a facade of normalcy, walking with measured steps and focusing on the unseen horizon beyond the city walls.

Relief washed over her as they emerged from the gate's shadow and navigated through the shanty town unnoticed. Eventually, they found the familiar wooded path they'd arrived on, offering a flicker of hope amid uncertainty. With each step, they moved farther from the city, closer to the freedom they desperately sought.

Night fell, but Elisabeth and David continued along the forest trail, their footsteps careful and silent. They dared not light a fire, fearing it would alert pursuers. Instead, they relied on the faint glow of the moon to guide their way.

Every rustle of leaves or crackle of twigs sent a jolt of fear through Elisabeth's veins, her senses heightened to the slightest sound. She cast furtive glances over her shoulder, half expecting to see shadows lurking in the darkness, ready to pounce at any moment.

David's hand found hers, his touch a silent reassurance. They moved as one, their breaths held in anticipation, their hearts pounding in unison.

After what felt like hours of tense, silent trekking, David stopped and listened. The forest was still, except for the natural sounds of the night. He turned to Elisabeth. "I think we can stop and rest until morning. It doesn't seem like we're being followed."

Elisabeth exhaled a shaky breath, relief mixing with exhaustion. She nodded, and they found a small, sheltered area beneath a cluster of trees. "I'll be right back," she said, reaching for her necklace while thinking of home.

****

In an instant, the quartz crystal's energy transported her to familiar surroundings. As she rummaged through the old camping supplies in the basement, her eyes skimmed over a couple of weathered fishing rods and Dad's old shotgun, barely visible beneath a tattered blanket. She wasted no time grabbing a sleeping bag and a small, battery-operated lantern.

****

"Miss me?" Elisabeth said when she reappeared in the forest, holding the bedroll and lamp in her arms—

although no time had passed for David.

He looked at her wide-eyed, a playful smile tugging at his lips. "You have no idea," he chuckled, shaking his head. "I don't believe I'll ever get used to that."

Elisabeth turned on the light and handed it to David, its faint glow illuminating their surroundings.

He marveled at the lantern; eyes wide with amazement. "This is similar to the lamps we wore in the mine," he said, shaking his head in wonder. He clicked the button, turning it off and on repeatedly. "And just as fun to toy with," he added, chuckling at his own antics.

Elisabeth smiled as David continued to fiddle with the light. She busied herself spreading out the sleeping bag and then climbed inside, unable to suppress a giggle as she straightened out her bunched-up dress, making sure it lay comfortably around her. When back home, she'd been tempted to bring her old childhood sleeping bag just to get a reaction out of David—a vibrant pink creation adorned with cartoon unicorns and glittery stars. Instead, she found herself nestled in her parents' old one since it was bigger. "We can share this."

With a mischievous grin, David set the lantern down, kicked off his shoes, and discarded the doublet beside the sleeping bag. He crawled in beside her, still wearing his white chemise and leggings. "Well, I hope you don't mind snuggling up with me then," he teased, wrapping his arms around her. "I'll keep you warm."

Elisabeth laughed, but the weight of exhaustion pressed down on her limbs. Snuggling closer to him, she let out a tired sigh.

David took a deep breath, seeming to savor the moment. "I could get used to this," he whispered, his breath warm against her ear.

Elisabeth managed a weary smile, her eyelids heavy with fatigue. "Me too," she admitted, her body relaxing against his.

As they lay in the sleeping bag in the quiet woods, the distant hoot of an owl filled the surrounding air. Elisabeth turned to David, her voice barely above a whisper. "We obviously can't go back to Lanchal's place. Any idea what we're going to do?"

David shifted beside her; his gaze fixed on the dark canopy above. His silence spoke volumes, heavy with defeat and frustration.

"Well, I've been thinking…" Elisabeth took a deep breath. "What if we return to Beatrice and Lancelot's village? There's a cottage available for rent there."

David turned his head to face her, his eyes meeting hers with a spark of interest. "There is, isn't there?"

"Yes, Lancelot and Stefan both mentioned it." Her smile grew wider. "What if we rent it and make ourselves a cozy little home in Lindenhart? Cato will *never* find us there, especially since the village is practically hidden in the woods."

As Elisabeth watched David's reaction, she saw his eyes widen with overwhelming emotion. She sensed his breath catching, his chest swelling with the significance of the idea. It was as if this simple notion encapsulated all his dreams and desires in life.

But then, a shadow crossed his features, and Elisabeth could almost feel the weight of reality crashing down on him. She saw the moment when excitement gave way to a more somber realization—

when practicality intruded upon the dream.

"I have no money, *cor meum*, nor anything to offer in exchange for staying there. You cannot risk trading spices again."

Elisabeth looked at him, a playful smile tugging at the corners of her lips. "I have a *really* good idea."

Chapter Eighteen

Mischievous thoughts flickered through Elisabeth's mind as she looked at David. "Seriously, I have a *really* good idea," she repeated.

David chuckled. His eyes, filled with both affection and a hint of resignation, met hers, conveying a silent acknowledgment of the familiar pattern of her misadventures. "I can only imagine."

She flashed him a bemused grin. "Aren't you even going to ask what it is?"

He pursed his lips in thought. "Do I dare?" Despite his playful hesitation, there was an undeniable twinkle of curiosity in his gaze as he awaited Elisabeth's response.

Her smile softened. "What if I told you we don't need to worry about money for renting the cottage?"

David quirked an eyebrow.

Elisabeth snuggled closer, her breath brushing against David's ear as she spoke in a hushed tone. "Remember the old mine?"

"Of course."

"You said there was lead in the walls, right?"

David's head flinched back slightly. "Yes...?"

"Well, do you think we can get some of it out?"

His brows furrowed. "Yes. Why?"

Elisabeth's smile widened. "The elixir is supposed to turn lead into gold, right?"

David's breath hitched as he processed her words. "And you have the elixir," he muttered, almost to himself.

"Just imagine it…" Elisabeth's pulse raced. "We'll extract some lead, melt it down, and add elixir to it. If it works, we'll have more than enough gold to rent the little cottage. It will definitely draw less attention than the nutmegs did. Nutmeg was too unusual, too exotic. But gold? It's valuable without raising too many eyebrows."

A slow smile spread across David's face, his doubts seeming to fade away in the wake of Elisabeth's infectious enthusiasm. "I have to admit, that's…incredible." He let out a spontaneous laugh and hugged her tighter.

Elisabeth snuggled into his embrace, head resting against his chest. "Tomorrow, we'll start fresh," she said with a yawn.

David turned off the little lamp and kissed her forehead. "Yes, tomorrow." His own eyelids grew heavy. "We'll make it work—*Pandora*."

As the forest whispered around them, they drifted off to sleep, cradled by the natural world, with dreams of a brighter future and the promise of a new beginning.

****

The morning light filtered through the canopy, casting dappled shadows on the forest floor as Elisabeth awoke. Stretching within the warmth of the sleeping bag, she blinked, slowly becoming aware of her surroundings. With a contented sigh, she sat up, feeling the chill of the morning air on her face. Beside her, David lay on the ground, having crawled out of the sleeping bag in the night.

They were surrounded by a profusion of late summer wildflowers. Along the forest path, delicate clusters of small, white blooms nodded in the breeze, their petals glistening with morning dew. Beside the path, tall spikes of purple blossoms swayed, attracting bees that hummed lazily in the warm air.

Listening to the melodic chirping of songbirds welcoming the new day, a sense of peace washed over Elisabeth. Even David had to admit her idea was *really* good this time. With a gentle smile, she slinked out of the sleeping bag, careful not to disturb him. After rolling it up, she reached for the lantern and then her crystal, thoughts of home on her mind.

Home.

****

In an instant, Elisabeth was back in her own time, the air around her still, as if it too had paused in her absence. With a contented sigh, she took the opportunity to shower and freshen up. Adventures in the fourteenth century were exciting, but the allure of modern luxuries like hot showers was undeniable. Moving about the bedroom afterward, Elisabeth spotted the canteen used in the mines and tunnels. Quickly filling it with water, she pulled the strap over her shoulder and then reached for the quartz crystal.

****

Back in the forest, a sense of calm enveloped Elisabeth and she bent down, brushing her fingers through David's hair. "Time to wake up, Aquarius," she whispered.

David roused from slumber, his eyes fluttering open to meet Elisabeth's gaze. Seeing her there, dressed and ready to go, a sleepy grin spread across his face.

"Good morning." He sat up, yawning, while stretching his arms above his head.

As Elisabeth snorted at his adorable drowsiness, he suddenly reached out, and with a mischievous smile, pulled her onto his lap, eliciting a surprised giggle from her.

Before Elisabeth could react, David's playful demeanor turned affectionate, and he peppered her face with kisses, each one accompanied by a quiet chuckle. Their laughter filled the forest as they shared a moment of gentle affection, the morning light casting a warm glow around them.

"We need to go now," she squealed through giggles.

David helped her off his lap. As they both stood up, he brushed stray leaves clinging to his clothes. "Absolutely." He grabbed his doublet and shoes, slipping them on with ease. Once dressed, they walked away, their steps light with lingering joy.

While walking through the dense forest, twigs and leaves crunched beneath Elisabeth's feet, echoing in the stillness. "I'm looking forward to seeing Lancelot again," she admitted. "He's nice."

David tilted his head. "What about Beatrice?"

Elisabeth's eyes widened in mock fear. "I'm kind of scared of her," she blurted out. "She suits her name—Bee, like a stinging bumblebee."

David suppressed an obvious laugh as he wiped at his mouth. "She's quite straightforward, isn't she?"

"Quite!" Elisabeth's posture perked up. "Hey, that reminds me, I've been meaning to ask—who's this Hannibal you and Lancelot were talking about? Because I can't believe that baby's name is Hannibal."

"Hannibal-Joe," David corrected with a grin.

Elisabeth shot him a knowing look, her lips fighting a smile. "Oh, that is *so* much better."

David led the way along the forest trail, the ground beneath them a patchwork of roots and fallen leaves. "Hannibal Barca was arguably the greatest general who ever lived. He was also the greatest threat Rome had ever seen—by the time he was twenty-six years old!"

Elisabeth, stepping over a thick root, looked at David with raised eyebrows. "At twenty-six? Really?"

He nodded, reaching out to steady her as she navigated a tricky section of the path. "He was from Carthage, Rome's powerful rival just across the Mediterranean Sea. Once, Hannibal led his entire army, elephants included, over the Alps and launch a surprise attack from the north."

"*Elephants?*" Elisabeth's voice was a mix of disbelief and amusement as she ducked under a low-hanging branch, which David held aside for her.

"War elephants," David confirmed, his eyes sparkling with the excitement of the tale. "Can you imagine the Romans' faces when they saw those colossal beasts, with men mounted atop them, charging down from the Alps?" He paused, shaking his head in disbelief. "I once saw an elephant during a *venationes* at the amphitheatre. It was a spectacle that will forever stay etched in my memory."

Elisabeth laughed, the sound mingling with the chirping of birds overhead. "I can only imagine," she said, accepting David's hand as he helped her hop over a mud puddle.

As they walked, his gaze scanned the forest floor. "Hold on." He crouched down to inspect some plants.

"These look like wood sorrel." Picking a few leaves, he added, "They'll make a satisfactory snack if you're hungry later." Retrieving a napkin from his belt pouch, the one Beatrice had given them, David wrapped the foraged wood sorrel in it. "Hopefully this will keep them fresh." With a smile, he tucked the napkin back into his pouch.

Elisabeth watched him with a mix of admiration and curiosity. "You really know your stuff."

"You never know when it might come in handy." A crooked smile spread across his face and he picked another small bundle of the wood sorrel and handed her a stem. "Try some."

Elisabeth eyed the leaves skeptically. They resembled clover, except with three heart-shaped leaflets per stem instead of circles. She hesitated, then nibbled a bit off one of the leaves.

Her eyes widened as she chewed. "It's…tangy. Almost like a lemon." She took another small bite, her expression a mix of surprise and cautious approval. "It's not bad. I didn't expect it to taste so fresh."

David chuckled and popped a leaf into his own mouth. "We'll save the rest for later."

They continued on, the forest sounding alive with the rustling of leaves and the distant calls of woodland creatures. David's stories of Hannibal Barca's exploits seemed to echo through the trees, bringing history to life amidst the greenery.

"And then there was the time Hannibal had his men collect venomous snakes from the surrounding countryside and placed them into clay pots." David paused, a mischievous twinkle in his eye. He reached for a low-hanging branch, pulling it back to let

Elisabeth pass. "Hannibal then launched the clay pots onto enemy ships. The pots would break on impact, and suddenly, angry, venomous snakes were everywhere."

Elisabeth gasped as David continued, his enthusiasm contagious.

"Picture it: the enemy's already tense, and then, out of nowhere, they're surrounded by hissing, slithering snakes on their ships. The chaos and panic disrupted their ability to maneuver, giving Hannibal's forces a huge advantage."

Elisabeth's laughter rang out. "That's ingenious! And terrifying." Her fingers entwined with David's as they walked side by side. She then glanced up at him. "When did all this happen?"

David smiled and squeezed her hand. "Oh, this was a couple hundred years before I was born, during the Second Punic War. The Romans were absolutely terrified of Hannibal. He was a brilliant strategist, almost Herculean in his ability to anticipate and outmaneuver them. Crossing the Alps with war elephants—a feat they thought impossible—made his reputation legendary. Hannibal repeatedly defeated larger Roman armies, not just with military skill but also by playing mind games that made them doubt their own strength and strategy. Parents would tell their children, 'Hannibal's at the gate,' to get them to behave."

Elisabeth's eyes widened in realization and then a smile spread across her face as she connected the dots. "Hannibal's at the gate. That explains Lancelot's joke when we left."

David chuckled at her sudden understanding and then paused near a cluster of bushes. "Blackberries," he said, changing the subject in a casual tone.

"Blackberries?" Elisabeth's stomach grumbled loudly as she dashed closer. Without a second thought, she plunged into the juicy bounty, devouring the ripe berries with gusto, her hunger driving her to indulge in their sweet perfection.

David plucked a few berries for himself. "Hungry, are we?" he teased, watching as she devoured the fruit.

Elisabeth glanced up with a sheepish grin while wiping berry juice from her lips. "Starving," she confessed between mouthfuls. "No offense, but that leaf of wood sorrel wasn't exactly filling. I didn't want to say anything in case you thought you'd barbecue *rat* again."

David chuckled, a twinkle of amusement in his gaze as he reached for another berry. "You'll never let that go, will you?"

"*Rat?*" She popped more ripe berries into her mouth and flashed him a knowing look. "Not a chance."

"Here." He offered her a handful. "They should keep us going until we find something more substantial." He then gave her a second glance. "You know, previously, you would have dashed back to your time for a meal without a second thought."

Elisabeth's hand hesitated for a moment before accepting the berries, her fingers brushing against his in the exchange. David's observation struck a chord, prompting a quiet reflection as she popped a berry into her mouth. He was right. In the past, she would have bolted back home to her own time at the first sign of discomfort or hunger. But now, as she savored the sweetness of the berry, she couldn't deny the growing sense of familiarity and even comfort in this medieval adventure.

She cleared her throat and offered David a timid smile. "I wonder why that is?" Her eyes darted away briefly before returning to meet his gaze.

He leaned closer and raised an eyebrow, a knowing smile playing on his lips. "It's undoubtedly because I am here."

Elisabeth's lips twitched, fighting back a grin as she shook her head.

He wasn't wrong.

"That being said, would it hurt to bring me some of your chocolate now and then, *cor meum*," he whispered with a playful pout.

She couldn't help but smile at David's request. "If we get that little cottage, I'll make sure you have a secret cupboard *filled* with chocolate."

David took Elisabeth's hand, lifting it to his lips to place a kiss upon her knuckles, causing her heart to flutter. He then led the way, their fingers entwined as they walked along the trail together.

The path wound deeper into the woods, the light filtering through the leaves, casting a kaleidoscope of shadows on the ground. David paused, helping Elisabeth navigate a steep incline. As they climbed, he spotted some wild mushrooms and picked a few, adding them to his pouch.

Elisabeth let out a shaky laugh. "You're sure they're not poisonous, right?"

David squinted with amusement. "I assure you, I'm no stranger to mushroom hunting, love. These are safe, I promise." He flashed her a confident grin as they continued along the trail.

"As remarkable as his tactics were," David continued, shifting seamlessly back to his monologue about Hannibal Barca, "it was Hannibal's ability to outmaneuver and out-think his opponents that truly set him apart. He was always outnumbered, yet he turned the tides of battle to his favor, time and time again."

Elisabeth watched David with an amused smile as he recounted the exploits of his obvious hero. She then pointed ahead at the fallen tree where they had shared their meal on the way to Ghent. "Hey, remember that spot?"

He reached down to pluck a few hazelnuts from the forest floor, dropping them into his pouch. "I certainly do."

As they approached the downed tree blocking the trail, Elisabeth ducked under it, this time lifting the hem of her dress to avoid snagging. When she emerged on the other side, David moved behind her, gently twirling her around before scooping her up by the waist and placing her onto the sturdy trunk.

Elisabeth squealed in surprise, her laughter bubbling over. "You never miss an opportunity to sweep me off my feet, do you?" she teased, swinging her legs playfully as she settled on the log.

"With you, it's always worth the effort." With a roguish grin, he settled next to her. Using a rock from his pouch, he cracked open a hazelnut and handed it to her. "Here."

She took the hazelnut, their touch lingering for a moment. "Thanks." She leaned into him, her shoulder pressing against his as they enjoyed their feast of wood sorrel, mushrooms, berries, and nuts. She drank from the flask and then passed it to him, their eyes locking in a tender gaze.

After a while, David hopped down from the log, extending a hand to help Elisabeth. She took it, and as she jumped down, he playfully pulled her close, their faces now inches apart.

Elisabeth bounced on her tiptoes, her lips meeting his in a tender kiss. "Ready to continue?"

"Lead the way, *Juliet*."

Hand in hand, they resumed their journey and David picked up where he had left off.

"Hannibal was the master of surprise and strategy. During another battle, he faced a Roman army nearly twice the size of his own. He created a diversion with oxen and brushwood, making the Romans believe they were up against a far greater force." David gestured to the expanse of the forest as if it were the battlefield itself.

Eventually, they reached the creek where the simple wooden board created a crude bridge. Elisabeth tilted her head to the side, smiling at the familiar scene.

David stepped onto the narrow plank first this time, flashing her a bemused smile. "I remember you making this look easy," he said, arms outstretched for balance.

Elisabeth giggled, but halfway across, David wobbled, trying not to lose his balance as his arms flailed comically.

Elisabeth gasped, her hand flying to her mouth. "Aquarius, be careful!"

David glanced over his shoulder, winked at her, then exaggerated his movements even more, causing Elisabeth to laugh out loud. When he reached the other side, he turned and bowed theatrically. "Made it." His eyes twinkled with mischief.

Elisabeth shook her head, still giggling as she crossed the plank with ease. "You're such a show-off," she said with a playful nudge once she was across.

As they reached the edge of the forest, the path curved alongside the serene lake. Vibrant yellow blooms stretched toward the water; their bright colors reflected on the calm surface. Dragonflies darted above, adding to the idyllic scene.

Hand in hand, they continued onward, veering around the lake instead of entering the village. The path narrowed and became overgrown, thick foliage making navigation more challenging.

Elisabeth looked around. "Are you sure this is the right way?"

"This *must* be the way." David stretched as he scanned their surroundings. He tilted his head to the side, and Elisabeth followed his gaze to an old tree with a small sign nailed to its trunk, partially obscured by undergrowth. They walked closer, brushing away leaves to reveal a simple pickaxe painted on the sign. "Look…" He pointed at the symbol. "I think we just need to follow these markers."

Elisabeth peered down the narrow path, remembering the disorientation they had felt upon exiting the mine. "We must have taken a roundabout way since we didn't know where we were going."

They walked amongst an array of wildflowers. Patches of deep blue mingled with cheerful splashes of orange and pink, creating a tapestry of colors that danced under the midday sun. Elisabeth couldn't help but smile, captivated by the surrounding beauty.

They followed the path, and soon enough, David pointed to a gaping hole in the side of a hill—the entrance to the mine. "Found it."

Elisabeth's breath caught in her throat, suddenly remembering what lurked inside. "I forgot about the bats," she whimpered.

David's gaze met hers with understanding and he wrapped his arms around her in a tender hug from behind. "Last time, it was nearly dusk, so the bats were waking up. Right now, they'll all be in a deep sleep." He pointed toward the midday sun, holding her close. "We made it in good time—there's still plenty of daylight left."

His warm breath brushed against her ear, sending a shiver down her spine in the most pleasant way.

Elisabeth sighed, feeling the tension ease as she leaned against him, cherishing the warmth of his body against hers and the steady rhythm of his heartbeat. David's presence alone was enough to dispel her fears; his reassuring words calmed her racing thoughts.

Until she glanced back at the entrance of the abandoned mine.

Despite her determination, a lingering sense of dread tugged at her. Set within the rugged hillside, the gaping hole yawned wide, its edges weathered and rough—stark reminders of their recent escape from the underground labyrinth, a journey she had vowed to never repeat. Nearby, an old wooden wheelbarrow lay abandoned, half-hidden by the tall grass, a quiet relic of the past.

Atop the hill, lay the remnants of an old smelting furnace. The stone and clay structure weathered by time. Overhead, heavy clouds gathered suddenly, casting a dim, foreboding light as if the atmosphere itself held its breath over this ominous place. Elisabeth felt a knot tighten in her stomach, a mix of fear and reluctant curiosity gnawing at her resolve. She exchanged a tense glance with David, seeing her own apprehension mirrored in his eyes.

Elisabeth shook her head. "I can't believe we're going back in there."

It was like descending into the underworld yet again.

A journey even Orpheus didn't undertake twice.

Chapter Nineteen

David dug out the old wheelbarrow, its weathered wooden frame a testament to years of neglect outside. With a determined effort, he freed it from its resting place and inspected it closely. "The wheels aren't in great shape, but they should do. And there are old tools inside the mine."

Elisabeth nodded. "I remember them. Can you take this for a minute?" She tried to keep her voice steady despite the knot in her stomach. From her leather purse, she retrieved a candle and matches brought from home. After handing a candle to David, she struck a match against the side of the small box.

His eyes widened with amazement as the flame flickered to life in her hand. Elisabeth bit down on a smile at his reaction to seeing matches for the first time.

"Ready?"

"No," she whimpered, her hand trembling as she took the candle from him. Elisabeth held it high, illuminating the dark entrance. "I just have to get past the flying rats." She took a deep breath and stepped inside, leading the way.

David followed close behind, pushing the old wheelbarrow through the narrow entry.

Elisabeth's heart raced with each step, knowing the *winged rodents* were waiting.

The flickering flame cast eerie shadows on the

damp walls as they ventured deeper into the darkness. She stifled a gasp, her breath catching as she noticed the bats hanging from the ceiling of the small alcove. They were twisted, nightmarish figures, their leathery wings wrapped tightly around their bodies like dark, draped shrouds.

Her grip on the candle tightened, her knuckles going white. The unsteady light from her shaking hand cast jittery shadows on the walls of the mine. As she retraced their steps, memories of being swarmed by those fanged creatures surged back, tightening the knot of dread in her stomach.

When they entered the narrow passage, leaving the *flying rats* behind, Elisabeth let out a huge breath.

They made their way down the pitch-black tunnel, finally reaching the spot she had likened to a birth canal. Setting the candle nearby, it cast a steady glow over their surroundings. She grabbed more from her purse, placing them strategically to illuminate the space.

Elisabeth then watched David inspect the walls, tracing the faint lines where lead deposits reflected the dim light. The sight triggered a sudden realization, and a nervous laugh escaped her lips. "Aquarius, once we mine the lead...do you know what to do with it?"

David glanced up, his brow furrowing slightly at her laughter. He paused, then smiled, understanding dawning in his eyes. "I know the basics." His tone was reassuring. "We'll need to melt it down, refine it. It's not too different from what I've seen before."

Elisabeth nodded, relief washing over her as David's confidence steadied her nerves.

Crouching beside the tools, she brushed away dust.

"What do we need?" She pushed aside a pail and shovel, holding up a sturdy chisel. "Will this do the trick?" The chisel's iron blade flashed in the candlelight, ready to carve through stone. She then picked up a large hammer, its wooden handle worn smooth.

David came closer to examine the tools. He took the oversized hammer and nodded. "These should do nicely."

Elisabeth walked over to a promising seam of lead, gripping the chisel. David pointed out where to position it, while he held the hammer ready. "On three," he said. "One, two—"

As he lifted the hammer higher, preparing to strike, Elisabeth flinched, her nerves suddenly on edge.

"Wait!" she shouted. "I think *I* should hammer instead."

David blinked in surprise, then his lips curved into a smile. "As you wish, my dear."

They swapped positions, Elisabeth taking hold of the large mining hammer, while David grasped the long chisel. She waited a moment, steadying herself, then began her own countdown. "Three, two, one—"

She swung the hammer with gusto, aiming for the chisel. However, in her eagerness, the hammer veered off course, almost striking David's arm instead. He jerked back, dodging the blow, his eyes widening in surprise as the hammer hit the rock with a loud clang. After a brief pause, he chuckled. "Close call there."

Elisabeth adjusted her grip on the hammer, exuding calm and focus. "Let me try again."

David lowered his chin and quirked an eyebrow. "You still love me, right?" He let out a shaky laugh.

With unwavering focus, Elisabeth swung the hammer again. This time, her aim was true, and it struck the chisel, splitting the lead seam with a satisfying crack. She turned to David with a satisfied smile. "Forever and always," she finally answered.

"Thank goodness." He reached over, easing the hammer out of her hands. "You did well, but let me take over now."

Elisabeth grinned, feeling the strain in her arms as she relinquished it. "Might not be a bad idea. That thing is *heavy*."

David winked playfully and then stole a kiss.

As they continued working together, they filled the wheelbarrow with lead-embedded rocks, the weight steadily increasing. Each strike of the hammer echoed in the cavernous space, punctuated by their occasional laughter and encouraging words to each other.

When satisfied with their haul, Elisabeth extinguished all but one candle, its steady glow meant to guide them out of the mine. Leading the way, she held the candle high while David pushed the heavy wheelbarrow through the narrow tunnel, the hammer, pail, and shovel resting atop the pile of rocks.

As the lone candle lit the path, eerie shadows danced around them, making Elisabeth's heart race. The inky blackness of the mine stretched on forever—a silent void that sent icy shivers down her spine.

The wheelbarrow creaked under the weight of the lead ore, accompanied by the growing flutter of bats as they neared the tunnel's mouth. Ahead, sunlight streamed through the exit, a welcome contrast to the dark mine. As they approached, the air warmed, and Elisabeth heard the faint flapping of wings.

She tensed and glanced back at David.

When he offered her a reassuring smile, she forced a watery grin into place.

Faint squeaking filled the air, and Elisabeth held her breath, desperate not to disturb the creatures as they passed—but the creaking from the wheelbarrow seemed to grow louder now too.

Her pulse raced, until they finally emerged into the open air. Stepping into the daylight, a gust of wind extinguished the candle, and Elisabeth let out a huge sigh of relief. "Oh my gosh, we did it."

David pointed to the crest of the hill. "We still need to wheel this up to that old smelting furnace."

Eager to assist despite David's apparent ease with the task, Elisabeth dropped the spent candle into her purse and then positioned herself behind him, her hands on his back, pushing him forward while bursting into giggles.

He maintained his grip on the handles of the wheelbarrow, steering it steadily up the hill. "Don't wear yourself out laughing," he teased.

"Too late."

Their combined effort stirred up clouds of dust and sent dried leaves swirling in a comical dance around them. Though Elisabeth tried her best, her contribution felt more symbolic than practical, like a small bird attempting to aid a lion.

"Almost there," Elisabeth encouraged, her determination matched by David's focused expression as he guided the wheelbarrow up the hill.

Upon reaching the furnace, he set the tools aside, and dumped the pile of lead ore onto the ground. David then wiped his brow and grinned at Elisabeth. "Well, that was an adventure."

Nearby, a wild rose bush with slender stems caught her eye. Its branches were adorned with clusters of bright, ruby-red hips, each one plump and vibrant against the backdrop of late summer foliage. The rounded hips, resembling tiny apples, added a splash of color to the serene hilltop clearing.

As Elisabeth cleared away the overgrown vegetation that covered the furnace, David inspected the structure, his hands moving over its contours.

"I need to clean out the interior." He brushed away cobwebs and debris. "And reinforce this section here," he added, pointing to a cracked segment of the clay lining.

Elisabeth listened as she continued uncovering the furnace from its leafy shroud.

David then grabbed the pail and shovel, tossing them into the wheelbarrow. He hoisted the handles and flashed a mischievous smile her way. "All right, love, we need to gather mud and clay from the stream to patch up these cracks."

Elisabeth's head jerked back, impressed by his knowledge and resourcefulness. "How do you know all this?" she asked as they descended the hillside, the sound of running water growing louder.

"Titus Sabinus." David snorted in amusement. "He was a jeweler I once knew. When I was freed in my father's will, I didn't know how to survive. Titus took me in, taught me the craft of making jewelry—amongst other things."

Elisabeth gasped. "You mean those *counterfeit* jewels you sold to Rufus that got you charged with fraud?"

"Led me to you though, *cor meum*." With a playful wink, he kicked off his shoes and shrugged off his jacket, revealing the plain white chemise underneath. Rolling up the sleeves, he crouched down at the edge of the stream. His strong hands dipped into the cool water, scooping up mud and clay, which he deposited into the wagon.

When Elisabeth crouched at the water's edge to assist, David shook his head, his hands already coated in wet clay. "I've got this. Why don't you gather some loose twigs and leaves to mix with the mud instead?"

She found a sturdy stick and began stirring the mixture, gradually adding water from the stream until it reached a smooth consistency. David watched, nodding in approval, then incorporated dried grass and leaves for extra strength.

Once their makeshift mortar was ready, David wheeled it up the hill to the furnace site, where he set to work applying the mixture to reinforce the cracked segment of its lining.

"That should do it," he said with a grin, glancing at Elisabeth who was inspecting his work. He then playfully inched closer; arms outstretched for an embrace.

Elisabeth looked up from the furnace, a smile tugging at her lips despite her attempt to appear serious. "Oh no you don't. Aquarius, you're covered in mud!" she said while backing away.

Undeterred, David continued forward, his grin widening. "Just a little hug?"

Elisabeth chuckled, ducking under his muddy arms as she stepped back. "Fine, fine! But you're washing up first." With a squeal, she turned and dashed down the hill as David gave chase. The grass rustled underfoot as they raced through the trees, laughter filling the air.

When they reached the stream, David kneeled by the water's edge to wash the mud from his arms and hands while smiling at Elisabeth. As she stood watching him, her heart fluttered for this young man who'd become her partner in every adventure.

"I'll get you next time," he teased, splashing water playfully toward her.

Elisabeth laughed and retaliated, sending a splash of cool water back at him. The sunlight danced on the ripples, adding a sparkle to their lively exchange.

"All right..." David shook the water from his hands before drying them on his trousers. He glanced around, eyeing the forest. "Now, we need to gather wood to make charcoal because it burns hotter. It's crucial for smelting the iron ore effectively. Let's find some dry, hardwood branches—oak would be perfect. It will burn slow and—"

"Why don't I just *bring* you some charcoal? Save some time," Elisabeth interrupted with a knowing grin.

David's eyes widened in surprise, a delighted smile spreading across his face. "Even better."

As he retrieved his leather shoes and slipped them on, Elisabeth crept closer with a sweet smile. She slid into his open arms, a perfect fit against his side. David instinctively wrapped one arm around her waist, drawing her closer.

"I finally get my hug." He leaned down to meet her lips in a tender kiss.

****

They stood by the old smelting furnace at dawn, having spent the night camped under a nearby tree amidst rustling leaves. With spirits high, they prepared to set their plans in motion under the morning sun's gentle light.

Elisabeth sucked in a quick breath. "Do you really think this will work?"

David rubbed the back of his neck. "I certainly hope so."

They had invested countless hours repairing the furnace, sealing cracks with mud, and gathering wood. Now, it was time to put their efforts to the test. David layered a substantial amount of charcoal and wood at the base of the chimney, creating a robust foundation for the smelting process.

"Time for the lead, *cor meum*."

"Finally!" Elisabeth bounced from foot to foot as David wheeled over the cart filled with heavy, dull-gray rocks he had broken into smaller pieces with the hammer. Carefully, he placed a cast iron pan, which Elisabeth had brought from home, inside the furnace, and arranged the chunks of lead ore on top of the layers of wood and charcoal, preparing for the next crucial step in their endeavor.

David leaned in and quirked an eyebrow. "Can I light it with one of those…?"

"Matches." Elisabeth smiled, digging into her purse to pull out a matchbox. "Of course."

With a slow, disbelieving shake of his head, David struck a match and ignited the dry tinder they had collected. Flames began to lick at the charcoal inside the sturdy walls of their smelting furnace.

As the fire grew hotter, David handed Elisabeth a hollow reed he had collected from the water's edge. She eyed it curiously as he placed one end of the reed in his mouth and positioned the other near the base of the fire. Elisabeth mimicked his actions.

"On three, blow," he instructed. "One, two, three."

She glanced at him, puzzled. "Why are we blowing on the fire?"

"It helps it burn hotter," he said, still focused on the flames.

"Oh." Elisabeth snorted in amusement. Together, they blew air through the reeds into the furnace. The stream of air surged into the flames, making them roar and dance with renewed intensity. The charcoal glowed brighter, and the temperature inside the furnace began to rise.

David kept a vigilant watch on the fire, ensuring the flames spread evenly across the charcoal bed. "Keep it going," he urged between breaths, his voice steady and encouraging.

The effort was demanding, sweat dripping down their faces as they maintained their rhythm. Driven by determination, they persevered. Gradually, the lead ore they had placed inside the furnace responded to the heat, softening and melting into a molten state.

Using a flat piece of wood, David skimmed off the slag—the impurities and waste materials that floated to the top. He cleared these aside, revealing the purer molten lead settling at the bottom of the cast iron pan.

He let out a throaty laugh. "It's working."

Elisabeth grinned, a mix of satisfaction and exhilaration coursing through her. She continued to blow air into the fire, her eyes fixed on the shimmering metal as it gradually collected in the pan.

After successfully refining the molten lead, David and Elisabeth turned their attention to the final step of their experiment. With a surge of determination, David reached for the napkin Beatrice had given them and used it to lift the cast iron pan from the furnace, its surface glowing with residual heat.

As he carefully set it down, Elisabeth retrieved the small vial containing the elixir of life—the most sought-after treasure in the history of mankind, also known as ambrosia or the philosopher's stone. They were one and the same.

Rumored not only to grant immortality but also to transmute lead into gold, Elisabeth knew the former to be true. Now, it was time to test the latter.

David ran a nervous hand through his hair, while Elisabeth held her breath and sprinkled a pinch of the red powder into the molten lead. She watched intently, observing how it merged with the shimmering metal.

Nothing changed.

Elisabeth's heart raced. She stole a quick glance at David, uncertainty clouding his expression. The air was thick with anticipation. Her gaze then returned to the cast iron pan, knuckles white as she twisted her dress fabric tightly.

They stood in silence, only the dying embers of the fire and their ragged breaths breaking the quiet of the clearing. Each second stretched into eternity while they waited, their hopes and fears intertwined in the air.

Chapter Twenty

Elisabeth held her breath as the molten metal shimmered, reflecting golden hues from the sunlight filtering through the trees. A soft gasp escaped her lips when the liquid lead began to change, its silvery surface transforming into radiant molten gold.

David's eyes widened in amazement as he watched the transformation. The air seemed to buzz with energy, and Elisabeth's heart raced. The once-quiet forest now felt alive with excitement, acknowledging their achievement.

She glanced at David, who looked equally stunned. The uncertainty on his face vanished, replaced by wonder. They stood captivated, seeing their experiment succeed, their hopes confirmed by the gold now resting in the large pan.

Elisabeth's fingers trembled as she reached toward it, hesitating before withdrawing her hand, the intense heat a vivid reminder of its reality. With a shaky exhale, she whispered, "It worked."

David's posture stiffened and he nodded. "It worked."

"Oh my gosh." Her voice rose in pitch. "What do we do now?"

"It's time to pour it into those molds you brought."

Elisabeth hurried to the sturdy oak tree, where she had placed a canvas tote near the trunk. From the bag, she pulled out a variety of baking items: mini-muffin tins, muffin tins, and a stack of candy molds shaped like coins that she'd ordered online. With a huge grin, she presented them to David. "Look what I have."

His smile widened as he examined the coin molds. "These are perfect."

David poured the liquid gold from the cast-iron pan into each cavity, starting with the coin-shaped molds. The molten metal shimmered as it flowed, gradually filling every crevice and forming delicate coins. He then moved on to the mini-muffin tins and muffin tins, the liquid gliding into the small, cup-shaped molds with a soft hiss.

"There." With a satisfied nod, he set the now-empty pan aside.

As they waited for the gold to solidify, David studied the newly minted pieces. "It appears we've struck quite a fortune, *cor meum*."

Elisabeth's hand covered her mouth. "Yeah."

"We should take only a small portion with us for immediate needs and bury the rest for safekeeping."

Her eyes widened, and a spontaneous laugh escaped. "We're going the buried treasure route, are we? A bit like Oak Island, isn't it? Remember I told you about that?"

David chuckled, nodding. "I do. But let's be practical—no booby traps for our treasure," he said with a mischievous twinkle in his eye.

Once the gold had solidified, they pried the newly minted coins from the molds, their surfaces reflecting a brilliant sheen. David picked up one, turning the coin over in his hand. "These are on the large side. I'd estimate they're worth at least a sou and a half, though in reality, they might fetch even more."

Elisabeth's head jerked back. "That much? Holy cow." She stacked the now-empty baking tins, molds, and cast-iron pan into her arms. "I'll be right back," she said, fumbling for her quartz crystal.

Moments later, Elisabeth reappeared before David, who took a startled step back and then snorted in amusement. From his perspective, the items had simply vanished from her arms.

David shook his head in wonder and grabbed a shovel. "Let's get this treasure buried. I found the perfect spot. It's easy to remember and feels fitting." As he began to dig a hole behind the rose bush filled with hips, a playful grin spread across his face. "We'll bury our treasure amongst your favorite flowers."

Even though the bush wasn't in bloom, it was clear that his choice was a silent way of connecting with something she loved, even in its off-season.

Elisabeth nodded, a smile spreading across her face. "That's a good spot. My mom told me there's a rosebush in Germany that's over one thousand years old. Our gold should be safe here if anything happens."

While humming a happy tune, Elisabeth tidied the area, smoothing over any disturbed ground and arranging fallen leaves to disguise their activity. The sun was starting to set, casting a golden hue over the landscape as shadows lengthened around them. "What should we do with the wheelbarrow and tools?"

David considered for a moment before responding, "We can hide them just inside the mine."

"Sounds good." Elisabeth nodded, her eyes scanning the horizon where the last rays of sunlight kissed the treetops. As they worked swiftly, driven by the fading daylight and the thrill of their clandestine task, Elisabeth finished tidying up the area.

With a satisfied sigh, she reached for the canvas tote and held it up. "I thought we could bury the gold in this."

David looked over, his face lighting up. "Absolutely."

Elisabeth sorted through the coins, her fingers dancing over the gleaming metal. "We need enough to rent a cottage and a little extra for other purchases." Her posture stiffened as she looked up. "Imagine all the things we can buy—pretty new clothes, soft bedding…"

David nodded, admiring the lustrous gold from afar. "Let's make sure we keep a good amount for immediate needs and future expenses."

Elisabeth's heart raced with excitement as she set aside a generous number of coins. "We have more than enough right here." She couldn't help but let out a delighted squeal as she transferred the larger gold pieces into the canvas bag. Once it was filled, she flashed David a huge smile.

He wiggled his eyebrows playfully. "Ready when you are, love."

Elisabeth carried the bag over, placing the canvas tote filled with gold into the hole.

David covered it with soil, patting down firmly to ensure their treasure was well hidden. "There," he said, brushing sweat from his forehead.

Elisabeth jumped up and down and then threw her arms around him. "You are amazing! I can't believe you did all that. I couldn't have done any of this without you."

David grinned while tucking a wayward strand of

hair behind her ear. "Truly, we are the perfect pair." He leaned in to steal a quick kiss. "It was all thanks to your 'really good idea', *Pandora*."

Elisabeth offered him a bemused smile. "I'll come up with the great ideas and you can implement them."

David's grin softened into a tender smile as he looked at Elisabeth. After a gentle squeeze of her hand, he gathered up the tools, placing them into the wheelbarrow. With care, he then loaded the gold coins into his leather belt pouch, which jingled softly with each movement. He gave Elisabeth a mischievous look. "Listen to that," he said with a chuckle.

She shook her head in disbelief while biting down on a smile.

As the sky transitioned from hues of orange and pink to deepening shades of blue, they began their descent down the hill. The darkness deepened, and stars began to emerge, twinkling against the encroaching night. From the mine entrance, bats quickly fluttered out into the dusk, their departure relieving Elisabeth's fears as they vanished into the night.

David wheeled the tools back into the mine and then pulled Elisabeth into a side hug. "We'll camp under the same tree where we slept last night. Tomorrow, we'll head straight to the village to see if we can rent that little cottage."

Elisabeth took a deep breath, savoring the moment. "Sounds perfect."

****

The next morning, Elisabeth stood in the comforting warmth of her shower, relishing the feel of hot water cascading over her. Downstairs, her and David's clothes spun in the washer, readying for their return to Beatrice's village. She couldn't help but chuckle thinking about David washing up in the stream, his clothes abandoned on the bank. Seizing the opportunity, she had snuck them away, knowing they needed a thorough cleaning.

After drying off, Elisabeth fixed her hair into a half-up crown braid, the strands weaving elegantly around her head. She donned the lilac dress once again, feeling the soft fabric settle comfortably around her. With a determined smile, she grabbed David's freshly laundered clothing in one hand, her quartz crystal in the other.

Elisabeth knew she should head to school, but the unfolding drama demanded her attention far more than her usual studies today.

****

As the pair approached the gate of Beatrice's village, they could hear bustling activity from the square just beyond.

"Something's going on," she whispered, her eyes wide with curiosity.

David nodded slowly. "It certainly sounds like it."

With the sun casting a warm glow, they pushed open the gate. After stepping inside, Elisabeth felt a rush of familiarity wash over her. To the right, tiny thatched-roof cottages stood with their wattle and daub walls. Ahead, the larger half-timbered building greeted them, its entrance ajar and shutters thrown wide this time.

From inside came loud voices, punctuated by shouts and heated exchanges. David glanced back, raising an eyebrow before leading the way closer.

Elisabeth's breath hitched as they neared the

threshold. Hesitating, she grabbed David's arm. "I think something important is happening," she whispered.

He flashed a reassuring smile. "We'll just take a quick peek. We don't want to draw any attention."

They leaned forward, craning their necks to get a better view through the doorway.

Inside was a makeshift courtroom—a simple yet dignified setting with benches for the villagers and a large wooden table serving as the judge's bench.

Brother Mattias sat at the front, his presence commanding respect. He raised his hand, calling for silence. "Order! Order!" The monk's voice carried through the room, quieting the murmurs of the assembled villagers. His kind eyes twinkled with wisdom from a gentle face framed by a crown of white hair on his balding head. "Henry, please continue," he said, his voice soothing but firm.

Henry, a middle-aged man with a sun-creased brow and a rough-spun tunic hanging loose over his shoulders, cleared his throat. "Brother Mattias, Beatrice exaggerates. My pig, she's usually gentle. At the time, she was pregnant, and perhaps she was more protective than usual. Or maybe Beatrice misunderstood. She's a nursing sow now, harmless to anyone who doesn't threaten her young." His hands fidgeted with the hem of his tunic. Henry's thinning hair was matted with sweat, and his gaze darted between the judge, the accusing Beatrice, and his pig—

Just then, Elisabeth's head jerked back when she spotted the pig—wearing a pale green dress and a white veil. The tiny gown, made from sturdy fabric, seemed oddly dignified yet entirely out of place on the animal's stout form. It snuffled and rooted from inside a small pen set up near the judge's bench.

Elisabeth's hand flew to her mouth, attempting to stifle a gasp at the absurd sight before her, forgetting the serious nature of the trial for a moment.

"But Henry, your pig is known to be aggressive," a middle-aged woman, with a stern expression shouted out, challenging Henry's defense of his pig. "It's a hazard to the village. Who's to say it won't attack again?"

Beatrice marched forward. "This pig is a danger! It attacked me without warning. What if it had been one of our children? Or one of our—?" Her eyes widened, and she paused mid-sentence, her mouth agape when spotting David and Elisabeth at the door. "My witnesses!" She waved them forward.

A collective gasp rippled through the crowd. Murmurs of astonishment filled the air as villagers craned their necks to get a better look at the unexpected arrivals.

Brother Mattias raised his hand. "Order! Order!"

Elisabeth exchanged a quick glance with David before they stepped forward, crossing the room to stand in front of the judge. She was still trying to process the sight of the pig in a green dress and white headdress, but composed herself, giving Beatrice a reassuring nod.

"Truly, the Lord works in mysterious ways," Brother Mattias said, a hint of a smile on his lips. "Your timely arrival must be no coincidence. Can you tell us how you happened upon this attempted attack?" His gentle voice contrasted with the tense atmosphere.

"Attack?" Beatrice's voice cut through the courtroom's silence. "Attempted *murder.*"

David stepped forward; his expression composed.

"*Dominus Praetor,* my wife and I were en route to Ghent when we heard a disturbance ahead. Through the trees, we observed Beatrice fleeing for her safety, pursued relentlessly by an aggressive pig."

Brother Mattias leaned closer. "Can you describe the pig's demeanor and behavior? Did it appear solely focused on Beatrice or did it react aggressively toward you as well?"

"When Beatrice stumbled and fell, I approached quickly, using my sling to hurl stones at it. The sow turned and chased after me as well, until I managed to drive it off with repeated strikes."

Brother Mattias considered David's account. "During the encounter, did you fear for your safety?"

David paused, choosing his words with care. "Not for my safety, but for that of my wife and Beatrice. The pig's aggression left little doubt about its intent."

A collective gasp rose from the crowd, whispers of alarm rippling through the assembly.

Brother Mattias nodded, acknowledging David's concern. "Thank you. Your bravery in protecting these women is commendable." He then turned to Elisabeth. "And you, my child, what did *you* experience during this event?"

Elisabeth took a deep breath before speaking. "The pig was so loud and ferocious that I thought it was a wild boar at first."

The crowd gasped again, the tension in the room heightening as they absorbed her words. Henry, visibly nervous, raised his voice to address the court. "How can you be so sure it was my pig?" His gaze darted around the room. "That young man," he pointed at David, "is an outsider. He doesn't know anything about our village or our animals. And that young woman," he added, gesturing toward Elisabeth, "is likewise an outsider. They have no place here, meddling in our affairs."

"We're *all* outsiders here," a man from the back of the room shouted with a touch of bitterness.

Several villagers murmured in agreement with the heckler.

Stefan, the stout man with a square jaw and a tunic that seemed too tight, who had bunked with them at Beatrice's cottage, spoke up. "Henry, we all know your pig can be aggressive. It's been a concern for some time now." The gap in his tooth caused a faint whistle with each word, yet his voice carried through the air with a note of certainty.

Henry shifted uncomfortably under Stefan's pointed gaze, casting a wary look around the room. The atmosphere grew tense as others nodded in reluctant agreement, their whispers adding weight to Stefan's accusation.

"He's right," one of them added. "I've seen that pig chase after other folks too."

As the trial continued, Elisabeth noticed a hunchbacked woman motioning for her and David to join her on the bench. She exchanged a glance with David, and they quietly made their way over, finding a spot amongst the villagers.

Brother Mattias cleared his throat and stood, signaling he was ready to address the assembled. "In the book of Proverbs, chapter 25, verse 26, it teaches us: 'A good person who gives in to wickedness is like a clean spring turned muddy.' Now, consider our pig here." He gestured toward the finely dressed swine. "It may not be evil at heart, but its aggression toward Beatrice and others shows it could harm our community. So, having carefully considered the matter, I find this pig guilty," he declared solemnly.

Mumbles of agreement rippled through the crowd. Heads nodded, acknowledging the wisdom in his words. The gravity of the situation seemed to settle on the villagers as they considered the implications of the animal's aggression on their small community. Some exchanged knowing glances, while others cast worried looks toward Henry and his swine.

"There are several options for sentencing," Brother Mattias continued. "We could exile the animal from Lindenhart once the piglets are weaned, ensuring it no longer poses a danger here. However, exiling the creature, while a compassionate gesture, poses risks to neighboring communities. Pigs are resourceful animals, and should it wander into another village or farmland, it could repeat its aggressive behavior. We cannot guarantee the safety of others elsewhere." He paused, clearly allowing his words to settle into the minds of those present. "Alternatively, we could impose punitive damages to compensate Beatrice for the distress caused and to reinforce the seriousness of the matter."

There was a buzz of agreement amongst the villagers, but Brother Mattias raised a hand to quiet them. "However, considering the aggressive nature of the attack and the risk to our community, I propose that the most appropriate course of action is *execution*."

Henry Gagneux paled, his eyes widening in dismay.

"In the book of Exodus, chapter 21, verses 28-29, it is written: 'If an ox gores a man or a woman to death, the ox shall be stoned, and its flesh shall not be eaten.' This principle underscores the seriousness of an animal causing harm and the need to protect our community."

Nearby, Beatrice nodded; her expression firm.

"Henry, you have until the piglets are weaned. After that time, the sentence will be carried out." Sensing the tension in the room, Brother Mattias added, "However, since no man or woman has died, I also decree that the pig be donated to the village for a community roast. This would not only serve as restitution but also foster communal unity and resolution." The monk's gaze then swept over the assembled villagers. "With that settled, I declare this trial concluded. Thank you all for your attention and thoughtful consideration today." He stood and raised his hands in a gesture of blessing over the villagers. "May the wisdom we have shared today guide our hearts and actions," he concluded, his voice carrying a gentle authority. "Go in peace, knowing that justice and community are upheld."

The villagers began to disperse, some exchanging solemn nods and quiet words of reassurance. Henry Gagneux paused, giving Brother Mattias a disappointed look before nodding and leading his pig, tethered on a leash, out of the courtroom. David and Elisabeth exited, casting one last glance at the scene before moving away.

Once outside, Elisabeth couldn't help but feel a pang of sympathy as she watched the well-dressed pig amble away, its trot deliberate and proud. The pig's small, curly tail poked out from beneath the hem of the green dress, swaying gently with each dignified step it took.

However, her sympathy wavered when the pig stopped and squealed, causing a nearby chicken to scatter in alarm. With a quick snap of its jaws, the pig lunged after the startled hen, pulling Henry, who was holding the leash, along with it.

Elisabeth, witnessing the display, couldn't help but feel conflicted—while she sympathized with the pig's fate, its unexpected aggression served as a reminder of the justice in the monk's decision.

Stefan must have sensed her empathy, because he walked closer. "It's a fair sentence. The pig wasn't a pet; it was meant to be slaughtered eventually. Henry is just forced to share the pork with the villagers now."

Before Elisabeth could answer, Beatrice bustled over. "Come, enjoy a hearty fill of my ale," she insisted, her posture perking up. "Then tell me why you two have returned and come to my rescue once again."

David smiled at Beatrice. "Thank you for the offer. We've actually returned to see about renting a cottage. Is one still available?"

Stefan chimed in. "Elias' place?"

Beatrice's head jerked back. "You're planning to stay?"

David considered for a moment before replying, "We wouldn't mind...*if* a cottage is available. With whom should we inquire?"

Stefan cleared his throat before speaking. "That'd be Beatrice. Elias put her in charge of renting his house. There's no one better at running things around here."

Beatrice nodded in agreement.

David and Elisabeth mirrored her gesture, acknowledging her with respectful nods of understanding. "Ah, I see," David said.

Beatrice clapped her hands together. "Come with me. I'll show you the place now while the babies are still with Lance."

A wide grin spread across Elisabeth's face. "Thank you." She exchanged a hopeful glance with David, noticing his eyes light up.

Filled with anticipation, they followed Beatrice. Elisabeth's heart raced; the possibilities of what Elias' cottage might offer as a much-needed sanctuary fueling her excitement.

As they hurried down the path, the air seemed charged with tension, each step bringing them closer to a new beginning.

Chapter Twenty-One

Just past Beatrice's cottage, the dirt road continued, winding its way between more cottages and outbuildings. To her left, Elisabeth noticed grazing sheep and a handful of goats in a fenced paddock. The village path meandered deeper into the surrounding forest, where the cottages thinned out and the sounds of nature became more pronounced. Birds chirped in the trees, and the rustling of leaves created a soothing background melody.

Beatrice pointed ahead toward a cottage. Positioned at the edge of the village, with the forest bordering it, the quaint home had an air of seclusion and peace that immediately caught Elisabeth's eye. Beyond the cottage, she could see the defensive wall of sharpened logs encircling the community and adding to the feeling of security in this hidden enclave.

The home was modest yet inviting, constructed of sturdy wattle and daub, with its whitewashed walls glossy in the warm afternoon sunlight. The thatched roof sloped gently to form a protective canopy over the front door, framed by rustic wooden beams.

A cobblestone path led from the road to the cottage's entrance, flanked by a small, overgrown garden hinting at its hidden potential. Lavender, daisies, and marigolds added splashes of color and fragrance, while a patch of what looked like herbs suggested the promise of fresh ingredients for their meals.

Nearby was a small tree, its gnarled branches loaded with small, brownish fruits that Elisabeth didn't recognize. The tree's leaves were a rich green, with some already beginning to show the first hints of yellow.

On the right-hand side of the cottage, a lean-to provided shelter for firewood and tools. Nearby, a rain barrel collected water from the roof, ensuring a steady supply for the garden and household needs. Adjacent to the lean-to, a stone fire pit with surrounding wooden benches served as a cozy gathering spot, ideal for warmth and cooking, and promising many evenings of shared meals and storytelling under the stars.

Beatrice nodded toward the door. "Elias is off on a pilgrimage to the Holy Land. He left just a few weeks ago."

The front door, made of weathered oak, bore the marks of time and use but looked solid and reliable. To the right of the door, a wooden bench invited one to sit and take in the serene surroundings, while above it, a painted birdhouse hung from a low-hanging eave, providing a home for several sparrows, their melodic chirps and occasional fluttering adding a lively touch to the tranquil scene.

As Beatrice ushered them inside, the oak door groaned and stuck halfway open. "I'll have Lancelot come by to fix that later this afternoon," she said, stepping over to assess the problem.

Inside, the cottage was a single-room abode, yet it felt spacious and welcoming. The walls were bare, save for a few functional shelves to hold necessities. At the heart of the room was a central hearth, its fire pit ready to crackle with a comforting blaze on cooler evenings. Suspended above the hearth was a metal pot crane, perfect for cooking stews and warming water.

Beatrice moved to one of the two small windows flanking the front door and opened the shutters, allowing a stream of natural light to filter into the room. The sunlight danced on the walls, casting a warm, inviting glow over the space.

"Over here, you've got your dining area." Beatrice gestured toward the simple wooden table and two chairs. "Perfect spot for meals."

Elisabeth nodded, smiling. "It's nice. Cozy."

Nearby, shelves and a sturdy wooden cabinet provided storage for household essentials.

"On the other side," Beatrice continued, "you've got your sleeping nook. The bed looks comfortable, doesn't it?"

Elisabeth approached the bed, noting its simple wooden frame. Beside it, a small table stood empty, ready for cherished possessions. A woven mat lay on the earthen floor, providing a warm spot for bare feet on chilly mornings.

Above the sleeping area, a loft offered extra space for storage or sleeping. A wooden ladder, leaning against the loft's edge, led up to it. The ladder had evenly spaced rungs and a handrail on one side for support.

"It does look cozy," Elisabeth said, admiring the loft.

David glanced around. "How long will Elias be gone?"

Beatrice opened the shuttered window beside the bed, allowing more natural light and fresh air to filter into the room. "He'll be gone for at least two years, probably longer."

As Elisabeth stood next to David, taking in the quaint appeal of their potential new home, a sense of peace washed over her, and she let out a satisfied sigh. The thatched-roof cottage, with its simple comforts and rustic beauty, felt like the perfect place to begin a new chapter together. Her mind raced with the possibilities of making it pretty, adding a feminine touch to transform this bachelor's abode into a cozy haven.

David looked at her, a hint of nervous anticipation in his eyes. "Do you like it?"

Elisabeth turned to him, catching the slight tremor in his voice and the earnestness in his gaze. She nodded, knowing exactly what this meant to him. "I love it," she replied with a hand over her heart. "It's perfect."

Beatrice glanced around the cottage, then back at David. "Elias was asking for five sous per year, but considering the repairs needed on the door and a bit of maintenance here and there, I could do it for four."

When he reached into his pouch and pulled out three gold coins, Beatrice's eyes widened. David held the gold pieces out to her, his expression calm and composed.

"This…this is worth a small fortune," Beatrice said, feeling the weight of the gold. She looked up at David with a mixture of confusion and skepticism. "How did you come by these? This is more than enough for Elias' cottage, and then some."

"I'm paying for the entire year upfront," David replied, his voice steady.

A cold chill ran through Elisabeth, causing her

muscles to tense. She watched the exchange, heart pounding as she tried to gauge Beatrice's reaction.

David hesitated for a moment, then flashed a charming smile. "You see," he said, his voice reassuring, "these gold coins are part of an inheritance from my eccentric uncle. He was always finding unique ways to secure our future. This gold was his way of preparing for uncertain times."

Intrigued by David's explanation, Elisabeth relaxed slightly, her confidence bolstered by his charisma. Glancing at Beatrice, she noted the skepticism still lingering in her expression.

"Your uncle, huh? And he left you gold?" Her tone indicated she was willing to entertain the idea. "Is it real?"

David nodded, maintaining his story. "Yes, absolutely real. He was quite the character, always fascinated by the enduring value of it."

Beatrice studied the coins for a moment longer. "In our little village, we don't typically handle these sorts of payments. Perhaps Elias can make up the difference when he returns?"

David nodded. "We're in no rush. We can arrange to settle the balance later when Elias is back. In the meantime, let's work out what we can for now."

Beatrice sighed, accepting David's suggestion. "That sounds reasonable. We'll manage as best we can until Elias returns to settle the rest. Just make sure you don't attract any unwanted attention with any more of those shiny pieces, if you know what I mean."

David smiled. "Thank you. We'll be careful," he assured her. Glancing at Elisabeth, he added, "You know, that's why we traveled to Ghent in the first place—to settle my uncle's affairs and retrieve this inheritance."

Elisabeth raised a subtle eyebrow at David's comment, a clandestine gesture to convey her amusement without drawing Beatrice's attention. She couldn't help but smile, realizing David was enjoying the moment despite the weight of their circumstances.

Beatrice nodded, her earlier suspicions melting into an air of acceptance mixed with a touch of curiosity. "Well, I'm sure you've had quite the journey," she said with a chuckle. "Feel free to make yourselves at home. If Elias has any luck, he'll return in a few years with a wife who'll appreciate the changes."

Elisabeth snickered, appreciating Beatrice's easy acceptance. "Thank you. We'll make sure to take good care of it."

"I'm sure you will," she said, stepping outside. "I'll send Lancelot over to fix this door for you right away. Enjoy settling in." As she turned to leave, Beatrice paused and looked back at them with a smile. "Oh, when you get hungry later, don't hesitate to come by for supper. I can see you've got nothing yet and we've got plenty. It's always better shared with neighbors."

With that, Beatrice disappeared down the cobblestone path, leaving them to savor the moment of finally having a place to call their own.

Without a word, they both burst into huge grins, Elisabeth giggling as David swept her into a spontaneous hug.

"We did it," he whispered, his voice filled with joy.

Elisabeth hugged him back even tighter, her heart racing with happiness. "Our own place," she squealed.

They danced across the dirt floor of the small

cottage, their laughter filling the rustic space. David spun Elisabeth gently, her skirts swirling as her laughter echoed in the cozy room they now called home.

When they stopped, David took Elisabeth's hands in his. "Here's to our new beginning," he said, his voice thick with emotion.

Elisabeth nodded, tears brimming in her own eyes. "To new beginnings," she echoed, leaning in to kiss him. She then bounced onto her tippy toes; senses heightened from excitement. "Aquarius, I have so many ideas! First, we'll cover this dirt floor with woven mats, like the ones Perenelle put in Nicolas' study—scented, of course, so it feels cozy and fragrant every time we step inside."

David chuckled. "That sounds perfect."

"I'll take this bed," Elisabeth insisted with a grin. "And up in the loft, we can make a second bedroom just for you."

With a playful smile, David shook his head. "I'll be sleeping down here." He gave her a mischievous wink. "But if you're set on sharing the bed, I won't object. It looks big enough for both of us."

Elisabeth's eyes widened. "Oh?"

David plucked at his jacket and then leaned closer, his voice gentle. "I need to be down here so I can keep an eye on things and respond quickly to any potential threats or sudden emergencies. It's all about keeping us safe."

Elisabeth let out a shaky laugh. "Well, I suppose that does make sense. I'll take the loft then."

David's smile grew as she settled into the idea; his eyes full of affection. "It's going to be perfect. We'll make it work."

"It's going to be *amazing*." Elisabeth's mind raced with ideas for the cottage, and David simply grinned as he took it all in.

"We can have pretty curtains for the windows, a beautiful tablecloth for our meals, and oh! We're going to need lots of lanterns and candles. We should also fix that garden outside, plant some vegetables and herbs, maybe even plant a rosebush, and have chickens in the—"

Before Elisabeth could finish, a voice called from the open front door. "Heard your door needs fixing. I'm…"

She spun around, spotting Lancelot standing in the doorway with a puzzled look. He clearly hadn't realized who had moved in.

Elisabeth's grin widened as she glanced at David, who was doing his best to stifle a laugh.

"It's us!" she called out, unable to contain her amusement. "Beatrice didn't mention it?"

Lancelot's eyes went wide as he set down his wooden toolbox. "No," he replied, looking between them. "Well, this is a surprise!"

David stepped forward and extended his hand. "Good to see you."

With an amused snort, Lancelot shook David's hand. "Likewise! What happened to Ghent?" he asked, rolling up his sleeves.

"Ah, the hustle and bustle of the big city didn't quite suit us after all." He exchanged a knowing glance with Elisabeth.

She nodded. "Then we remembered there was a cottage available here in Lindenhart. It felt like the right place for us to settle down. We just need to get some supplies and make it a home now."

"Glad you're here," Lancelot said, rummaging through his tools. "This door won't take long. Afterward, if you want, Romeo, you could join Stefan and me on a trip to Oudenaarde. He's hauling a load of thatch there in his wagon. It's the nearest town—not as grand as Ghent, but you should find what you need. Stefan won't mind if you come along, and you can bring back supplies once the wagon's emptied."

Elisabeth's pulse raced with excitement as she turned to David. "I don't mind staying here. You should definitely go and get everything we need for the cottage."

David smiled. "Sounds like a plan."

As they spoke, Lancelot removed the door from its hinges and carried it outside, beginning to plane the bottom to ensure it fit better in its frame. His movements were deft and practiced, a testament to his skill as a carpenter.

Alone again inside the cottage, Elisabeth couldn't contain her excitement as she rattled off a list of things David could look for to buy. Her voice alternated between animated exclamations and whispered suggestions; her enthusiasm obvious as she envisioned their new home taking shape. "Look for new bedding, dishes—oh, and definitely a vase for the table." She bounced from foot to foot. "Maybe a broom, I didn't see one. Oh, look for some nice baskets…"

David grinned widely. This was obviously a dream come true for him, and seeing Elisabeth so thrilled seemed to add to his happiness. "Absolutely. I'll get everything you want. It's going to be perfect."

As they wrapped up their conversation, Lancelot

returned to hang the repaired door back up. "Oh, before I forget, did Beatrice show you the gate?"

Elisabeth's brows squished together. "Gate?"

Lancelot gestured for them to follow. "I'll show you."

He led them to a section of the protective log wall a short distance from the cottage. "You'll like this," he said, lifting a wooden latch hidden amongst the timbers. With a smooth motion, several of the log panels swung open on simple hinges, revealing a discreet gate leading to a nearby stream.

"Most people fetch water from the stream near the bridge, but this spot is closer for folks at the back of the village. Just lift the latch and push the panels aside whenever you need water."

"Oh, that's handy," Elisabeth said, thinking of all the times she'd lugged heavy pails from the well in Ghent.

"It's mainly for emergencies, but now you know where it is." With a smile, Lance let the latch fall back into place. "Just make sure it stays closed."

With that, they headed back to the cottage. Lancelot picked up his toolbox and glanced at David. "Ready to go?"

David nodded and turned to Elisabeth. He took her hands in his, his gaze tender. "I'll be back before you know it," he whispered, pressing a gentle kiss to her lips.

Chapter Twenty-Two

The late afternoon sun dipped lower, a reminder that evening was not far off. Elisabeth quickened her pace as she neared Beatrice's house. Her heart raced with growing worry.

The young mother was outside, playing with Jemra and Hannibal-Joe, their laughter filling the air as she encouraged them to toddle toward her.

"Beatrice?" Elisabeth called out while wringing her hands.

Beatrice looked up, breaking her smile. "What's got you so worked up?" she asked, raising an eyebrow.

Elisabeth glanced nervously down the road. "Romeo—" She hesitated, the name feeling foreign on her lips. "He's with Lancelot and Stefan. He said they'd be back soon, but it's been hours."

What if something had gone wrong?

What if they were ambushed on the road or stumbled into a trap?

He might have been captured by Cato, or maybe they'd run into one of Guglielmo Tartare's mercenaries.

The thought of Tartare's greasy blond hair and calculating eyes sent a chill down her spine. She imagined David injured, cornered, or worse—unable to escape. The thoughts swirled in her mind, each more dreadful than the last.

Beatrice let out a snort, her expression reassuring but blunt. "Don't worry. Men always take longer than they think. They'll be back when they've had their fill of whatever nonsense they're into."

"But what if—"

Beatrice cut her off with a wave of her hand. "No need for 'what ifs'. Sit yourself down and I'll get you some ale. They'll show up when they show up."

Elisabeth hesitated, but the warmth in Beatrice's eyes and the aroma of ale wafting from her cottage were comforting. She sat while Beatrice stepped inside the cottage.

A moment later, she placed a cup on the table. "Drink up. It'll settle your nerves."

"Thanks." Elisabeth took a sip of the ale, noting its earthy flavor and comforting warmth. It seemed this beverage was enjoyed by all ages for its nourishing qualities rather than any intoxicating effects, more akin to a meal. Unlike beer, Elisabeth thought, this ale was about wholesome sustenance rather than alcohol.

As Elisabeth sipped, her gaze drifted to little Jemra, who had made her way over to the table. Feeling a momentary respite from her worries, she reached out to tickle Jemra's cheek, eliciting a delighted giggle.

Beatrice bustled about, juggling random chores while keeping an eye on the babies. "They'll be back. Lord knows Lancelot will," Beatrice muttered, her gaze flicking toward Hannibal-Joe. "Always underfoot, poking his nose where it doesn't belong."

Her tone held a hint of bitterness, betraying a deeper hurt that lingered from their past.

Elisabeth, sensing the tension, proceeded with caution. "You and Lancelot…there seems to be more to your story."

Beatrice's shoulders tensed before she let out a heavy sigh, setting aside her tasks for a moment. "Oh, there's a tale all right, but not one I care to dwell on," she admitted, her voice tinged with unresolved emotion.

Elisabeth cleared her throat. "Sorry. I didn't mean—"

Beatrice waved off Elisabeth's apology and gathered the twins. "Let's get you settled." She lifted them into wooden walkers and handed them handmade toys. Once they were content, Beatrice took a seat across from Elisabeth, a cup of ale in hand.

"You're curious to hear my tale of woe?" She took a deep drink. "I grew up in Ghent. Lost both my parents when I was young, but an innkeeper and his wife took me in."

Elisabeth leaned forward, her eyes wide with curiosity.

"Life wasn't easy, but they were kind. That's where I met Lance. He was required to travel and find work after his apprenticeship, but he'd stop by the inn often." A bittersweet smile played on Beatrice's lips. "He always had a charming presence and a story to share."

Elisabeth nodded in agreement, recalling how he'd captivated her with tales of fire-breathing dragons, to the point where she *almost* believed they were real.

Beatrice's expression grew somber as she took another sip, her voice tinged with pain. "Lance left for a temporary job, promising he'd return in a few months. And he did come back. By then, I was heavily pregnant with his baby."

Elisabeth's brows lifted in surprise.

"He was so happy. Everyone was. We started making plans—talking about a small home and raising our family. We never exchanged vows, but in my heart, I felt we were already committed."

Elisabeth, listening closely, thought back to her own elopement. She remembered Brother Jacques explaining that, for common people, marriages were simply verbal promises made between a man, a woman, and God—no ceremonies, priests, or written documents were needed.

Beatrice paused to take another drink from her cup. "At first, he was happy—but everything changed after I gave birth to twins. The innkeepers turned against me, saying I had brought shame upon them. People started whispering—and Lance accused me of being unfaithful."

Elisabeth's eyes widened in shock as Beatrice's voice grew more intense.

"The betrayal was a knife to the heart. I had nowhere to go. I'd heard about Lindenhart from a customer and thought it might be a place where I could start anew."

Elisabeth's posture perked up. "Wait…then why is Lancelot here now?"

Beatrice let out a bitter laugh. "He followed me, claiming he forgives me. But what's forgiveness worth when I did nothing wrong? He shattered my heart. How can I just forget that?" She drained her ale, hands trembling. "Lancelot says he accepts both babies and already loves them no matter what. But it's not that simple." Her voice cracked as she fought back tears. "He shattered my heart by doubting me. I loved *only* him, and he repaid me by accusing me of being unfaithful."

Elisabeth sat in stunned silence, absorbing Beatrice's pain. The contrast between the charming man she had admired and the one who had hurt Beatrice was jarring. Lancelot's actions overshadowed his previous charm, leaving Elisabeth questioning the true nature of someone she thought she knew.

Beatrice set down her empty cup, shoulders slumping. "Now, he's just another paying customer at *my* alehouse. He can pay for a drink, pay for a meal, and earn his keep around here. But he's not welcome in my heart. He broke something in me that can't be mended. How can I pretend like everything's fine when it's not?"

Her eyes filled with tears as she looked away. "I'm here trying to build a life for my babies—a place where they're loved and accepted. But every time I see him, I'm reminded of the unjust pain and betrayal that haunts me."

Elisabeth's heartbeat slowed. She understood now why the situation was so complicated. "I...I'm so sorry." Her voice was barely above a whisper. "I can't imagine what you've been through. It's just...unbelievable."

Beatrice took a deep breath, her gaze distant and pained. "The truth is, I don't even understand how I had twins. We were only intimate once." She let out a heavy sigh and changed the subject. "So, what about you two? Lots of babies now that you've settled into the little cottage?"

Elisabeth took a sip of ale, only to choke and sputter at the unexpected question. "Oh, um...no. Not for *quite* a while," she insisted, her voice strained and eyes wide. After all, she was still in high school. Being technically married was wild enough for now.

"Well, in that case, let me give you a board for your bed." Beatrice took a deep breath, her expression turning melancholy. "You know, it's strange how one moment can change everything. But despite that, I love my babies more than anything." She let out a heavy sigh and then straightened up, her expression firm as she stood. "I best get things ready for the villagers. They'll want their ale soon."

Elisabeth nodded, relieved that Beatrice was focusing on her duties instead of past grievances. "I should head home," she said with a faint smile. "Thank you for the drink."

Walking to the cottage, Elisabeth clutched a long, narrow board tucked under her arm. Measuring about four feet in length, the wood was awkward to carry and just wide enough to be cumbersome. Though not heavy, it pressed uncomfortably against her side as she quickened her pace, urged on by the darkening sky and the threat of rain. She had no idea what it was for—its purpose shrouded in mystery since it had been handed to her without explanation. Yet, out of politeness or perhaps some unspoken instinct, she had accepted it, and now it weighed on her mind as much as her body.

Just as Elisabeth reached her new home, she heard the steady thud of hooves and the creak of wheels against the dirt. The sounds were coming from behind her, growing louder with each passing second.

Chapter Twenty-Three

Elisabeth stepped aside as Stefan's wagon approached, pulled by an ox moving at a steady pace. Her eyes widened at the sight of David and Lancelot, their laughter echoing through the quiet village. They were clearly enjoying themselves, their jovial shouts and hearty guffaws filling the air.

As the wagon slowed, Lancelot leaned out, waving. "Juliet!" he hollered with a broad grin, his words slurring slightly. "Romeo bought us a fine meal!"

David, grinning ear to ear, held up a cloth bundle. "Don't worry, Ju-lie-ette!" he bellowed, dragging out the name with exaggerated flair. "I brought you some too." His eyes crinkled with mischief. "See? Thought of you the entire time."

Elisabeth couldn't help but laugh at their antics, shaking her head in disbelief.

Stefan, older and more composed, chuckled as he adjusted the yoke on the ox before descending from the wagon and stretching his legs. "It was quite the adventure, I must say." The faint whistle from the gap between his teeth punctuated his words.

David and Lancelot followed, hopping down from the wagon with broad smiles and lighthearted banter. They stumbled but caught themselves, laughing even more.

As David approached Elisabeth, his expression

softened, though she could see a slight unsteadiness in his steps. "Let me help you with that." He took the cumbersome board from her and leaned in close, his breath carrying a faint scent of wine. "I love you." His voice was a soft whisper meant only for her. "I've never been this happy in my entire life." He then kissed her forehead.

Elisabeth smirked at David's unguarded affection as she took the cloth bundle of leftovers in exchange. She watched him adjust the board, feeling the lingering comfort of his words.

Lancelot burst into laughter when he noticed the object, pretending to look sorry for David. "Oh, mate." He shook his head. "Looks like you've got your work cut out for you tonight."

David glanced at the long, flat piece of wood, puzzled. "What is this?" he asked, turning it over in his hands.

Elisabeth giggled, unable to contain her amusement. "I've no idea. Beatrice insisted I take it," she said, grinning at David's perplexed expression. "Apparently, it's a board for the bed?"

David's head flinched back as he tried to make sense of the strange object. "For the bed?"

Lancelot's laughter intensified at their innocent ignorance. "A chastity board!" he finally managed to say between laughs. "You put it down the center of the bed as a divider. To keep your love life under control."

David's cheeks flushed with embarrassment, but he couldn't help joining in the laughter, shaking his head in mock dismay. Meanwhile, Elisabeth felt her face grow warm and joined them with a nervous chuckle.

As the laughter settled, David, Lancelot, and Stefan

began unloading the various items David had bought, retrieving them from the back of the wagon. They pulled out sacks of grain, bundles of herbs, a few clay pots filled with preserved food, along with specific items from Elisabeth's list: new bedding, a new mattress, dishes, cups, linens, a vase, a broom, and scented woven rugs for the floor.

Elisabeth joined in, helping to carry the lighter items. She first set the bundle of leftovers on the table inside the cottage. Her eyes widened with surprise as each new item was brought in. "Did you buy out the entire market?" she asked, half in jest and half in genuine amazement.

David set down a stack of linens. "I wanted to make sure you had everything you could possibly need."

Lancelot, struggling with a heavy sack of grain, grinned at Elisabeth. "Your husband has quite the eye for provisions," he teased. "At this rate, he'll blow through his inheritance in no time."

Stefan, shaking his head, added with a smirk, "However, you'll be dining like kings until the coffers run dry."

Elisabeth couldn't help but laugh at the sight of their new friends working together amidst the mountain of supplies. Despite the overwhelming amount, she felt a warmth in her heart knowing that David had put so much effort into making their new home comfortable and welcoming.

As the tasks wound down, Lancelot and Stefan climbed into the wagon.

"Until next time, Romeo and Juliet," Lance called out with a lopsided grin.

"Take care," Stefan said with a friendly wave while guiding the ox.

Side by side, they watched the wagon until it disappeared around a bend in the road. "I've never seen you so happy before," Elisabeth said with a gentle smile.

David nodded, his gaze lingering on the empty road. "It feels like a new beginning." Wrapping his arm around her shoulders, he led the way back to the cottage. Inside, he went straight to the bed, a tired chuckle escaping his lips as he pulled Elisabeth down beside him. "I just need a moment to rest." His arm settled comfortably around her waist.

Elisabeth laughed, giving in to his playful tug. "There's still more stuff to bring in," she said, although unable to resist settling down beside him.

David let out a contented sigh, his eyes closing. "In a moment," he murmured as he pulled Elisabeth closer.

She smiled and brushed a lock of hair from his forehead. "Fine." Her hand rested on his chest. "We've got all the time in the world now."

David nodded, a peaceful smile spreading across his face. "With you, it's perfect."

After a few minutes, Elisabeth nudged him. "We *really* should bring everything in before it starts to rain."

David sighed and sat up. "All right, let's get to it."

They set to work, organizing the items for the cottage. Elisabeth unrolled the woven rugs, laying them on the floor, while David busied himself in the loft. He stopped to hang a sheet across the front, obscuring her view of his activities.

She glanced up with a furrowed brow. "What's

with the sheet?"

David peeked out from behind it, a mischievous grin spreading across his face. "It's a surprise. You'll have to wait and see."

Elisabeth clapped her hands, feeling a surge of excitement. "I *love* surprises!"

She continued arranging the rugs, her thoughts momentarily distracted by David's secretive project. "Oh! You won't believe what I found out about Beatrice and Lancelot." Her voice bubbled with excitement while smoothing a woolen blanket over a bench.

David's head peeked out from behind the sheet again, making her giggle.

Elisabeth glanced around, ensuring no one was approaching the cottage. "They were once madly in love," she said in a low, hurried whisper, as if Beatrice or Lancelot might appear at any moment. "They had *one* night together, if you know what I mean, and that's when she ended up pregnant."

"Really?" David asked, a note of surprise in his tone.

"Yep." Elisabeth's voice rose with indignation. "But here's the twist—when Lancelot found out she was pregnant, he was overjoyed at first. Then, *after* the twins were born, he suddenly didn't believe they were his."

David let out a sympathetic sigh. "Poor Lancelot. That must be incredibly hard to deal with."

Elisabeth's head jerked back in surprise. "Poor *Lancelot?*"

David shrugged, his face visible but his body still obscured behind the hanging sheet. "Well, if Beatrice had two babies, it's clear she must have been with someone else. Lancelot has every reason to feel betrayed."

As Elisabeth's eyes narrowed in confusion, disbelief set in. "Wait. What?" The first drops of rain drummed softly on the thatched roof. Quickly, the gentle patter turned into a steady downpour. Elisabeth moved to close the shuttered windows, the rhythmic sound of the rain echoing her growing perplexity. "You think having twins means she was unfaithful?"

David nodded, still puzzled. "Well, if Beatrice had *two* babies at one time, it would suggest she must have been with another man. Plus, they were only together once. It makes sense Lancelot might think at least one of them isn't his. Why do you think he asked us which baby looked more like him?"

Elisabeth froze, her eyes wide with shock as the gravity of the misunderstanding sank in. Her hand flew to her mouth, and she struggled to find words. "No, oh my gosh, no! That's not how it works at all."

Still up in the loft, David's head tilted to the side, his uncertainty evident. "How else do you explain *two* babies at one time? Twins are pretty unusual."

Without answering, Elisabeth sighed and rubbed her temples, gazing out at the storm through the open front door.

She was determined to resolve the misunderstanding between Lancelot and Beatrice, but had to do so without relying on modern explanations. She needed to convince Lancelot that twins came from the same father and that Beatrice had indeed been faithful.

"How can we fix this?" Elisabeth muttered to

herself.

"We?" David's voice was now directly behind her, teasing. "Oh no, *cor meum*, don't drag me into another one of your *really* good ideas when it comes to matchmaking." He leaned in close, his warm breath caressing her ear, sending a shiver up her spine. "I can practically hear those wheels spinning in that head of yours."

Elisabeth turned, trying to suppress a grin. "Oh, come on. I can totally fix this. They're angry with each other over a complete misunderstanding."

David chuckled, shaking his head. "Here we go again. If you're so confident, what's the truth behind all this? I'm curious. How are twins made?"

How are twins made?

Heat rushed to Elisabeth's cheeks, and she fidgeted with her hands, struggling to find the right words. "Oh, um, well, it's actually a bit awkward to explain." *To you.* "Trust me, twins come from the same father. And Beatrice has been faithful, I swear." She gave an awkward little laugh. "I just need to figure out how to explain it to Lancelot without, you know, making it sound like I'm from the future or something."

Elisabeth cast a final glance at the rain pouring down outside before closing the door. The cottage grew darker, and David moved to the new lanterns, suddenly holding a small piece of flint and a steel striker. Striking them together, he created a shower of sparks, catching the flame on a bit of tinder and transferring it to the lanterns. The warm glow began to push back the encroaching darkness.

Elisabeth tapped her lips with a finger. "Somehow, I'm going to have to get Lancelot to come over."

David raised an eyebrow, his expression a mix of curiosity and skepticism. "Oh? And what's your plan this time?"

She smiled, starting to figure out a strategy. "Well, we'll say we need him to *fix* something in the cottage."

David laughed, continuing to light the remaining lanterns. "What do you need fixed? I'll do it."

Elisabeth shook her head, her expression turning serious. "No, it has to be something only a *carpenter* can fix." Her gaze wandered around the room until it landed on a wooden chair. "That chair is wobbly."

David glanced over at it and then snorted in amusement as he latched the front door. "It's not."

"It totally is. Look." Elisabeth marched over and rocked the sturdy chair back and forth with exaggerated effort. "And it's not just that. We also need him to check—uh—the door latch? I think it might be loose, too."

David eyed her with a knowing look, a smirk playing on his lips. "You're making this up as you go along, aren't you?"

Before Elisabeth could respond, David flashed a playful grin, shook his head, and then swept her up and over his shoulder. She squealed in surprise, her hands gripping his back as she laughed. "Wha—?"

"I had a really good idea myself."

Navigating the steep, ladder-like staircase, David carried Elisabeth with a theatrical swagger, drawing giggles from her with every step. At the top, he set her down and gave her a playful spin.

When he pulled down the sheet concealing the loft, Elisabeth's eyes widened in astonishment at the scene before her.

The tiny space had been transformed into a charming, feminine retreat beneath the gentle curve of the arched roof. The sloping ceiling, formed by exposed wooden beams, gave the loft a cozy, intimate feel. A simple pallet on the floor was covered with an embroidered burgundy coverlet, adding a touch of elegance. Neatly arranged linen sheets peeked out from beneath the coverlet, with overstuffed pillows in linen cases completing the inviting look.

David pulled in a deep breath and pointed to a delicate iron lamp. Its glow cast a soft light over the space.

Elisabeth's eyes filled with tears as she took in the scene. "Oh my gosh, I…I'm speechless for once."

A sachet of dried lavender hanging from a hook filled the air with its subtle, soothing fragrance. Elisabeth closed her eyes for a moment to savor the calming scent. "This is amazing."

A tapestry depicting a pastoral scene was mounted beside the bed, its colors contrasting beautifully with the whitewashed walls of the half-timber cottage, adding warmth and charm to the cozy loft.

David chuckled. "The tapestry was a bit of a splurge, but it reminded me of you."

Nearby, a wooden chest carved with floral designs stood waiting. David's grin widened. "I'm told this is from a craftsman in Lille. Go on, open it."

Elisabeth's posture perked up. "Open it?"

David nodded, trying to hide his smile. "Open it."

With a burst of laughter, Elisabeth kneeled beside the chest and flung it open. Her hands trembled with excitement as she peeked inside. When she saw the contents, she squealed and sprang to her feet. "Oh my gosh! This is so amazing!"

David snorted in amusement as he watched her.

Elisabeth took a deep breath to steady herself and kneeled down to peek inside the chest again. Inside, she discovered a soft white nightgown crafted from delicate linen and edged with fine embroidery. Alongside it were several more garments: a simple yet elegant woolen gown in gentle blush pink, a soft pale blue linen dress with embroidered detailing, and a light cream-colored tunic. Each was neatly folded and ready-made, reflecting the vibrant textile trade of the time.

Elisabeth's heart raced as she explored the garments. Her grin grew wider with every new discovery. "Oh my gosh, these are incredible. I've been wearing this same dress for weeks, and now I have these beautiful choices." She glanced around again. "This whole space is like a fairy tale. I can't believe you did all this."

Elisabeth, overcome with joy, leaped into David's arms with such enthusiasm that she sent him sprawling onto the soft pallet. They tumbled into a heap, Elisabeth clinging to him with giddy laughter, their shared happiness lighting up the space.

David wrapped her in a tender embrace. "Hopefully, you'll never want to leave."

Elisabeth's heartbeat slowed at his words, understanding he wasn't just referring to the cottage but to the period they were living in. She looked at him, her voice soft and trembling. "I wish it could be that easy."

His smile faltered as he held her close, the weight of their star-crossed fate settling between them. "Just keep looking forward," he said, the gravity of his words clear. "Orpheus looked back, and it cost him everything."

Chapter Twenty-Four

The next morning zipped by in a whirlwind of activity. David threw himself into work, digging in their new garden and chopping wood for the colder months. The rhythmic thud of his axe striking the wood mixed with the distant chatter of villagers. With his shirt off, his strong, tanned arms glistened with sweat under the sun. Elisabeth's heart fluttered with each swing, her thoughts wandering back to the gladiatorial arena where she'd last seen him in a similar state.

Inside the cottage, Elisabeth busied herself with chores, but her focus was frequently pulled outside. She couldn't help sneaking glances at David as he worked, her eyes darting back to her tasks whenever he turned. Each time she peeked, she found herself smiling like a lovesick fool.

As the sun dipped lower into the sky, Elisabeth watched David pause to wipe the sweat from his brow. He turned toward the cottage, a satisfied smile playing on his lips. "How about we call it a day and get some ale from Beatrice's place?" he called out.

Elisabeth perked up at the suggestion. As she opened her mouth to respond, she realized she'd been standing in the doorway, completely engrossed in watching him. Caught in the act, she blinked and averted her gaze, cheeks burning with embarrassment. "That sounds perfect," she managed to say after clearing her throat.

David chuckled, noticing the obvious flustered look on Elisabeth's face.

He washed up, splashing cool water from the rain barrel over his face and arms. After drying himself with a piece of linen, he pulled on the white chemise, looking like something out of a Jane Austen novel she'd once read.

Elisabeth fanned herself with her hand, trying to calm the unexpected warmth in her cheeks. "Must be the weather," she muttered to herself, stifling a giggle. Her eyes kept drifting back to David, and she shook her head, amused by her own silly, fluttery feelings that she hoped he wouldn't notice.

"Ready?"

"Yep!" She skipped over the threshold, already dressed in one of her new gowns—a pale blue linen dress cinched at the waist with a leather belt. As usual, she had left her head uncovered, a small rebellion against the customs of the time that she managed to get away with. "Ready when you are."

David reached for her hand. "You look lovely."

"Thanks to you," she replied with a grin, entwining her fingers with his and glancing down to admire the light, airy dress.

They walked together down the dirt road, the air filled with the scents of early autumn and the sounds of laughter and conversation. By the time they arrived at Beatrice's, the sun had dipped below the horizon, leaving a twilight that gently illuminated their path.

The flickering light from the lanterns cast dancing shadows around the yard. At the large wooden table, Lancelot, Stefan, Brother Mattias, and several other villagers enjoyed their evening, mugs of ale in hand.

Elisabeth eyed the lively scene, spotting Jemra and Hannibal-Joe playing nearby. She gasped, realizing she'd completely forgotten about her plan for Lancelot and Beatrice. Was it really a matchmaking scheme, or just a matter of clearing up a misunderstanding?

"Look who's here," Lancelot called out with a wide grin, raising his mug in greeting. "Romeo and Juliet, just in time to join the festivities."

The villagers turned to them with warm smiles and curious eyes.

"We're just getting started." Stefan gestured to an empty space at the table. "Come. Sit. We were just talking about how you two have settled into Elias's cottage."

Elisabeth bit her lip, trying not to laugh at the string of "s" sounds that whistled through Stefan's teeth, as she and David took their seats.

David glanced around, appreciating the lively atmosphere. Just then, Beatrice emerged from the cottage, struggling to balance a precarious tower of ale cups on a wooden tray. With a grimace, she distributed them, one to David and another to Elisabeth.

"Glad you're here," Beatrice said, her voice a bit strained from balancing the load.

David accepted his cup with a smile, slipping a coin into Beatrice's hand. "Thank you. This ale is just what we needed."

Beatrice took the coin with a grateful nod, and then distributed the remaining cups.

The hunchbacked woman, her wrinkled face framed by a wimple that covered her graying hair, exuded an air of wisdom and experience. She had been observing from her seat and now cast Elisabeth and David a curious look. "How're you finding the cottage? Hear you've been quite busy."

Elisabeth took a sip of her ale. "It's wonderful. We're still adjusting, but we're making it our own."

Beatrice stepped in to introduce the woman. "This is Maria, the best baker in the entire village. She keeps everyone well-fed with her delicious pies."

As the woman nodded modestly, Elisabeth's posture perked up at the mention of pies. "Do you make *fruit* pies?"

Maria smiled. "Ah, yes, I do. When the fruits are in season, there's nothing better. Just let me know when you're ready for a treat."

David chuckled. "I think my dear Juliet is already planning her visit to your table, Maria."

Before she could respond, Lancelot chimed in with a grin. "It's almost time for your medlar pies, isn't it?"

"Medlars." A middle-aged man with a rugged face and a wooden leg, laughed heartily. "Ah, those wrinkled little things. They look like they've seen better days, don't they? Some say they resemble a dog's—"

"Mind your manners, Maarten," Maria interrupted with a mock-stern tone, though her eyes sparkled with amusement. "It's true, they're a bit... unusual, but that's what makes them special. Once they've ripened to perfection, there's nothing sweeter."

Elisabeth leaned in with a curious smile. "I've never heard of a medlar before."

"They're like a fine wine when aged just right," one of the villagers replied with a wink. "A little tart, a little sweet—just don't judge them by their appearance."

"Because they look like a dog's arse," Maarten said, earning another round of laughter.

Maria nodded, clearly enjoying the banter. "I'll be sure to save a slice for you both when the time comes. There's a medlar tree on Elias' property—those brown fruits you might have seen. Don't let the look of them fool you; they're worth the wait."

Elisabeth's eyes widened as she made the connection. "Oh, I did see them! I had no idea what they were."

Maria grinned. "That's the one. They're not much to look at, but once they're ripe, they're perfect for pies."

Just then, Jemra and Hannibal-Joe giggled while reaching for each other's toys. Their innocent babble drew everyone's attention.

As the twins' antics brought smiles and laughter, Elisabeth cast a hesitant glance at David before turning to the group. "I've been thinking about how fortunate Beatrice and Lancelot are. In my town, twins are considered a sign of great fortune. So, I suppose they've been favored by the fates," she said with a shy smile while fidgeting with the rim of her mug.

Beatrice looked up, her eyes narrowing. "Is that so? Not everyone shares that view. Some folks here believe twins are a sign of infidelity." She shot a pointed glance at Lancelot, her voice tinged with bitterness.

The chatter around the table slowed, and curious glances turned toward Beatrice and Lancelot.

Elisabeth swallowed hard. "Really? That seems like an old-fashioned belief. From what I understand, twins definitely come from the same father. It's not a sign of infidelity but rather a completely natural occurrence."

As she spoke, Elisabeth noticed Beatrice's eyes soften, directed right at her. The stern expression eased, and with a hint of appreciation, Beatrice gave a subtle nod of approval.

Lancelot, maintaining his gentlemanly demeanor, raised an eyebrow with genuine curiosity. "And what makes you say that?"

Elisabeth offered a thoughtful smile, knowing she was telling a little white lie. "My mother is a midwife, and she's always said that such beliefs are rooted in old superstitions rather than reality. Between a man and a woman, twins are *just* as likely to be a blessing as any other child—perhaps even a double blessing."

Just then, Brother Mattias, who had been quietly sipping his ale at the end of the table, cleared his throat. "It's a fascinating topic. The Scriptures offer insight into the matter. Consider the story of Esau and Jacob, twins born to Isaac and Rebekah. Their birth was part of God's plan and not viewed as a misfortune. The Bible often portrays twins as a sign of God's favor and purpose, rather than as a symbol of wrongdoing."

The table grew quieter as the villagers absorbed the monk's words. Stefan leaned in, intrigued. "I've heard of those stories, but they never seemed to be about blessings in this context."

Brother Mattias nodded. "It's true that the Bible sometimes uses twins to demonstrate divine intention. Children, including twins, are depicted as gifts from God. Misinterpretations about their origins should not lead to suspicion or judgment."

Lancelot, who had been listening intently,

furrowed his brow in thought. His expression shifted as he seemed to consider the monk's words. He glanced at Elisabeth and then at Brother Mattias, his mind clearly wrestling with the implications.

He said nothing, but his face revealed a mix of surprise and introspection. The realization that his previous beliefs might have been mistaken appeared to weigh heavily on him.

He took a slow sip of his drink.

Feeling a sense of victory, Elisabeth savored the moment with a sip of her own ale. It seemed that her plan was proving successful. As she set her cup down, she allowed herself a small, satisfied smile, hopeful that her subtle influence would continue to make a difference.

Chapter Twenty-Five

David led Elisabeth out of their cottage at the edge of the village, his hand warm around hers as he whistled a happy tune. With a grin that had been growing all morning, he tossed her a playful wink as they stepped onto the well-trodden road. In the weeks since their arrival, the trees in the forest surrounding Lindenhart had transformed into a vibrant tapestry of gold and crimson. The crisp autumn air was laced with the scent of damp earth and pine, while the distant sound of a woodpecker kept time to the cheerful rhythm in their steps.

As they walked, David's excitement became more apparent. He bumped Elisabeth lightly with his shoulder. "I've got a little surprise for you," he said, his eyes twinkling with mischief.

A wide grin spread across her face. "I knew you were up to something." She nudged him back, her heart fluttering with anticipation. "You're going to keep me guessing all day, aren't you?"

He flashed a roguish smile. "Absolutely."

Elisabeth bounced along beside him. "That's all right…because I *love* surprises." Her gaze then fixed on Beatrice's cottage as they strolled past, noting its quiet and empty appearance.

When they reached the picturesque bridge in the center of the village, the afternoon sun filtered through the weeping willow branches, casting a warm, golden light as they crossed. Elisabeth let out a satisfied sigh. "This spot is so romantic." Her gaze drifted over the serene view of the stream below. The play of light on the water and the tranquil surroundings made the moment feel truly magical.

David's eyes met hers. "It is." He leaned in and brushed a soft kiss against her lips.

Elisabeth giggled, her cheeks growing warmer as she returned the kiss, their shared affection lingering in the air like a sweet secret.

Suddenly, the rhythmic clunk of wood on wood echoed across the bridge. Startled, they turned to see Maarten, the blacksmith with the wooden leg, approaching. His wooden leg made a steady rhythm with each step, and a knowing grin was plastered across his face.

"Well, well, aren't you two just making the rest of us look bad with all this sweetness?" His hearty chuckle was accompanied by the steady clunk of his leg. "You've set the bar pretty high for the rest of us, you know." His voice carried a mix of amusement and mock sternness as he gave them a playful nod.

Realizing they'd been caught in their private moment, they quickly pulled apart. David rubbed the back of his neck, a sheepish grin spreading across his face. "Uh, sorry about that."

Elisabeth's laughter bubbled up, her cheeks growing even hotter. "We didn't see you there," she managed between giggles.

Maarten gave them a hearty laugh as he hobbled away, leaving them to exchange amused and slightly embarrassed glances.

David winked at her. "Come on," he said, his voice laced with playful mischief.

Hand in hand, they soon reached the village gate and left Lindenhart behind. The sun-dappled road led them through the forest, where the autumn colors painted the canopy above. The air was crisp, and the soft crunch of leaves underfoot accompanied their steps, while the occasional rustle of small creatures in the underbrush added a gentle background noise to their journey.

Elisabeth's excitement grew with every step. "Where are we going?"

"We're almost there," he replied, keeping the destination a secret.

When they emerged from the trees, less than an hour later, Elisabeth's eyes widened in surprise at the sight of the imposing city walls in the distance. The high stone ramparts, topped with battlements and dotted with watchtowers, enclosed a bustling town that seemed far larger than she had imagined. The town's gates, framed by sturdy wooden structures, marked the entrance to the city.

"Is that Oudenaarde?" she asked, her voice tinged with awe.

"Yes." David squeezed her hand. "And we're going to the faire."

Elisabeth let out a spontaneous laugh. "Really?"

"Really."

As they rounded a bend, her eyes widened at the sight of a large field bustling with the lively faire. Colorful tents and stalls filled the grassy expanse, and the distant hum of festivities hinted at the vibrant scene awaiting them. Elisabeth had expected Oudenaarde to be modest, but as they walked across the grassy fairgrounds, the scale of the fortress-like city and the size of the event exceeded her imagination.

The air was rich with the scents of freshly baked bread, roasting meats, and sweet pastries, mingling with the earthy aroma of autumn leaves. Laughter, clinking mugs, and the chatter of vendors and townsfolk created a festive atmosphere.

Colorful banners fluttered in the breeze as they passed entertainers playing lively music and performing daring acrobatics. Children darted between stalls, clutching bright ribbons and sweets, while traders showcased their wares—spices, fabrics, and intricate handcrafted goods.

David guided Elisabeth through the crowd, their hands still entwined as they navigated between bustling stalls and excited visitors. With a mischievous grin, he glanced at her. "So, where's the first stop on our grand adventure?"

Elisabeth's breath hitched as she took in the sights. "Let's see everything! How about some of those roasted chestnuts first?" She pointed to a vendor whose stall was surrounded by a tantalizing aroma.

They made their way to the vendor. After David paid with a small coin, the man handed them a cloth pouch filled with warm, roasted chestnuts. A slow smile spread across Elisabeth's face, relieved to see that David had used change from the large gold pieces they had minted—a reassuring sign that they were blending in with the locals and no longer standing out.

She bit into one of the chestnuts, savoring the rich, nutty flavor. "They're delicious." She held out the pouch to David. "Here, try some."

As they wandered further, they stumbled upon a juggler performing an impressive routine with flaming torches. Elisabeth clapped and laughed. "Wow, look at that. Almost as good as Theresa," she said, nudging David playfully.

He chuckled, flashing her a cheeky grin. "You know what? I'm planning to enter the archery contest while we're here."

Elisabeth's eyes widened as she met his gaze, a smile spreading across her face. "Really? I have a feeling you're going to be quite the competitor. Or are you just trying to steal the spotlight?"

David's grin grew. "Maybe a little of both."

As they wandered through the faire, they came across a group of dancers in colorful costumes performing a vibrant folk dance. Elisabeth's feet started tapping to the rhythm, her excitement hard to contain.

When spectators began to join in, David quirked an eyebrow and shot Elisabeth a knowing glance before pulling her into the action. Surprised but laughing, she grasped his fingers as he twirled her around.

Everyone joined hands and moved in a spinning circle, stepping, hopping, and clapping to the infectious rhythm, their faces glowing with joy.

David held on to Elisabeth, doing his best to keep up. His hops were offbeat, and his claps came at unpredictable intervals, adding a charmingly clumsy twist to his dancing.

Elisabeth couldn't stop laughing as she tried to match David's enthusiastic but awkward rhythm. She nudged him with her elbow, her laughter spilling out in waves. Every time David missed a beat, her smile widened, and she had to take a deep breath to compose herself, thoroughly enjoying the carefree moment.

He flashed a boyish grin. "I'm doing my best," he said, still slightly off rhythm with his claps and hops. "Though it seems I might be inventing a dance of my own!"

Elisabeth's heart swelled with happiness and a hint of longing. Her gaze swept over the lively faire and then back to David's awkward attempts, making her smile grow even wider. "This isn't prom," she shouted over the noise, "but I'll take it."

David's eyes softened, and with a gentle tug, he pulled Elisabeth out of the dance. Drawing her closer, his expression conveyed an unspoken promise. "What is this pr—"

"Juliet! Romeo!" a familiar voice called out, breaking the spell.

Elisabeth turned, her surprise melting into a big smile as she spotted Beatrice making her way through the crowd, with Lancelot following close behind.

Beatrice approached with a wry smile. "I didn't know you were here," she said, her tone both blunt and amused. "Lancelot insisted I needed a break. I'd have joined you two *instead* if I'd known."

Lancelot flashed Beatrice a rueful smile. "Well, *I'm* glad you're here."

"Where are the babies?" Elisabeth asked.

"With Maria," Beatrice replied. "I'm already looking forward to next year when they're walking and can actually enjoy all of this. They're still too little for it now."

As Beatrice spoke, David's attention was drawn to a three-legged race nearby. Pairs of contestants stood with their legs tied together, hopping and stumbling their way down a makeshift course. The cheering spectators added to the energetic atmosphere.

David's eyes widened as he took in the scene. "Let's try that next."

While Beatrice and Lancelot were bickering about the best way to navigate the faire, Elisabeth leaned in with a grin. "And unlike your old life, these games aren't played to the death," she whispered.

David's lips curled into an amused smile. "No life-or-death stakes here. Just the risk of looking foolish in front of a crowd."

As Lancelot caught the tail end of their conversation, he glanced over at the nearby race. "Ah, you're talking about the bound race. It's all about teamwork and balance—though judging by those teams, they might end up more tangled than you expect."

David's face lit up. "We must try that next. It looks tremendous."

"Tremendous?" Elisabeth laughed and raised her eyebrows. "Seriously? Are you planning to try every single game?"

Lancelot grinned and squared his shoulders, matching David's enthusiasm. "Up for the challenge, Romeo?"

Elisabeth mockingly clasped her hands together. "Please, don't encourage him!" she begged.

David planted his feet in a wide stance, biting down on a smile as he and Lancelot locked eyes. "Challenge accepted."

Lancelot nodded, clearly enjoying the competition. "Let's do it."

As Elisabeth and David made their way to the

starting line of the three-legged race, the boisterous organizer waved them over. "Welcome! You'll be racing against two other fine pairs. The prize for the winning team is a lovely posey of flowers for your better half. Ready to prove your mettle?"

Elisabeth's eyes widened with excitement at the mention of flowers. "I'm in!" She squeezed David's hand, eager to participate.

Beatrice, however, seemed caught off guard. "Two other pairs? I thought it would be just Lancelot and Romeo racing."

Lancelot, surprised but quickly regaining his composure, offered a reassuring smile. "Come on, it's just for fun, Bumble Bee," he whispered.

Elisabeth noticed Beatrice's stern demeanor soften as she sighed and gave a resigned nod. "Fine." Her tone carried a hint of reluctant amusement. "Let's see how this goes."

With anticipation fluttering in her stomach, Elisabeth and David moved to the starting line. David adjusted their tied legs, and they wrapped their arms around each other for balance, their connection steady. David's playful smirk met Elisabeth's excited grin as they stood ready. She nudged him with her elbow, laughing as their shoulders touched in a silent promise of victory.

On their left, a pair of teenagers, around fourteen and brimming with youthful energy, waited. Their faces were bright with excitement as they prepared for the race. Beyond them, an older couple, with movements slower but spirits just as high, adjusted their own tied legs.

Beatrice, meanwhile, looked unimpressed as she

and Lancelot took their positions. She stood stiff, reluctant to let Lancelot's arm touch her, in stark contrast to the easy camaraderie between the other teams. "This isn't what I had in mind when I agreed to come to the faire," she muttered in a monotone voice.

Elisabeth watched as Lancelot, determined to lighten the mood, adjusted their tied legs. He placed his hand on Beatrice's arm, trying to bridge the distance between them. "It's all in good fun, Bee," he said with a hopeful smile.

Beatrice shifted slightly, still holding her composure but letting his touch linger. "All right," she said with a small nod. "I suppose I do want those flowers after all."

David, catching the exchange, grinned at Lancelot. "You hear that, Lancelot? I hope you're ready to lose," he teased, his tone light but competitive.

Elisabeth flashed David a confident smile as the whistle blew. They sprang into action, their bound legs moving in perfect sync. Their laughter rang out as they raced down the course, their coordination seamless.

Beatrice and Lancelot, however, shot forward with a burst of speed. Beatrice's expression was fierce, her eyes set on the finish line. The younger teenagers, quick on their feet, darted past, adding to the race's intensity.

Elisabeth, her leg tied to David's, stumbled slightly as they pushed ahead. Out of the corner of her eye, she noticed Beatrice and Lancelot tumble into a heap, their legs tangled awkwardly. Lancelot flashed a roguish grin and held out his hand. "Come on, Bee, we've got this."

Even as she focused on her own steps, Elisabeth saw Beatrice pause, her frustration evident, before she accepted Lancelot's hand. For a brief moment, their fingers lingered together, and something in Beatrice's gaze seemed to thaw before she quickly pulled away. Elisabeth caught the exchange, a flicker of curiosity sparking in her mind—were old feelings bubbling up, despite everything?

David's steady pace pulled Elisabeth's attention back to the race, and together they pushed forward, determined to win. But their momentum was interrupted when the teenagers zipped past in a final burst of energy. Elisabeth laughed, breathless but exhilarated, as she and David tried to regain their lead.

But then, Beatrice and Lancelot, spurred by sheer determination, found their rhythm again. With a coordinated effort, they edged ahead, crossing the finish line first. Elisabeth and David, neck-and-neck with the quick-footed teenagers, crossed just behind them, their faces flushed with the thrill of the race. The old couple brought up the rear, finishing last but still beaming with the joy of participation.

The crowd erupted in cheers, but it was the sight of Beatrice and Lancelot that held Elisabeth's attention.

As soon as their legs were untied, Beatrice threw her arms around Lancelot. He lifted her off the ground in a joyful spin, their faces flushed with excitement, their laughter filling the air before realizing what they were doing and stepping apart awkwardly.

But for that fleeting moment, Elisabeth could see that their past grievances seemed distant and irrelevant, overshadowed by the happiness of their shared victory.

****

As the day wound down, the four friends made their way home, their spirits high and the festive energy of the harvest faire still vivid in their minds. They had enjoyed pastries, roasted meats, and lively games, with Beatrice carrying the small posy they had won. David, triumphant, bore a new quiver of arrows from the archery contest, just as Elisabeth had predicted.

As they traveled the winding trail, the sun hung low in the sky. They chatted excitedly, David adjusting his bow as he reminisced about the competition, mindful of the need to reach the village before the gates were locked for the night at dusk.

But—

As they entered Lindenhart, the cheerful banter faded, replaced by an unsettling silence.

The vibrant memories of the day dissolved into a heavy, oppressive quiet. Broken barrels and scattered debris littered the path, and the once-warm glow of the village was now overshadowed by a chilling emptiness.

Elisabeth's heart pounded as a cold wave of dread surged through her. Her hands trembled, the stark contrast between the day's joy and the sudden, eerie stillness making her breath catch in her throat.

The village lay eerily still, as if holding its breath, and a sense of foreboding settled over them.

Chapter Twenty-Six

Beatrice's face went pale, her gaze wide with fear as she locked eyes with Lancelot. The moment seemed to freeze between them—a silent acknowledgment of the terror gripping them both.

The twins.

Without a word, they sprinted through the village, their movements fueled by raw, desperate emotion.

Elisabeth and David raced after them, their footsteps pounding through the quiet streets. Her gaze flicked to the chaos all around—doors left swinging, belongings strewn across the dirt paths. The silence that followed felt ominous, pressing in on them as they ran.

Elisabeth's breath came in ragged gasps, heart pounding not just from exertion but from the gnawing dread. When they arrived at Maria's cottage, the door was ajar, and the sight of the empty interior sent a jolt of panic through her.

Beatrice and Lancelot's faces twisted with fear.

"Maria! Maria, where are you?" Any composure Beatrice held onto shattered as she called out Maria's name, her voice rising in desperation. "Please, answer!"

Lancelot stood behind, his hands on her shoulders, trying to offer some semblance of comfort despite the obvious strain in his own eyes. "Bee," he said gently, though his voice trembled, "maybe she took them home to put them to bed." His words were meant to soothe, but the worry etched into his features revealed the anxiety tormenting him. "We'll find them, I promise."

Elisabeth's heart ached with worry. She and David dashed alongside Beatrice and Lancelot, racing toward the cottage. Their voices cut through the stillness of the village, calling out for Maria, their desperate cries echoing with the weight of their fear.

The sound of crying babies reached their ears from a distance, causing the tension to spike even further.

Just then, Maria came shuffling down the road as fast as her bent frame would allow, her steps uneven but determined.

She was empty-handed.

"They're safe! Don't worry, they're safe!" Maria's breathless voice called out, carrying a note of reassurance despite her exhaustion.

Elisabeth let out a shaky laugh, though it was mingled with lingering concern. She could see the same relief spreading across Beatrice's face, her breath hitching as she absorbed the news. Beatrice's voice trembled as she whispered, "Thank God," but her eyes remained clouded with worry. "Where are they? Where are my babies?"

Before she could respond, Maarten appeared, his wooden leg thumping with each step. His shoulders were tense, and he held the crying twins close to his chest, their tiny hands reaching toward their parents.

Beatrice let out a shuddering sigh as she rushed to take Hannibal-Joe from Maarten. As soon as she had him in her arms, he clung to her, his cries of relief mingling with her tears. At the same time, Lancelot, his face etched with intense concern, took Jemra. The baby reached for him, and Lancelot's hands trembled as he held her close, his expression a mixture of fierce relief and overwhelming emotion.

Elisabeth swallowed the lump in her throat as she watched Lancelot. Despite his initial doubts and fears—fueled by the mistaken belief that Beatrice had been unfaithful—his unwavering devotion to the twins was evident. He had been a constant presence, showing his love for them day after day.

As he drew Jemra close, his eyes brimming with tears and his breath coming in ragged gasps, Elisabeth saw the profound depth of his love and the strong bond he shared with his family. She felt reassured that any misunderstandings between him and Beatrice would be resolved, and that their enduring love would guide them through.

Maria looked both relieved and exhausted. "With the ransacking earlier, we hid the babies to keep them safe." Her voice was trembling. "There was so much commotion, and I wanted to make sure they were out of harm's way."

David squeezed Elisabeth's hand. "Thank goodness they're all right," he murmured, his voice reflecting the weight of the fear they had all felt.

Elisabeth nodded, her heart still racing. She glanced around at the gathered villagers, the tension slowly dissipating. Despite the relief, the sense of unease lingered, a stark reminder of how fast their world could shift from peace to panic.

Just as they began to make sense of the situation, Stefan and Brother Mattias appeared, weaving their way through the crowd. Stefan's face was drawn with worry, while Brother Mattias looked solemn. "Romeo, Juliet," the monk greeted them. "Thank goodness everyone is safe."

Stefan nodded in agreement. "It's fortunate that most of the village was at the faire," he said, his voice carrying the faint whistling sound from the gap in his teeth. "They searched every house and corner, asking questions we could not answer. It seemed they sought someone in particular."

Elisabeth froze, rooted to the spot.

Maria looked up, her eyes bloodshot. "A group of men came through here, tearing the village apart. They were searching for someone and asking about gold, overturning everything as if they thought we were hiding something of great value."

A cold chill ran down Elisabeth's spine. She exchanged a quick look with David, who had gone rigid beside her.

Stefan straightened, his posture growing alert as he shifted his gaze between Elisabeth and David. "I overheard them talking about a nobleman's daughter—Lady Elizabeth, was it? And the young man she eloped with—apparently, he's accused of abduction, theft, and disrupting a noble contract." His brow furrowed as he focused on her, curiosity evident in his expression.

Elisabeth felt the color drain from her face and she swallowed a lump in her throat.

Stefan's expression softened with understanding as he looked at David. "You're the ones they're searching for, aren't you?"

A murmur of confusion swept through the crowd. "Who, Romeo and Juliet?" Maarten asked, trying to make sense of the revelation.

A stunned silence fell over the group as the villagers exchanged uneasy glances.

David's shoulders slumped, his resolve crumbling under the weight of the truth. He took a deep breath, his voice heavy with resignation. "Yes," he said, meeting the shocked eyes of the villagers. "We are."

Elisabeth glanced around uneasily. "My father, Lord Cathon, is a ruthless man," she said, her voice unsteady. "He wants my husband dead so he can force me to marry Guglielmo Tartare, a mercenary leader, in order to form an alliance." As she spoke, Elisabeth reached for David, her fingers entwining with his in a desperate grip, the slight tremor in her hand betraying her fear. A murmur of shock rippled through the villagers at the mention of Tartare's name, some gasping audibly. "By doing this, he'll have a huge army that will be entirely loyal to him."

Beatrice, with Hannibal-Joe still in her arms, remained calm. "Well, would you look at that," she said, unfazed. "I had a feeling you weren't quite who you claimed to be. Figured you were hiding something, but kept my suspicions to myself. Everyone in Lindenhart's got their secrets."

David took a deep, pained breath. "I'm *truly* sorry for everything. We never meant to bring trouble here. We'll leave right away."

Lancelot, shaking off his initial shock as he held Jemra, stepped forward with a firm yet reassuring stance. "You've faced enough already. The searchers came through, ransacked the village, and left without finding you. If they didn't locate you here, then you're safe for now. Lindenhart may be small, but we protect our own."

Beatrice nodded. "You're part of our village now. We may be outcasts, but we look out for each other.

They've moved on, so the immediate danger has passed. Stay here with us, and we'll do everything we can to keep you safe. You've nowhere else to go, and *we* won't turn you away."

The villagers murmured in agreement. The belief that the immediate threat had passed brought them renewed unity.

"Tartare's mercenary army is growing." A sharp voice cut through the conversation.

The crowd turned to see Henry Gagneux, the reserved pig farmer, had joined them. His quiet demeanor was replaced by a look of serious concern.

"This matter extends beyond Tartare," Henry said with grave concern. "A lord gathering a mercenary force is a dire threat. I've heard rumors spreading through neighboring towns and villages—whispers of soldiers for hire, growing in number and brutality. Should we allow his power to grow unchecked, he will endanger not just Romeo and Juliet," —he gestured toward them— "or whatever their true names may be, but all who oppose him. A nobleman's army is seldom employed for any cause other than his own gain. We must act swiftly to curtail his growing influence and prevent his mercenaries from becoming an indomitable force."

A tense silence followed Henry's words, the weight of his message sinking in. The villagers exchanged worried glances, their initial relief giving way to renewed fear. The realization that their small village could be caught in a larger conflict was sobering.

Henry twisted his tunic, clearly uncomfortable in the midst of the crowd. "I'll be straight with you," he said with a wry smile, "I don't enjoy the company of most of you. Given the choice, I'd prefer to be back at my farm, with my pigs and my peace. But isn't that what being part of a village is about? You may get on my nerves now and then, but I won't stand by and let anyone threaten you without stepping up."

The group chuckled, the unexpected humor breaking some of the tension. The laughter was brief but enough to lift their spirits.

One by one, the villagers found their voices, each word carrying growing resolve. "We can't just stand by," Lancelot insisted. "If Tartare's army keeps growing, we'll be overwhelmed. We need to act now."

Maarten nodded. "This isn't just about Romeo and Juliet. It's about stopping a powerful nobleman from taking too much control and putting us all in danger. We've seen it before—like in Ghent, where folks are already rising up against unfair lords and pushing back against Burgundy's grasp."

The murmurs of agreement grew into a strong chorus. "We've got to stand firm," Stefan said with conviction. "It's not just about keeping ourselves safe; it's about making sure no lord can rule us unchecked."

The air crackled with new determination as the villagers, stirred by Henry's warning, readied themselves to face the threat together. "We need to keep the balance of power," Lancelot added, "and protect the common people from those who think they can control our lives from their high towers, whether they're in Flanders or far beyond."

As the weight of their determination settled over the gathering, Beatrice stepped forward, her voice cutting through the charged atmosphere. "It's been a long day for everyone, and the little ones need their rest." Her gaze shifted to Hannibal-Joe. "Let's all get some sleep and regroup in the morning."

Despite the lingering tension, the villagers said their goodbyes. Their voices, though weary, carried a warmth that contrasted with the danger looming on the horizon. One by one, they bid David and Elisabeth goodnight, their farewells a quiet reminder of the community's strength and solidarity.

"Rest well," Beatrice whispered, her eyes betraying a flicker of concern as she gave Elisabeth a reassuring squeeze. "We'll be here if you need us."

Lancelot gave a curt nod, his expression solemn. "Get some sleep. Tomorrow is another day."

Stefan's gaze lingered on David and Elisabeth for a moment longer before he spoke. "You've faced enough for one night. We'll talk more in the morning. Goodnight."

As the last of the villagers departed, David and Elisabeth walked back to their cottage. The night air was cool and crisp, a sharp contrast to the warmth of the day. Their home, once a sanctuary, now felt like a ghost of their former peace, a stark reminder of the danger that always seemed to loom just beyond the horizon for them.

They pushed open the door to find the cottage in disarray. Drawers hung open, and belongings were scattered across the floor.

Elisabeth's heart sank as she took in the mess. "They've ransacked everything," she said, her voice trembling. She moved through the room, checking the contents of the drawers and the scattered items on the floor.

David's jaw tightened as he joined her in surveying the chaos. His gaze then hardened. "We need to leave *now*. It's too dangerous to stay here. They'll be back."

Elisabeth cast a heartbroken look around their small cottage, knowing he was right. Through watery eyes, she took in the cozy loft, the small garden visible through the window, and the well-worn path leading to the door. Though they had only been here for a matter of weeks, the time had been filled with simple joys and intimate memories.

Elisabeth let out a long, low sigh, and then sprang into action. She filled a canteen with water from the barrel, then retrieved a loaf of bread and a bundle of dried meat from their small cupboard. David joined her, grabbing a sturdy leather traveling bag. Together, they packed the essentials, working with focused efficiency.

As David draped a cloak over her shoulders, Elisabeth's teary eyes met his. "I know this is difficult," he said in a soothing tone. "We've just begun to build a life here. I hate to leave it behind, but as long as we're together, we'll build a new life wherever we go."

"I know, it's just…" Elisabeth leaned in, needing a hug.

David wrapped his arms around her, pulling her close. Her head rested against his chest, and she could feel the steady beat of his heart. After a few moments, he tilted her chin up, his eyes searching hers. With a tender smile, he leaned in and their lips met in a soft, reassuring kiss—a fleeting moment of peace amid the chaos.

When they parted, Elisabeth's eyes lingered on his. "Let's stop and dig up the gold. We can eventually melt it down and recast it into smaller, unmarked pieces. We have to be more careful not to leave a trail."

David nodded and brushed a stray tear from her cheek with his thumb, then entwined his fingers with hers, his touch warm and reassuring. He kissed her again, his lips conveying a promise of a future yet to come. "We'll build a new life, a safe one, where we can be free."

"Where will we go?" Elisabeth asked, her voice trembling.

"Somewhere out of Cato's reach," David vowed, his grip firm. "A place where we can start fresh. We'll find it together, I swear."

Chapter Twenty-Seven

As twilight settled and the first stars emerged, David and Elisabeth prepared for their departure. David secured the leather bag of provisions over his shoulder, his new bow and quiver resting on top. Just as they completed their preparations, a sharp shout from within the village shattered their quiet moment.

"To arms! To arms!" The sound was urgent, desperate.

David and Elisabeth exchanged wide-eyed looks and rushed outside.

Stefan burst into view, his face pale, gasping for air. "Men…lots of men," he panted, his chest heaving. "They're setting up camp outside the fence."

Elisabeth's blood ran cold, her heart pounding.

From their cottage on the edge of the village, they could now hear the low, ominous hum of voices and the occasional clinking sound, revealing the presence of an army on the other side of the fortified timber wall.

The realization hit hard and Elisabeth gasped.

The village was surrounded.

David grabbed her hand. "We need to move."

But Lindenhart was already in turmoil.

"Everyone is assembling in the meeting hall," Stefan shouted, his voice nearly lost in the rising commotion. Without waiting for a reply, he dashed toward the next cottage, calling out for more villagers to join them. "To arms! To arms!"

David and Elisabeth sprinted down the road. The path was a whirlwind of movement and noise. Villagers rushed past, their faces etched with fear.

Outside the meeting hall, the chaos intensified. Inside, dim lanterns cast flickering shadows over the crowded space, where frantic chatter and hasty commands filled the air. As they neared the entrance, Elisabeth's gaze was drawn to a frantic mother who was clutching her two small children, one in each hand.

"Théodore!" the woman yelled; voice sharp with anger. "Théodore!" Her fierce eyes scanned the crowd with a mix of frustration and worry.

The scene inside was a blur of frantic energy as David and Elisabeth burst through the door, gasping for breath. A moment later, Lancelot arrived, guiding Beatrice and a small wooden cart with the twins nestled under blankets. His imposing figure and authoritative voice quickly cut through the clamor.

"Quiet!" Lancelot commanded, his tone firm and unyielding. The room fell silent as the villagers turned to him. "Listen to me. We need to stay calm and focus on a plan. We have the strength to face this threat—together."

His presence, combined with David's resolute stance, brought a sense of order to the room. The villagers, seeing their confidence and determination, began to steady themselves. The frantic energy eased as they gathered around Lancelot and David, ready to follow their lead.

Suddenly, a deep horn blast echoed through the village, reverberating through the thin, half-timber walls of the meeting hall. The sound sent a chill down

Elisabeth's spine. Inside, the tension thickened as the clattering of weapons and heavy footsteps grew louder. Elisabeth could feel the fear creeping in, the earlier resolve of the villagers beginning to waver.

She exchanged a worried glance with David, her stomach knotting with fear.

"Someone's coming!" The muffled sound of a boy's voice reached them, strained and urgent, as he called out from somewhere above. "A man with a torch!"

As Elisabeth looked up, trying to find the source of the voice, Brother Mattias stepped outside, turned around and glanced at the roof. "Théodore, dear boy, come down and join your mother inside. She needs you close."

While Brother Mattias turned his attention back to the imminent threat, the villagers inside the meeting hall waited uneasily.

A voice from the besieging force rang out with chilling authority: "By order of Lord Cathon, surrender his daughter and the fugitive by dawn, or every soul within these walls will be slaughtered!"

Murmurs of panic spread through the crowd, fear taking hold.

Elisabeth's breath caught as the dim light from the lanterns flickered, casting anxious shadows around the room. She could feel the tension in the crowded space, the oppressive weight of uncertainty bearing down on them all.

David took a deep breath and closed his eyes for a moment before addressing the gathered crowd. "I'm truly sorry." His fingers instinctively fidgeted with his rope sling. "We never meant to put this village in

284

harm's way, but the situation has spiraled beyond our control. There's no option to stay; we will leave immediately. Lord Cathon will stop at nothing to see me dead, and he'll come for us here if we remain. We are leaving to protect everyone, including my wife and myself."

His gaze swept over the villagers, his expression firm. "Cathon is only after us. Staying here means risking *your* lives, and I cannot allow that. We have to move quickly to ensure everyone's safety."

"You can't leave," Beatrice cut in, her voice tense. "The village is completely surrounded. There's no way out."

David nodded, fully aware of the gravity of the situation. "I have a plan," he said, his voice low and measured. He glanced at Lancelot. "Do you remember how Hannibal used oxen to mislead the Romans?" He reached into his new quiver, pulled out an arrow, and used its tip to draw a strategy in the dirt floor.

Lancelot's eyes lit up with excitement, seeming to understand where David was going.

"I have an idea that could be just as disruptive." David stood tall, planting his feet in a wide stance. "And we have a certain aggressive pig that might help us create the diversion we need."

A wide grin spread across Lancelot's face, and the villagers exchanged whispers of intrigue. The anxiety in the meeting hall lifted as they realized the potential of David's plan.

Elisabeth felt a flutter of excitement in her stomach.

It just might work.

Chapter Twenty-Eight

Once the sky had darkened to a deep indigo, David climbed onto the thatched roof of the meeting hall. Elisabeth stood below, gripping the ladder firmly, her heart racing in the cool night air. Shadows blanketed the village, and the only sounds were the rustling of leaves and the distant voices from the enemy forces that surrounded them.

From his elevated position, David scanned the area beyond the village's timber wall, noting the positions of the enemy. After a few minutes, he descended, his expression grim but controlled. He took a deep breath, lowering his voice as he spoke. "There's a command post set up just outside—large tent, central fire. The perimeter's guarded, but I saw gaps we can exploit."

Elisabeth's pulse quickened, her eyes flicking toward the village gate. She could see the tension etched into Lancelot's face as he absorbed David's words.

David turned to Stefan, speaking in a low, urgent tone. "Stefan, we need your ox waiting near our cottage as soon as possible. And bring a lantern—it'll help make the diversion convincing."

Stefan's eyes widened, but he nodded without hesitation. "I'll be there. I'll get the ox now," he whispered, and then turned and moved into the shadows, understanding the gravity of the task.

David's gaze swept over the small group of villagers nearby, all keeping their voices hushed. "Henry," he called quietly, motioning the man over. "You and Lancelot, get your pig and her piglets. Bring them to the meeting hall."

Henry blinked in surprise. "All twelve?" he asked, his voice just above a whisper.

David gave a firm nod. "Yes, all twelve. If this works, I'm sure Brother Mattias will pardon your swine."

Henry glanced at Lancelot, who met his eyes with a silent agreement. Without another word, they slipped into the night to gather the animals.

David turned to the remaining villagers; his tone calm but filled with determination. "Find a cart—something light enough for a pig to pull. And gather whatever you can that'll burn fast—straw, wood, oil. We need to load it up as soon as possible."

The villagers exchanged brief glances of understanding before disappearing into the shadows to search for supplies.

David then spotted the blacksmith with the wooden leg. "Maarten," he called, striding over. "I need a small bucket of pitch. Can you find some for me?"

"Of course," he replied, already moving toward the storage area. "I'll have it ready for you in a moment."

David turned back to Brother Mattias, who was organizing the villagers. He spoke softly, pointing toward the edge of the village. "There's a tree near the fence, not far from the enemy camp. I need a hole dug under it—just big enough for a piglet to fit through. Can you manage that without drawing attention?"

Brother Mattias nodded. "I'll get it done. How

soon?"

"As soon as possible."

Brother Mattias, without another word, grabbed a shovel and headed toward the designated spot.

After the monk slipped away, David took Elisabeth's hand. "We'll get through this."

Together, they sprinted toward their cottage, their footsteps rustling through the fallen leaves in the darkened village.

When they arrived, Stefan was already there, his ox tethered to a post, the lantern in hand.

David signaled for him to follow, leading the stout man and the ox along the shadowy path toward the hidden gate in the timber wall. Elisabeth walked beside them, her body tense with anxiety. The distant sounds of the enemy camp reached them through the dark, making each step feel fraught with danger.

"Stefan, listen carefully," David whispered as they reached the concealed gate. "When you hear the commotion from the front—when the uproar begins—I need you to wait until the men here become distracted or leave their posts. Only then should you let the ox out through this gate. Once it's clear, shut the gate again immediately and secure it."

Stefan's eyes widened, realizing the importance of the hidden exit. "I'll do it."

David continued in a low voice, "Hang the lantern from its horn. We need them to believe it's Elisabeth and I making our escape through the back."

Stefan glanced at David with a dawning realization. "Elisabeth," he repeated, testing the name. "And I take it your name isn't really Romeo."

David's smile softened, a bittersweet warmth in his

gaze. "I'm David," he said quietly.

Stefan met David's eyes, a new understanding in his gaze. "David and Elisabeth," he whispered, the names now holding deeper meaning. "We'll do everything we can to help you. I'll wait for the right moment—you can count on me."

David placed a hand on Stefan's shoulder, the gesture both reassuring and final. "Thank you. Your help is something we'll never forget."

Stefan's eyes glistened. "Godspeed," he said with a small, solemn smile.

With one last look, they all knew it was a final goodbye. David and Elisabeth exchanged a brief, poignant glance before slipping back into the night, leaving Stefan to his task.

They sprinted down the darkened path. As they neared their small cottage, Elisabeth noticed David's pace falter. His gaze lingered on the familiar, comforting sight—a dream come true for him, a place of solace and happiness.

Noticing his pause, Elisabeth pulled him to a stop. She looked up at him, her vision blurred with unshed tears. "I didn't realize how much I'd miss this place either," she whispered, her voice trembling.

David, still focused on the cottage, took a deep breath. "It was everything I hoped for." His posture stooped with the weight of his emotion.

Elisabeth stepped into his embrace, and he enveloped her in a tight, protective hug. "I won't let anything happen to you," he murmured fiercely into her hair. "I promise."

She clung to him, drawing strength from his presence. "I know," she whispered back.

They held each other for a few heartbeats longer, both aware it might be their last moment of peace together. With a final squeeze, David released her. "It's time," he said, his voice steady but tinged with sadness.

Elisabeth nodded, blinking back tears. "Let's finish this," she said as they turned and picked up their pace toward the meeting hall.

Once there, David wasted no time. "Lancelot, Henry, it's time."

Lancelot nodded, pulling a sturdy wagon that carried a wooden crate packed with the piglets, their soft squeals and wriggles barely contained.

Henry, with the ornery pig harnessed to the cart loaded with flammables, prepared to lead her toward the gate. "Mama's all set."

David nodded, his mind clearly focused. "Good. Lancelot, bring the crate and be ready to release the piglets as soon as I give the signal."

Henry tugged on Mama Pig's tether, guiding her toward the gate. Lancelot and another villager lifted the crate of piglets, carrying them to Brother Mattias' newly dug hole. The piglets squealed, but the crate's sturdy construction kept them secure.

When they reached the designated spot, David gave a soft whistle. In response, Lancelot tipped the crate, releasing the piglets through the small gap under the fence.

They all listened, catching the first signs of commotion from the enemy camp—laughter and shouts erupted, mingling with the frantic squeals of the piglets. The chaos on the other side of the fortified fence grew louder as the piglets scattered, causing a ruckus amongst Tartare's mercenaries.

Mama Pig, her maternal instincts in overdrive, began to panic. She thrashed violently against her tether, her hooves pounding the ground with increasing urgency. The sound of her distressed grunts and the frantic squeals of her piglets filled the air.

"Open the gate!" David whispered loudly.

Maarten yanked the gate open, and Mama Pig burst through with a forceful surge. The cart, bumping and jostling, trailed behind her as she charged into the enemy camp. Her massive frame crashed through the fray, the cart clattering against soldiers' legs and scattering supplies. The enemy, already disoriented by the piglets, were thrown into further disarray as Mama Pig barreled through them, her rage unstoppable.

The gate slammed shut once more, and Elisabeth raced to catch sight of the commotion through a narrow gap between the fence's wooden planks.

The camp erupted into turmoil, soldiers stumbling and shouting in every direction. Mama Pig, her sides heaving, tore through the camp, the cart clattering and bumping through the disorder, her enraged squeals piercing the night. The soldiers, shocked by the sudden onslaught, fumbled and shouted in alarm. Their attempts to regain control were futile against the relentless fury of the massive pig.

Piglets squealed in disarray, amplifying the pandemonium.

Elisabeth sucked in a quick breath. The distraction was working. She watched as Mama's rampage continued, the confusion escalating. With every passing moment, the enemy's disorientation grew, creating the perfect cover for their escape.

But then, Guglielmo Tartare, with his greasy blond

hair, scrambled to respond. With a fast stride, he unsheathed his sword and made his way toward Mama.

Elisabeth's heart raced as she observed Tartare approach the sow; sword raised. He struck at the ropes, slicing through the harness with swift, practiced movements.

Mama Pig, already in a frenzy, reacted violently to the sudden tug of her restraints being cut.

Elisabeth's breath quickened as Mama Pig's rampage reached its climax, throwing the camp into chaos. She glanced anxiously at the cart filled with flammable material, now positioned dangerously in the heart of the turmoil.

She turned to see David sprinting toward the ladder, his face set with determination. "Maarten!" he shouted, intensity clear in his voice. Elisabeth quickly spotted Maarten, his wooden leg clacking as he hurried over with a bucket of pitch.

This was Elisabeth's signal. She grabbed a lit torch and dashed over to the ladder, holding it steady while David dipped an arrow into the thick, black pitch. With a quick nod, David began climbing. As he reached the top and started to scramble onto the lookout roof they had been at earlier, Elisabeth climbed up the first few rungs, extending the flaming torch toward him.

"Be careful," Maarten warned, his voice laced with concern. "That thatch will ignite in an instant."

Elisabeth's hands trembled with anxiety, heart pounding as she held the torch high. David lit the arrow's pitch-coated tip, and as the flame flared to life, the intense heat and flickering light only deepened her fear.

David positioned himself on the rooftop, his focus

unyielding. He took aim, and with a steady release, sent the flaming arrow streaking through the night air. It struck the cart filled with flammable material, and within moments, a fierce blaze erupted, engulfing the cart in roaring flames. Thick black smoke billowed upward, spreading rapidly into the dark sky.

Suddenly, Maarten, his wooden leg clacking, hurried over. He took the torch from Elisabeth's trembling hands, his face etched with concern. "Can't be too careful," he mumbled, carrying the torch away.

Elisabeth's eyes widened as she listened to the scene erupt into turmoil. The fire's heat reached her even from a distance, and she heard the enemy scrambling, their plans thrown into disarray. The commotion grew louder as shouts filled the air. "They're at the back! They're getting away!" the men yelled, voices echoing with confusion and panic.

She couldn't see what was happening, but from the frantic cries and sudden shift in the enemy's focus, she knew the ox had done its job. The lantern dangling from its horn must have fooled them into believing they were chasing her and David.

Elisabeth felt a flicker of hope, realizing the enemy was now hunting shadows.

David scrambled down the ladder and grabbed Elisabeth's hand. A mischievous grin spread across his face. "Stefan let the ox out." His eyes twinkled with satisfaction. "Let's move!"

They dashed toward the front gate, their footsteps quick and determined. As they neared, their new friends gathered.

Maarten, his face etched with concern, grasped David's shoulder. "Be careful out there."

David nodded in reply.

"May the heavens protect you. You're in my prayers," Brother Mattias added solemnly.

David gave a slight bow. "We appreciate that."

Maria, eyes full of tears, held Elisabeth's hands. "Please promise me you'll stay safe."

Elisabeth hugged Maria tight. "Believe me, we'll try our best."

Henry, his gruff face softened with worry, gripped David's arm. "Listen…" His rough voice betraying a rare hint of emotion. "They'll be after you for sure. Stay sharp and don't trust anyone you don't know. I may not like people much, but…just be careful out there."

David squeezed Henry's shoulder. "Thank you. I'll keep that in mind."

Beatrice and Lancelot, standing close together, looked at them with deep concern.

"You've done much for us," Beatrice said, blunt as ever. "And seeing you go breaks my heart. Stay sharp and avoid risks."

Elisabeth nodded. "We'll be careful."

Lancelot, his worry evident, added, "Stay safe out there. We'll be thinking of you."

David and Elisabeth exchanged a final look before Elisabeth pulled her hood up and they slipped out the front gate.

Chapter Twenty-Nine

Outside the village, chaos reigned, flames flickering against the night sky. The front entrance had been left unattended amid the turmoil as Tartare's men—paid mercenaries rather than trained soldiers— raced toward the rear perimeter, misled by the distraction of the ox. David had warned Elisabeth earlier about their lack of discipline, and now it showed. This oversight created a crucial window of opportunity as they slipped out of Lindenhart.

Slinking through the darkness, they hurried away from the village. The forest road loomed ahead, a shadowed refuge from the glow of the burning camp. Crossing the small bridge, its wooden planks creaked beneath their steps. The dense trees closed in, the darkened path offering a brief sense of safety.

Elisabeth removed the hood of her cape as she and David hurried hand in hand down the overgrown trail to the mine. Her heart pounded when David let go, disappearing inside to grab the shovel. Moments later, he reappeared, and they sprinted up the hill to where the gold was buried. The cool evening air brushed her face, a sharp contrast to the heat of their escape.

David went to work, plunging the shovel into the earth beneath the rosebush, its bare branches still dotted with red hips. Elisabeth stood close, her breaths quick and shallow. The night was quiet here, shattered only by the frantic clink of metal against dirt as they neared their buried treasure.

David pulled out the canvas tote filled with gold, pausing to brush off the clumps of dirt clinging to it. Slinging the bag over his shoulder, he gave Elisabeth a quick nod, and they began their hurried descent down the hill.

He pulled Elisabeth closer. "We'll stay off the roads and follow the stream."

She nodded, a small smile tugging at her lips, the flutter in her belly growing as the realization hit—they were actually going to slip away unnoticed.

When they crossed the clearing outside the mine entrance, a chilling sound reached Elisabeth's ears—the unmistakable crunch of approaching footsteps.

Her breath hitched, cold panic flooding her veins. She scanned the darkness until her eyes locked onto a familiar silhouette creeping from the shadows.

David halted mid-stride, his body going rigid as the figure sharpened into focus.

Neither of them dared to move as Cato stepped into the clearing; his face bathed in the pale glow of the moonlight.

His gaze, though calm, was sharp and unsettling. "I'm impressed," he said smoothly. "Originally, I thought you'd disappeared…for good." He snapped his fingers for emphasis. "But when you resurfaced in Ghent, foolishly registering with the guild, I realized you must have used the mines beneath Paris instead. Then I discovered there was an old one on Flamel's property."

He gestured theatrically toward the mine entrance behind them. "Well, would you look at that—another mine."

Elisabeth felt the blood drain from her face as the full weight of their blunder sank in.

Cato's eyes narrowed, a shiver of something almost like fear crossing his face. "I know what lurks in those dark places below. I'm surprised you'd risk so much." He stepped closer, his voice dropping to a chilling whisper. "So, the real question is, *why* are you still here?"

Elisabeth's stomach churned at the harrowing reminder. She *could* use her crystal to pull them both through time, but the thought terrified her—what if she lost David somewhere along the way, separated from him forever? Her grip tightened on his hand, her fingers trembling under the weight of that possibility.

She only ever brought "things" through time, and her one desperate attempt to save David in Pompeii had ended with him here in the 14th century, instead of back to her home in Mahone Bay.

Cato let out a low, mocking laugh and directed his gaze at David. "You're *stuck* here, aren't you?"

"Why can't you just let us be, Cato?" David's words were laden with the weight of old wounds. His eyes, filled with a deep, unspoken sorrow, searched Cato's face. "We were once close as brothers."

Elisabeth held her breath, hoping for some flicker of humanity in Cato's hardened expression. But as the silence stretched on, she saw nothing—no trace of the bond they'd once shared, only cold, unrelenting indifference.

Their former friend scoffed; his smile bitter. "Cato is long dead."

"H-how did you find us in Lindenhart?" Elisabeth

managed to squeak out.

"Let's just say certain…information has a way of reaching me." He took another step closer, his gaze menacing.

David drew Elisabeth in.

"I was expecting nutmegs, yet instead, strange gold coins began circulating in Oudenaarde—coins of an unusual value."

Elisabeth's stomach sank. She had feared this might happen. Her shoulders slumped and her head dipped, betraying a sense of defeat.

David began to guide her away. "Come on," he whispered. "We need to move."

When Cato let out a sharp wolf whistle, Elisabeth's body went rigid.

From the shadows stepped Guglielmo Tartare.

His stringy blond hair, calculating gaze, and long, pointed nose were unmistakable. Anger radiated from him, his face twisted in fury, as he locked eyes on David. "You're an unfortunate fool," he spat. "That woman was promised to me—my bride by arrangement. You think you can just take what is mine?"

David's demeanor shifted instantly. He pushed Elisabeth behind him, his body tensing into a defensive stance. "Find another way to form your alliance," he growled, his voice low and dangerous, each word carrying the weight of barely contained fury.

Tartare sneered, stepping closer with a dark, threatening expression. "You think you can defy me without consequences? You're mistaken if you believe you can simply walk away from this."

David's rage flared. He threw his gear to the

ground with a resounding thud, the sound echoing his anger. His fingers curled around a rock in his pouch, muscles flexing as he readied his rope. His eyes blazed, locked on Tartare like a predator about to strike. "My wife is not a pawn, and she was never yours."

Tartare's hand moved to the hilt of his sword, his eyes narrowing as his fingers curled around the weapon. "You're mistaken if you think you can stop this. You alone stand in the way of a powerful alliance with her father." He gestured toward Elisabeth, his grip tightening on the sword. "She is the key to that pact."

David's nostrils flared as he knotted the rock to the end of his rope, his movements quick and sure.

Tartare took a step closer. "This marriage is a matter of strategy, not affection. If need be, I'll remove you to secure this deal."

"Elisabeth, wait for me behind our tree, love," David instructed, his eyes never leaving the enemy. As he spoke, he began to whirl the rope beside him with increasing speed. "This won't take but a moment."

Elisabeth's breath came in quick, uneven bursts as she sprinted toward the nearby tree, where they'd spent two nights beneath its leafy canopy while making the gold. Heart pounding, steps unsteady, she pressed herself against the trunk, struggling to steady her trembling hands.

Tartare's eyes flicked briefly toward Elisabeth before returning to David. "A shame your foolish devotion will cost you everything." He lowered his voice, leaning in slightly. "While I have no desire for her myself, I'll still take great pleasure in claiming her—in every sense."

David's neck corded with rage. "You will not lay a

finger on her. She is my bride, and I'll protect her with my last breath."

Tartare unsheathed his sword. "Bold words for a man who's about to lose it all."

At that moment, David lunged forward, flicking the rope with precision. It lashed out, wrapping tightly around Tartare's sword arm before he could react. With a swift pull, David yanked the sword from his grasp, sending it skittering across the ground.

Tartare's eyes widened in surprise, but he quickly regained his composure. With a snarl, he lunged at David, fists clenched. David sidestepped, his movements fluid and precise. He swung the rope in a wide arc, aiming for Tartare's midsection.

The mercenary blocked with his forearm, but the impact sent him staggering back.

They clashed again, trading powerful blows. David's agility and fierce determination drove him forward, while Tartare's brute strength and relentless fury made him a formidable foe.

Ducking under a wild swing, David retaliated with a sharp kick to the side, forcing his opponent to double over.

Roaring in anger, Tartare grabbed a heavy branch from the ground and swung it wildly. David ducked and rolled to the side, narrowly avoiding the makeshift weapon. Springing to his feet, the rope still coiled in his hand, he lashed out again, catching Tartare's arm and pulling him off balance.

With a frustrated growl, Tartare charged once more, but David was faster. He hurled the weighted rope, which coiled tightly around Tartare's legs, sending him crashing to the ground. Struggling, the mercenary managed to pull a hidden dagger from his boot and started slashing at the rope.

David, spotting the threat, quickly kicked the dagger from Tartare's hand, sending it flying several feet away.

Despite losing his weapon, Tartare's rage only intensified. He lunged again, but his movements were frantic and uncoordinated. David, now fully focused, dodged and countered with a series of precise strikes that drove Tartare to his knees.

Breathing heavily, David stood over him. "You're finished, Tartare. This ends now."

Tartare glared up at him, his greasy hair matted with sweat, his eyes burning with rage. "You think this is the end?" In a sudden move, his eyes darted to a small pouch hidden under his cloak. With a swift, calculated motion, he retrieved a second dagger.

Without hesitation, Tartare lunged forward, the dagger shining in the dim light. The blade sliced through David's flesh, causing his eyes to widen in shock and pain. Staggering back, he clutched his side, the sudden injury draining his strength.

Elisabeth's scream pierced the air as she sprinted toward him, shaking her head in denial.

Desperately, David swung a fist, catching Tartare's arm and knocking the dagger out of his hand. The blade clattered to the ground as David fought to stay on his feet.

As he staggered and fell to one knee, Tartare's relentless blows pounded him with brutal force. Each punch landed with crushing impact, his fists raining down mercilessly. Elisabeth's sobs tore from her, heart breaking at the sight of the young man she loved enduring such violence.

Desperation clouded her thoughts while she frantically searched for a way to intervene.

But Cato's voice, cold and sinister, sliced through her anguish. "You have the power to end this. You know how. Just say the word, and we'll become like the gods of old, wielding boundless power and control. Even your elixir, with its true potential, surpasses mine. You're clever enough to unlock its secrets."

Her eyes darted between David's battered form and Cato, her breath coming in shallow, ragged gasps. Fear and determination clashed within her as she struggled to focus.

Cato's voice grew sharper, more insistent. "Only *you* can stop this with a single word. Save Aquarius and seize your destiny. Agree to my terms, and I'll send Tartare away. Don't let your emotions cloud your judgment—take control and shape your future."

With a final, furious roar, Tartare grabbed his sword, lifting it high above his head. The blade glinted ominously in the moonlight, hovering over David's helpless form.

The moment seemed to stretch into eternity, each second laden with the terrifying certainty that this was it—Tartare was about to deliver the fatal blow.

Elisabeth's hand shot to her crystal, her fingers trembling uncontrollably as she clutched it. Tears streamed down her face, her breath coming in uneven gasps.

Thoughts of home on her mind.

Home.

Chapter Thirty

Elisabeth's chest hitched as she stumbled through the house, the elixir of life now tucked into her belt pouch. She darted toward the basement door, heart pounding as she wrenched it open and plunged into the cool, musty air of the lower level.

Her parents were in the kitchen, their voices drifting down the hallway as they chatted over breakfast, oblivious to her frantic movements. Elisabeth had to keep herself hidden from them, her old-fashioned clothing and tear-streaked face a stark contrast with the modern world around her.

The basement, illuminated by sunlight streaming through a small window, was cluttered with old camping gear and dusty shelves. Elisabeth's eyes darted around the room as she moved quickly, careful to avoid making any noise that might alert her parents.

In the corner, next to the stack of fishing rods, lay her father's double-barreled shotgun, wrapped in an old blanket. She unwrapped it hastily, revealing the sleek, polished wood and shiny barrels. Her fingers shook as she examined it, trying to understand its mechanics. She noted the two barrels, the triggers, and the lever for breaking the gun open, struggling to remember *anything* she'd heard about using a shotgun.

Elisabeth glanced toward the basement stairs, her ears straining against the distant murmur of her parents' voices in the kitchen. She couldn't afford to be discovered.

Desperation pushed her to focus on finding ammunition. Scanning the basement shelves and cupboards, she spotted a small box labeled "Shells" on a top shelf, partially obscured by dusty fishing gear. She grabbed the box and opened it, finding a few cartridges inside.

Elisabeth took a deep breath, trying to steady her shaking hands as she figured out how to load the gun. Her mind raced with the gravity of the situation—she had mere *seconds* to save David's life once she returned.

Each creak from above made her flinch, a reminder to work fast and silent.

Finally, Elisabeth cradled the shotgun across her chest, her grip firm and ready. She wrapped her fingers around the quartz crystal hanging from her neck and thought of David, preparing herself for what was to come.

****

In a moment, Elisabeth emerged back into the chaos, her eyes darting to Tartare, still poised above David with his sword, ready to deliver the fatal blow. David, though in pain, was conscious and watching intently, his face contorted with fear.

With a surge of determination, Elisabeth lifted the shotgun, her hands trembling as she braced it near her shoulder. The weapon felt heavy and unfamiliar, but her resolve was unwavering. She aimed with a shaky breath, then pulled the trigger.

The blast was deafening. The recoil of the shotgun threw Elisabeth onto her bottom, the shockwave rattling through her body. As the report echoed through the night, Tartare staggered back, clutching his arm where the bullet had grazed him, blood seeping through his fingers. His sword fell from his hand and clattered to the ground.

David's eyes widened. Despite his injuries, he tried to move, his strength waning but his tenacity strong. He attempted to crawl closer to Elisabeth, but his movements were slow and painful.

Elisabeth fought to stay focused, scrambling as fast as possible to her feet despite the disorienting force of the blast.

Tartare, bloodied and in agony, glared at her with a blend of rage and disbelief. His eyes widened. "What in the name of all that's holy *is* that?" he bellowed; his voice thick with shock. With one final, desperate surge of fury, he lunged for the sword, clutching it tightly with his uninjured arm, even as a growl of pain escaped his lips. With the weapon now back in hand, he charged toward her, sword raised high.

"Elisabeth!" David's voice, hoarse but fierce, cut through the chaos.

Elisabeth's heart pounded, but her grip on the shotgun steadied. She planted her feet and braced for the recoil. With one bullet left, she took a breath, aimed, and fired.

The shotgun roared again, the blast ringing out with a deafening crack. Tartare crumpled to the ground instantly, the force of the shot ending his attack with brutal efficiency. His sword fell from his hand, the metal clanging sharply on the rocky ground.

Elisabeth's entire body shook as she lowered the weapon. Her breath was ragged, her gaze fixed on the now lifeless body of Guglielmo Tartare. With adrenaline still coursing through her veins, she ran to David and dropped to both knees beside him, tears streaming down her face.

She placed the shotgun beside her, her focus shifting entirely to David. "How bad are you hurt?" Her hands trembled as she examined his wounds.

His eyes met hers, filled with a mix of relief and lingering pain. "What was *that*?" he asked, his voice gravelly with awe.

Elisabeth gently hushed him, her own voice trembling with emotion. "It's nothing. Just stay with me, Aquarius. We're safe now." As her pulse raced, she fumbled for the elixir, her movements clumsy. She administered the red powder, knowing it would heal him within hours.

"Is that…Jupiter's thunderbolt?" Cato asked, his voice trembling.

Elisabeth's head jerked up, heart pounding. In her anguish, she'd somehow forgotten Cato's presence. With a gasp, she grabbed the shotgun, her hands shaking as she sprang to her feet and pointed it at him. It wasn't loaded, but he had no way of knowing that.

Cato stood frozen, his eyes wide with a blend of dread and fascination. "I *knew* it," he whispered. "Your weapon is like Jupiter's thunderbolt. Just as his could summon divine fury from the heavens, your weapon wields a power so overwhelming, it seems to command the very force of the gods."

Elisabeth's eyes narrowed as she kept the shotgun aimed at Cato, her mind a storm of worry. David, now regaining his strength, was slowly becoming more alert, his breaths steadying.

"Listen carefully," Elisabeth warned. "I don't want any part of your schemes. But I do want you out of our life. *Now*."

Cato's face twisted with frustration, but the sight of the shotgun and Elisabeth's determined stance made him hesitate. "Elisabeth—"

She cut him off, her grip on the shotgun tightening. "I will *kill* if you come near us again." Her tone deepened. "Leave now and order your mercenaries to withdraw from the village. If you don't, I promise you'll regret it."

Cato's expression darkened as he took in her words, and for a moment, Elisabeth could almost feel the tension between them crackling in the air. With a last, intense gaze, he took a step back, his hands raised in surrender. "Fine. You've checkmated me." His voice was laced with a disturbing fascination.

As Cato retreated into the shadows, Elisabeth let out a deep breath and lowered the shotgun, savoring the triumph of their narrow escape. She turned her attention to the scattered supplies, including the gold, and heaved the weight onto her back, the load straining her shoulders but manageable. Pulling David's arm around her neck to help him walk, she guided him toward the stream.

With each step, her knees shook under the strain of everything she carried, yet the burden of their situation seemed lighter as her confidence grew.

Outnumbered—like Hannibal Barca had been—they'd just won the battle, defying all odds.

Chapter Thirty-One

By morning, the elixir had worked its magic. David walked alongside Elisabeth, their load carried easily on his back, their hands clasped together.

Elisabeth's gaze wandered dreamily ahead. "Let's return to Paris. You can resume your apprenticeship with Nicholas, and we can use the gold in smaller amounts this time, so it doesn't attract too much attention." She squeezed David's hand, her eyes widening with excitement. "We'll have a cozy little cottage just outside the city, down the road from Perenelle and little Colette, with roses climbing up the walls and a garden filled with flowers. We'll finally have a place to call our own, and I can have Rosamund with me again." She bounced from foot to foot, thinking of her sweet old mare. "No more hiding, no more running. Just a simple, joyful life together." She bit her lip gently and turned to him. "With Tartare dead and Cato running scared…what do you think?"

David's face seemed to shine as he met her gaze, his eyes reflecting the hope and love between them. He came to a stop, pulling her close. With a soft smile, he brushed his lips against hers in a tender kiss. "That sounds perfect."

****

As they walked on, the golden light of hope seemed to envelop them. Elisabeth, immersed in dreams of a new life ahead, didn't know that while Hannibal Barca, the legendary general, won many battles—he ultimately lost the war.

To be continued...

Author's Note

In the Middle Ages, animals were sometimes put on trial, much like humans, for crimes such as theft or murder. This bizarre legal practice stemmed from the belief that animals, like people, were morally responsible for their actions. Pigs, in particular, were frequent defendants due to their close proximity to humans in rural life.

Throughout Europe, such trials were not uncommon, but some of the most notable cases occurred in France. One such case happened in 1386, where a pig was tried for killing a child. The animal was dressed in human clothes, brought before a court, found guilty, and executed by hanging.

In 1494, also in France, a swarm of bees was put on trial for stinging a man to death. A lawyer was appointed to defend them, arguing that the bees were acting in self-defence. Ultimately, they were excommunicated and driven out of their hive.

In 1522, rats were summoned to court in the French town of Autun. Accused of destroying barley crops, they were assigned a defense lawyer who argued that the rats couldn't attend the trial because they were scattered and in danger from cats on the way to court.

The trial was delayed indefinitely.

****

In the medieval period, the birth of twins often led to superstitions and misconceptions. One common belief was that twins were fathered by two different men. This idea arose from the twins' physical similarities and the unusual nature of their birth. The lack of understanding of human reproduction and a tendency to view strange occurrences through superstition fueled this belief, causing twins to be viewed with suspicion.

A word about the author...

An adventurer at heart, Tammy has explored ruins in Rome, Pompeii, and Istanbul (Constantinople) with historians and archaeologists.

She's slept in the tower of a 15th century castle in Scotland, climbed down the cramped tunnels of Egyptian pyramids, scaled the Sydney Harbour Bridge, sailed on a tiny raft down the Yulong River in rural China, dined at a Bedouin camp in the Arabian Desert, and escaped from head-hunters in the South Pacific.

I suppose one could say her own childhood wish of time traveling adventures came true...in a roundabout way.

http://www.tammylowe.com

Thank you for purchasing
this publication of The Wild Rose Press, Inc.

For questions or more information
contact us at
info@thewildrosepress.com.

The Wild Rose Press, Inc.
www.thewildrosepress.com